I0673907

THE DARK - BOOK 3

To save his daughter, Cain has to fight an army
— they're going to need more than that to *stop him!*

In the third installment of this heart-pounding series, Cain Haight — a drunk ex-soldier, his opportunist ex-wife, her redneck mother, and a sweet Amish woman are on a desperate mission to save his daughter from the clutches of rebel soldiers. But the group becomes separated, leaving each member to fend for themselves against bloodthirsty monsters and ruthless humans. Cain's only thought is to reach his daughter, who is held captive in an army base overrun by enemies. With a reckless disregard for his own safety, he charges into battle against impossible odds, ready to do whatever it takes to save his child - even if it means sacrificing his own life in the process. The stakes have never been higher in this rollercoaster ride of courage and redemption.

THE DARK 3, by *New York Times* bestselling author Christopher Greyson, is a relentless, pulse-pounding descent into a world where humanity stands on the edge of extinction. Packed with jaw-dropping twists, devastating betrayals, terrifying monsters, and heroes pushed far beyond their limits, this explosive thriller never lets up.

Praise for Christopher Greyson's
The Dark

You can't shackle talent like Christopher Greyson's. He finally stepped out of his comfort zone and wrote one of the best dystopian novels I have ever read. I really enjoyed the terror and the suspense. I am certain you will too!
— Dan Santos — Author of the Insurrection Series

If you're captivated by a novel that launches surprises and eerie happenings with practically every turn of the page, this is it! Wild, so filled with never-ending twists and turns that it's impossible to put down! Once again, Christopher Greyson has written a thriller that will have you on the edge of your seat for the entire page-turning ride!
— Robert Tolich — Amazon Review

Mr. Greyson gifts readers with a frightening window into the ramifications of the enduring isolation of a global loss of power. With unexpected twists, our reluctant hero tackles unknown creatures, corrupt leaders, diabolical plots, and so much more in this edge-of-your seat, white-knuckle visit to the Highland Plateau town of Ridgecrest. — Micki Wiersma — Amazon Review

ALSO BY CHRISTOPHER GREYSON

The Girl Who Lived 1

The Girl Who Lived 2

One Little Lie

The Woman Beneath the Stairs

Pure of Heart

The Detective Jack Stratton Mystery-Thriller Series

The Case Files of Detective Charlie Westbrook

Kiku - The Rogue Assassin Series

The Dark - A Post-Apocalyptic Thriller Series

The Adventures of Finn and Annie - A Mini Mystery Series

This book is dedicated to Kevin Bowling. He opened his home to me in my time of need, and his friendship, fellowship, and example have been a wonderful blessing.

A Post-Apocalyptic Thriller Serial

THE DARK
Book 3

by
Christopher Greyson

1

THE GOOD GUYS

Cain Haight

I'm lying on a cot, waiting for the first hint of sunlight so I can get moving. A couple hundred people are sleeping in the darkness around me—men, women, and children—all that's left of the city. Everyone else has fled, is holed up someplace else, or died. From the carnage left in the street and what Bob told me, most were killed by the monsters. They overran the city and butchered everyone in their path.

How had Ridgecrest gone so untouched? Something had kept the creatures out. What, I've got no idea. None of it made sense to me, but I've got five priorities higher on my mental to-do list that I'm trying to figure out. At least four of them are in the same location. Unfortunately, that's a former U.S. Military base. Fen took Bri and Jacob to Fort Burgess. Lucy and Sadie got captured and brought to the base in the back of a truck.

But what happened to Mercy?

Images of the Amish woman slowly play through my mind like I'm watching a rerun of *Little House on the Prairie*. I was alone, getting ready to eat a can of tuna fish before it expired.

But when I looked out the window, I saw Mercy carrying a tray of food down the path to my cabin. It was spring, and in the field behind her, the wildflowers were bending in the wind. She's wearing a blue dress and black hat, smiling like the happiest woman in the world. Why? What could possibly make anybody that happy?

And what was with the black hat? Growing up, I remember the bad guy always wearing a black hat in Westerns. But as far as the Amish went, women wore a black hat until they were married and then switched to white.

Mercy's green eyes are bright, taking everything in. She's smart and hyper-observant. But she's good, so she's not ruining what she sees, like I do. I look at a field of flowers and see they're pretty, and then I start thinking, how soon are they gonna die and rot? She doesn't do that. She's as beautiful on the inside as the out.

I don't know how she stood being around me. Most people won't look me in the eye. And the good ones usually head in the other direction when I'm around. But Mercy was different. She not only looked me in the eye but treated me nicely. Was it pity or mercy?

I'm back to picturing her heart-shaped face. I'd never seen her with makeup on, and I would never want to. It would be like painting over the Mona Lisa. She's got a natural glow. Makeup would ruin it.

Those thoughts are pushed aside by the memory of her before we left Ridgecrest. We're standing beside the canoes, her eyes filled with concern for the children, yet hard as emeralds with determination. She was scared out of her mind but determined to march into hell on a suicide raid to rescue someone else's kids. That's a true hero—someone who does something even when they're scared.

I need to find out what happened to her. To do that, I have to get to Lucy and Sadie, which means I need to get into that

Army base. I'm going to that Army base anyway to save my daughter and her friend, Jacob.

I'm not going to solve my problems by staying in bed. What was that proverb? A little sleep, a little slumber, a little folding of the hands to rest—and poverty will come on you like a thief, and scarcity like an armed man.

That gets me on my feet. I grab my guns and backpack, then head for the exit. The hum of over a hundred people breathing in the same room is loud enough to cover any noise I make.

I reach the bottom of the escalator and stop when I hear the guard at the top. Pete took over for Linda at midnight. Linda told me both their names before she headed off to bed. That's a problem you get when you press civilians into playing military roles. They're undisciplined, untrained, and too trusting.

I silently climb the steps and peek over the top of the escalator. Pete is sitting in a folding camp chair with his chin on his chest and his shotgun at his feet. He lifts his head slightly at the sound of my boots, but it settles back down like a bobber with a fish nibbling on the end of the line. He's not fully asleep, so there's no use trying to sneak by.

Creeping across the floor, I reach the side of Pete's chair. He blinks and glances up at me.

My right-hand covers his mouth, and I hold up my left hand. "Hey, Pete. Linda asked me to get you. She said Angel wants to meet with both of you. I'm supposed to replace you on watch, and you and Linda are to report to Angel's office. Something big is going down. You need to hurry."

Pete rubs his eyes, mumbles, "Thanks," and heads for the escalator.

"Hold up," I say, reaching down and grabbing the shotgun he left behind. "You don't want to forget this."

Pete exhales, rushes back, and takes the weapon. "Thanks. Angel would have handed me my head if I forgot this."

I smile and nod. At least he won't get chewed out for leaving his post and forgetting his gun.

As his boots echo down the stairs, I rush to the door. Three large bars hold it shut, but there's also a two-foot by two-foot portal cut through the metal they use for checking outside. It's large enough for me to fit through.

Down in the basement, multiple boots echo off the escalator as at least a few people run upstairs.

I grab the latch and pull. The portal swings open.

"FREEZE!" A man shouts behind me.

I ignore him and grab the bottom of the portal.

"Stop, or I'll shoot!"

I recognize Bob's voice. He was a cop before the Dark, and even without an official department, he's still a cop. He's also what's left of the good guys. He won't shoot me.

I'm halfway out the window when I feel two stings—one in the back, the other in my right butt cheek. Before I can figure out what bit me, a spike of electricity courses through my body. My muscles stiffen, my head bangs off the top of the portal, and I fall backward onto the floor, twitching like a wet French fry dropped into hot oil.

Bob runs up and stops a few steps to my right. He stands over me, covering me with his pistol.

Angel marches forward. Even upside down, she looks really mad. She raises her pistol, and I raise my hands.

"Can I ask why you tased me for going for a walk?" I ask as Bob takes my shotgun and pistol from their holsters.

"Shut up, Cain. My office. Now." Angel snaps.

A short guy with a bushy beard runs up behind Bob. His lips disappear into his beard as he grins. "Don't that beat all! I knew it would work."

The man's Southern accent is as thick as his beard. He holds up a taser in his hands, the wires still connected to my backside. "Don't go fidgetin', boy. Keep your butt in the air and stay on your stomach so I can get them needles out."

Feeling like I sat on a fishing lure as the man hovers over me, I ask, "How did your Taser work? It's got a computer chip in it, right?"

"Atticus here built his own Faraday cage," Bob says.

"I told ya it would work." Atticus sticks his thumb against his puffed-out chest. "And you all saw the way it lit him up!"

"I had a front-row seat," I mutter as he removes the probes.

Atticus helps me to my feet, and Bob takes out his cuffs.

"Are those necessary?" I ask.

He, standing to my left, laughs. "So asks the man who just tried to escape."

It would have been impossible for me not to have noticed the mountain of a Marine if I hadn't just been tased.

"I think there's been some miscommunication," I say as I stare at Angel. "No one informed me that I'm a prisoner, and I couldn't leave."

Angel motions toward the staircase. "We're not having this discussion here. Take him to my office."

H grabs my right arm and Bob my left. As they lead me downstairs, I relax my shoulders. This isn't the time to fight. Another opportunity will come later. I may be their captive now, but I won't stay that way. These are the good guys, and I doubt they've ever dealt with someone like me.

2

USELESS

Lucy Green

Lucy lay on her cot, glaring at the ceiling. Barefoot and wearing a drab green set of Army coveralls, she tried to remain perfectly still. Her head throbbed from getting clubbed by the stock of a rifle, but it was her road rash that was driving her up a wall. The scrapes along her side itched like she'd slept in the woods, and the chiggers had feasted on her all night long. And since the coveralls were as comfortable as panties made from a potato sack, every time she moved, the fabric chafed her raw skin.

But she didn't scratch. Instead, she let the pain fuel the anger inside her. She let all that rage build and then played with the ideas that danced in her imagination. The men who captured her were part of the group who stole her little girl and dragged her into hell. Lucy would make them pay for that. How? She didn't know yet, but thinking of the different possibilities was fun.

Lucy shut her eyes. Part of her had hoped that the army

base would be different. When Fen and Nicholi came to Ridge-crest, Lucy had seen their offer to take her to the base as her last chance to leave that Godforsaken town. But now that she was here, it wasn't what she'd expected. Naively, she pictured an Army base out of a movie with handsome soldiers marching by and other shirtless ones playing volleyball and drinking beers in the rec hall. Instead, gaunt, shell-shocked men and women scurried like rats from cover to cover.

This was no place for her or Bri. But how could she escape?

Lucy smiled. Everyone had gifts. If she were Sadie, she'd use her brain to devise an escape plan. If she were Cain, she'd use her brawn and fight her way out. At the thought of her ex-husband, she lifted her chin, letting the pain of his death burn white hot and forge itself into her determination.

Seeing how she lacked neither of their positive attributes, she needed to work with the assets she did possess. Brushing back her blonde hair, she crossed to the sink and dipped her fingers in the cup. She sprinkled a few drops on her eyes but decided that, in this case, more was better. Holding the cup, she let the water drip down her cheeks and run down her neck until it dampened the front of her shirt, accentuating her cleavage.

Taking a deep breath, she burst into fake tears and rushed to the door. In her thickest Southern Belle accent, she cried, "Help! Help! Help me, please!"

Boots sounded in the hallway.

Lucy moved back, closer to the cot.

The door handle rattled, and two thin Chinese soldiers stepped inside. They eyed Lucy suspiciously. One held a black rod in his hand.

"Thank you! Thank you!" Lucy stepped forward.

The men moved back. The one with the baton raised it to waist height.

Lucy gasped and pretended to swoon. The men made no motion to catch her, so she stumbled to the cot and flopped down. "Thank you for saving me," she said, holding her hand toward the closest guard. "I don't know what I would have done if you hadn't rescued me on the road."

The two men exchanged puzzled glances.

"Do you speak English?"

The man closest to her scowled. "Perfectly."

"I didn't mean any disrespect," she said, grasping the fabric on the leg of his fatigues. Laying on the bed, she batted her eyes and poured on the act. "You have my eternal gratitude, sir."

"We did not rescue you," The other guard said. "We know who you are and why you came here."

"You never should have come." The one with the baton said. "Now you're trapped too."

The hopelessness in his eyes made Lucy's stomach clench.

The first guard said something in Chinese that angered the one with the baton. They went back and forth for a full minute, arguing in Chinese, their voices low and bitter.

The one with the baton turned back to Lucy. "Is it true about Ridgecrest? Is it safe there? Do you have food?"

Lucy stood and changed tactics. "We do, and we are safe. I can bring you there."

"Ha!" The first guard laughed dismissively.

Lucy ignored him and met the man holding the baton's desperate stare. "I made it here. I can get you there."

"Don't listen to her. Tianzi said we're not to speak with her." The first guard said.

The other man's shoulders sagged. He stared at Lucy and shook his head. "You never should have come."

"Who is Tianzi? What are you talking about?"

The first guard said something in Chinese, and the other one nodded. There was a finality to it. Even if Lucy didn't understand the language, she knew her chance of getting one of these men on her side was slipping away.

"Let Tianzi stay here and die. Come with me if you want to live."

The first guard's face scrunched up, and his lip curled. "You are the one who will die after he speaks with you. There's not enough food, and you are useless."

Lucy turned to the other guard, but he stared guiltily at the floor.

Useless.

All the rage pressed down inside of her ignited. Like she was making a field goal attempt from the fifty-yard line, she kicked the guard in the groin with all her might.

Spit and air shot out of his mouth. His arms raised as he doubled forward.

Lucy ripped the baton from his hand and brought it down on the other guard's head. It sounded like she'd hit a coconut with a golf club, and he crumpled to the floor.

The guard she'd kicked in the groin stumbled forward and grabbed hold of the wall to keep from falling.

Lucy smashed him across the back with the baton.

Whimpering, he crashed onto the tile and writhed in pain.

Holding the club high, she scanned both men. Neither had a holster or a gun or weapon other than the one baton. She backed to the door and peered out.

The room sat at the end of an empty, long hallway with doors on either side. She reached back into the room and snatched the doorstop off the floor. Pulling the door closed, she wedged the doorstop underneath and straightened up. Panic gripped her chest. She had no plan or clue where Bri or Sadie were being held. She glanced at the half dozen doors. Was it possible her captors kept all the prisoners together or at least close by? There had to be a chance. But how could she locate Bri before someone noticed the missing guards?

Lucy's hand shook. She had no idea why, but an image of Mercy appeared in her mind. That Amish woman stared at her with those green eyes and bowed her head.

Lucy gritted her teeth and started walking. She wasn't about to get down on her knees and beg God for help. He was the one who got her into this mess in the first place.

3

SHAME

Evan Green

Evan Green stood at the end of the boat dock, watching the water sparkle in the morning light. He'd spent another night in an empty bed, staring at the ceiling and wondering where Lucy was now.

Guilt slapped him upside the head like a backhand from his father. Only in his mind his father was yelling at him, not for being a coward, but for wanting to throw his life away for a woman.

A scrap of paper floated on the water, followed by another. They were small, like a quarter of a page. He raised his eyebrow as more appeared. They were slowly being swept closer to him by the river.

Puzzled, he crossed the deserted parking lot. The usual bustle of people fishing, even after the Dark, was absent today, adding to the silence.

Evan's shoulders slumped. Everyone else in town was busy doing something to prepare for the monsters' attack except him. His father didn't trust him enough to make decisions, but he didn't want him putting up barricades because that was beneath the mayor's son.

Turning onto the footpath, Evan followed the natural curve of the river. The trail was well worn by fisherman's boots and easy to walk. He glanced at the water as additional pieces of paper floated down.

Ahead, someone softly cried.

Evan slowed. He craned his neck and scanned the path. A woman knelt on the rocks in a little natural nook where the large stones went a few yards into the river. She was hunched over and scribbling in a book. After a moment, she carefully tore a piece off the page, folded it, and tossed it toward the river.

The wind caught it, blowing it sideways. It landed in the branches of a tree growing beside the rock. She dropped the book and scrambled to her feet. Rushing over, she stopped at the side of the rock, stretching up to retrieve the note, but it was out of her reach. Covering her face, she burst into tears.

Evan raced forward. He easily leaped onto the rock with his long legs and crossed to her side.

Sarah Yoder was startled and stepped away. She stared at him with red-rimmed eyes. "Oh, hello, Evan. I'm sorry, I..."

"It's all right, ma'am. I saw the papers, then heard you crying and wanted to make sure you're okay."

"I'm fine," Sarah took a trembling breath and forced a smile. "Fine."

Evan stretched out and plucked the paper from the tree. He handed it to Sarah, and she smiled as if he had just given her a box of chocolates.

"Oh, the Lord sent you here today." Fresh tears wet her lashes.

"I doubt that," Evan rolled his eyes, then quickly added. "No offense."

"None taken," Sarah crossed to the river and tossed the paper into the water.

Evan rubbed the back of his neck. "If you don't mind my asking, why did you get so upset about the paper getting stuck in the tree if you were just going to throw it in the river?"

Sarah blushed and crossed her arms. "It's a silly habit I picked up from my older sister. I don't know why, but when I was little, I had a hard time praying. So Mary told me to write my prayers down and send them to God by way of the river. I don't know if it's the physical act of writing or letting them go, but doing it made me feel good." She closed her eyes and inhaled deeply. "I haven't done it since I was a little girl, but I needed to feel closer to the Lord." Her green eyes sparkled like the river when she opened them. "Do you know what I mean?"

"No."

Sarah stood there blinking. She opened her mouth and closed it. "I'm sorry. I assumed... Your mother was a believer."

"You knew my mom?"

Sarah gave him the pitying smile he'd gotten his entire life when people spoke of his mother. "You were young at the time of the accident."

"Nine." Evan said, rubbing the scar on his elbow. He shrugged. "Funny thing. My arm itches every time I remember it. We were going food shopping."

"Your mother was such a sweet woman. She bought one of my Amos' signs. 'As for me and my house, we will serve the Lord.'"

"My father smashed it in two and pitched it in the fire. After." Evan admitted.

Sarah swallowed. "I don't know what to say."

"I didn't mean to offend you. It's just that I kinda agree with him. "My mom was sweet. And kind. She took me to church every Sunday, but God didn't stop the truck from T-boning us, did He?"

"No. And He didn't stop the Dark. Or me losing my little Abraham. But that doesn't mean He doesn't love us or them."

"No offense, Mrs. Yoder, but how does a loving God let your son bleed to death in a field?"

Sarah stood straighter. "I wondered that for a while, myself. It pulled me down into a darkness that I'd never known. But then I realized two things: The first is the most important. Abraham is much better off now, and I believe that with all my soul. The second was that so much good came out of Abraham's death. It was the third year of the drought. The community was splintering. Families were giving up. That's why Abraham was alone in the field. No one would go with him to work. If they had, they may have been able to help when he was injured. Instead, he died alone. The guilt and shame of the people had made them turn around. They came back together and worked."

Anger boiled up inside of Evan. His hands balled into fists. "Guilt and shame aren't good things."

"Who says!" Sarah shot back. "The fluffy people in this world tell you that pain is bad. It's not. It serves a purpose. If you put your hand on a hot stove, it burns. Guilt and shame are the same. If a man breaks his vow, leaves his wife, and deserts his family, he should feel guilt and shame. If he does, he may come to his senses and correct his error."

Evan reeled back like she'd slapped him. "I deserted my wife." He whispered the words, seemingly ripped from his chest.

Sarah gasped. "I wasn't referring to you staying here when Lucy left. I wasn't. I was talking about infidelity. I used the first sin that popped into my head. I wasn't trying to guilt you."

Evan grinned. For the first time in a long time, he felt alive. "I know. But I should feel guilty. And you're right. I should do something about it. Thanks, Mrs. Yoder." With his newfound energy, Evan leaped down from the rock and marched back on the path.

"Evan?" Sarah called after him. "What are you going to do?"

"What I should have done the first time. Go get my wife."

4

A DICTIONARY

Cain Haight

H and Bob lead me downstairs and then along a corridor on the right. Angel brings up the rear. She's short, five feet two inches tall, and has a slender build. She's got a hard face and cold eyes. Her nose is thin, and her cheekbones are high. She could be in her early thirties. Her real name is Angela Florez, but she goes by Angel. She's ex-Homeland Security and the one in charge.

Judging by the way her hand is resting on her pistol grip in the holster on her hip, she's also the paranoid type. Being paranoid is probably how she caught me. There's no way the guard could have alerted them so fast. Someone must have been watching for me to make a move.

H is a Marine who is built like a bulldozer. He is six feet tall, has a thick neck, a broad back, and scarred arms. Judging by his cauliflower ear and broken nose, he knows how to fight.

Bob is all cop. His hair is cut short, and he's clean-shaven. Considering we're a year into the apocalypse, that tells me he's all business and won't drop his guard easily.

In a way, I feel bad. All three are play-by-the-rules types, and I've always been a color-outside-of-the-lines kind of guy. I will have to hit them hard, fast, and ruthlessly. I don't want to, but my girl is counting on me.

We pass some restrooms and a door labeled breakroom, and I'm led through another door where the word OFFICE had been vandalized to look like orifice. I'm tempted to crack a joke but hold my tongue and chuckle instead.

Angel must have noticed. She rips a good-sized knife out of a sheath on her thigh and, with a single swipe, scrapes all traces of the word off as H pushes me inside.

The medium-sized room has a desk and two old file cabinets shoved against the wall. There's an assortment of mismatched chairs scattered about. From the blanket peeking out behind the couch, I assume Angel sleeps in here.

"Sit." Angel orders as she marches to the back.

I look at the low-back chair and look at Bob. "Do you mind switching my cuffs to the front?"

"I mind," Angel says as she walks around the desk and sits down. "Leave them."

"Really? What do you think I'm going to do? Try to over-power both H and Bob and make a play for their guns?" That's precisely what I have in mind, but I figure a little reverse psychology is worth a shot.

Both H and Bob smirk, but Angel doesn't fall for it. She fixes me with a cold stare. "Do you want me to order them to make you sit?"

"I was hoping you'd be the one to try to make me, but because you asked so nicely," I sit. "Since when am I a prisoner?"

"You're not."

I turn to Bob. "Do you have a dictionary? If you do, could you please look up what you call a guy who can't leave and is handcuffed?"

H coughs.

Angel glares. "When I allowed you to come with us, you promised to hear me out. This is my house, my rules. No one leaves and comes back without my permission."

"Knock yourself out with your rules. You don't have to worry about me breaking them if I'm not here. And I wasn't planning on coming back. Can I go now?"

Bob sits in a chair on my right. His brow knits together. "Don't tell me you were thinking about going to the fort alone?"

"Are you crazy, or do you have a death wish?" Angel asks. "I'm sorry about your daughter and friends, but now that they've been taken to Fort Burgess, there is no helping them."

I crack my neck and keep my mouth shut. My back is tensing up, and with my hands cuffed behind me, my shoulders are starting to burn. "If aliens took my daughter to the moon, I'd build a rocket to get her. Either way, it's not your concern."

Angel slams her hand on the desk. "But those people out there are. Have you considered what would happen if the soldiers ever came into the city looking for us?"

"Are you saying the soldiers in the fort don't know you're here?"

"That's exactly what I'm saying. And if you give me a chance to explain, maybe you'll understand."

"You're right. I said I'd listen, but all I've thought about was helping my daughter. Go ahead and talk. You've got a captive audience." I try to lean back in my chair, but I don't make it far with the handcuffs.

Angel points at Bob, "Uncuff him."

Bob stares at her, and they have a silent conversation for a second. The way his eyebrows knit together, I know Bob isn't fond of that idea. Despite his hesitation, he stands and moves behind me.

I lean forward.

Bob unlocks the handcuff on my left hand but relocks it around the arm of the chair before I have a chance to react.

"I believe she said *remove* the handcuffs," I say.

"No offense, Cain." Bob sits back down. "But I've got a feeling that if you're unhappy with how this conversation goes, you'll try to leave anyway. So you stay cuffed."

I nod. I wouldn't have taken the cuffs off if it had been me. And the arm of the chair looks like it will break easily enough. I'm halfway free, so I settle back to listen.

Angel sets her arms on the desk and stares at me with brown eyes. "I was stationed in the city. H was one of the few who made it out of the fort. I'll let him start."

H sits ramrod straight, shoulders back and chin out. "I had been stationed at the fort ten years ago but haven't been back since then. My unit was in Africa when I got called in and grilled by some CIA spooks about Fort Burgess. They raked me over the coals, but I didn't know anything they were talking about. That night, we got the order to ship out to Fort Burgess. All I knew was something big must have happened at the base."

"Why do you say that?" I ask.

"Because my commander hand-picked five platoons to go. Every unit was assigned a soldier who had been stationed at the base before. It felt wrong from the start. Bad juju all around." H met Cain's eyes.

He didn't need to say anything more about the feeling of impending doom. As a soldier, Cain knew it well. It was like a cloud that enveloped everyone. It had a presence. You felt that if you turned fast enough, you'd see the reaper waiting there.

"When we got to the base, Fort Burgess was on edge." H continued. "Everyone seemed to be on a war footing. It was a joint op. Russia and China each sent five special ops platoons, too. Everyone was gearing up for something, but no one was talking. Before we found out what was going on, the first EMP wave hit. All communication goes down. It went from tense to chaos. We've got backups of everything in Faraday cages, but everyone was freaking out trying to determine what happened. When we got coms back online, we found out that Russia was launching nukes."

"At who? Who set off the EMP?" I ask.

Angel set her elbows on the desk. "I don't think anyone did. I was stationed in the city. We had equipment in a Faraday cage, too. After the first EMP pulse, I initiated emergency protocols and contacted Washington. No nation or terrorist group had claimed responsibility, and it was a global event. Scientists were all saying it was caused by solar activity, but Russia didn't believe the denials and launched their nukes."

"Once the nukes started to fly," H continued, "several other countries followed suit, including us. We lost communication with Washington before the second pulse hit. That pulse was ten times stronger than the first. It destroyed everything we took out of the cages and any equipment that survived the first wave. After that, all hell broke loose—literally. That's when the spotters noticed what was happening in the city..." H pales, and his voice trails off. He's staring at the wall, but from the horrified look in his eyes, he's re-seeing what happened that day.

Bob clears his throat and starts talking. "I was on duty that day. Most people thought it was a blackout, but since everything electronic shut down, I knew it had to be some kind of EMP. At first, it wasn't that bad. Everyone was scared, but they all pulled together, trying to figure out what happened. Then survivors came running from the direction of the Cook Caverns. The monsters were chasing them. It was something you see in nightmares—thousands of white rat-like things. You must have seen them."

"Bone rats." I nod.

"That's what we call them, too. Then came the wolves, bears, and apes. Everyone ran out of ammo. My partner and I grabbed everything we could at a sporting goods shop. But they overran us with sheer numbers. They poured into the city, killing everyone in their wake. They broke into buildings and dragged people out of cars. We thought we were saved when the Army rolled out of Fort Burgess."

H stood up and paced. "We brought the heavy equipment that survived the first EMP. We kept it underground in a special bunker. We rolled up on the city. All the animals retreated to Cook Caverns. We followed them, but it was a trap. The ghouls were waiting for us. I noticed the frontline troops dropping their guns and grabbing their heads. Once they were unarmed, the rats took them down. The ghouls even affected the helicopter pilots. When those crashed, everyone was ordered to fall back."

"Did these ghouls look like a man with grayish-white skin?"

A pained look crossed H's face. "Yeah. But I don't think they're men. They eat humans and animals—the bones, not the meat. You've seen them?"

"One killed a friend of mine." I swallow as I remember Adam dying in the cave. "They messed with my head. It didn't have a weapon, so I don't know how, but it hurt like hell."

"We don't know anything about them." Angel smacked the desk in frustration. "We've cobbled together some theories about the ghouls and their capabilities, but we're running blind. We were hoping you knew something more."

"Before a few weeks ago, we only knew about the wolves. It wasn't until we left that we saw the other monsters."

Angel motioned to H. "Continue."

"When the Army retreated for the base, the people in the city followed. A flood of refugees rushed to the safety of the fort. But the soldiers had blocked the road. They ordered everyone away, but there was nowhere to go." H's hands balled into fists. "I don't know why, but the base opened fire. It was a slaughter. Everyone returned to the city and held up here with our group."

"But this can't be all that's left." I lean forward, and my handcuffs rattle. "I saw you out on patrol. There must be other groups that survived."

"That's who we look for," Angel said. "After the initial attack, the monsters tore the city apart, looking for survivors. I don't know why they didn't find us. After a week, the creatures left the city. We still see them from time to time, but we're careful. We use spotters to look for them and other survivors. Occasionally, we find people who've run out of supplies and come out of hiding. That's what we thought you were."

I settle back in my seat as reality slams me upside the head like a club. I glance at the wall to my left, picturing the people on the other side. "That's all that's left?"

"Yes." Angel sighs. "That's why I can't have you jeopardizing their safety by wandering around."

I stare back into her brown eyes and see the concern there. She's right. "I get it. But you have to understand, I'm going to get my daughter."

Angel smacks her forehead and runs her hand over her brown hair. "Did you just hear a word we said? You can't get into the base. They opened fire on civilians. They will kill you."

"We also don't know who's in charge," H says. "With the amount of Chinese and Russian troops, one of those factions could have taken over."

"You two have it all wrong. I'm not going there to ask for my daughter back. I'm taking her."

Angel laughs.

Bob leans over and uncuffs my hand.

"What are you doing, Bob?" Angel asks.

"Do you see that expression on his face?" Bob points at me. "Unless we kill him, which I won't do, he's not going to stop until he gets out of here."

H walks in front of the desk and snaps to attention before Angel. "I beg your pardon, Ma'am, but he can't just walk in there blind. He needs recon. I'm requesting permission to help."

"I am, too," Bob says.

Angel fixes me with a hard stare. She's debating, and from the look on her face, it isn't going my way.

I stand up and move between Bob and H while I plead my case. "Look, if you're worried about me stirring up a hornet's nest by going to the base, you don't have to be. The soldiers who took my girl know me. If I do get caught or killed, they won't think I came from the city. They'll know I came from Ridgecrest and why I'm there. This isn't a threat, but I'm going with or without your permission."

Angel stood up. "Don't be so quick to throw your life away. We'll do some recon first and then decide. If I agree, do I have your word you won't try anything and will follow my rules?"

I look at the three people who've just volunteered to risk their lives to help me and nod. "I'll agree to go on recon and come back here—*if* you agree, I can leave when I want to leave." I hold out my hand.

Angel shakes it with a surprisingly strong grip.

I crookedly grin. "Great. Let's go figure out how to take on an army."

5

USELESS

Lucy Green

Beginning with the door across the hall, Lucy started checking every room. Her hopes rose and fell a little further with each door when she discovered they were empty. Standing at the last one in the hall, she clenched her jaw. Her palm, slick with sweat, slipped on the knob. She tightened her grip, turned the handle, and pushed open the door.

The room lay empty.

The last flames of adrenaline sputtered inside Lucy, and she hung her head. Her shoulders slumped, and she leaned against the doorframe.

Where was Bri? Where had they taken Sadie? If the soldiers had moved them to a different building on the huge army base, she'd never be able to find them unless...

An idea sparked in her brain, kindling the adrenaline fumes back into an inferno. She'd make them tell her where her daughter was.

She marched to the end of the corridor and peered around the corner. The hallway ran along the side of the building. On the right, windows let the overcast sun through. On the left, a solid wall without a trace of doors stood.

Holding the baton slightly behind her leg, Lucy jogged down the hallway. In the growing shadows outside, the army base stretched out before her. It looked like a war zone with burned-out vehicles, sandbag bunkers, and barbed wire barriers.

As she neared the end of the hall, footsteps rang off the tile.

Lucy stopped, her mouth so dry she couldn't swallow. She moved over to the wall and hunched over. "Help." She called out in a soft voice. "Anybody? Please!"

A soldier ran around the corner, his pistol drawn. He was of average height and thin, with blond hair. He aimed his gun at Lucy and eyed her suspiciously.

"Who are you?" He asked in English, his voice thick with a Russian accent.

"They killed them." Lucy pointed down the hall. She let her voice lower to a whisper and repeated, "They killed them."

"Who killed who?" The soldier moved cautiously closer.

Lucy cradled her stomach, hiding the baton along her side. "They got inside. How? How did the monsters get inside?"

The soldier's eyes widened in terror. "They've breached the base? How many? What kind? Where?"

Lucy let her head sag forward like she was about to fall over.

The soldier turned to look back in the direction he'd come from.

Lucy pounced. She raised the metal baton over her head and gripped it with both hands. She slammed it down on the soldier's back.

The soldier cried out in pain. He dropped his pistol and stumbled forward.

Lucy snatched the gun off the floor but still kept hold of the baton in her left hand. "Don't move!"

The soldier's blue eyes narrowed in confusion. "The monsters! We must go." He pointed to the end of the hall.

"I'm the only monster you need to worry about." Lucy aimed the gun at his chest. "Where is my daughter?"

He shrugged and winced.

"A little girl came in here yesterday." Lucy threateningly held the baton out a little higher than her waist. "Blonde. Small. She was with a boy."

"Children? I don't know."

Lucy raised the baton over her head.

The man held out his hand. "I don't know."

"Two children! A boy and a girl."

His mouth fell open. "Was the boy dark-skinned with blue eyes?"

Lucy didn't know the color of Jacob's eyes and didn't care. "Yes. Where are they?"

"If it is that boy, they would have taken him to the Den." The soldier lowered his arm.

"The Den? What are you talking about?" Lucy stiffened. "Put your hands over your head."

The soldier raised his left arm, but his right arm hung limp at his side. "I can't. I think you dislocated my shoulder."

"Where is this Den?"

"It's another building. Outside. It's in the center of the compound."

Lucy aimed the gun at his face. "They took my daughter. She means more to me than my life, so she certainly means more to me than you do. You try anything, and I will kill you. Understood?"

The soldier nodded.

"There was another woman with me. She was injured. Do you have an infirmary?"

His brow knit together.

"A hospital. She was hurt."

He nodded. "Next door."

Lucy ground her teeth. She didn't know how badly Sadie was hurt but couldn't chance trying to get her before getting Bri. "You're going to take me to the Den. Start walking." When he turned, Lucy pressed the baton against his back and nudged him forward.

They traveled down one hallway to another with more closed doors on each side. The building was quiet except for the sound of their steps. He took a sharp right, and they reached the glass exit doors.

The soldier stopped. "They won't let you go. You don't know what you're doing. Even if you could escape, there's no place left to go. Everything is gone."

"Let me worry about that. Do what I say, and you live. Don't, and I'll get a soldier who listens. NOW MOVE!"

The soldier opened the door, and they both walked out. The sun was about an hour away from setting, and the shadows were getting long.

Someone shouted, and soldiers ran from all directions.

"Back off!" Lucy yelled. "All I want is my daughter, and then I'm out of here."

A crowd gathered around them. It quickly grew until it must have numbered nearly a hundred. They were mostly Chinese and Russian, but also at least twenty Americans. Men and women dressed in combat fatigues. All appeared to have seen more than their fair share of fighting. They were gaunt with dark circles beneath their eyes and stared at her with haunted expressions.

Lucy prodded her hostage forward, and he walked toward a plain white, one-story building.

The crowd moved along with them, keeping their distance. All sorts of weapons were aimed at her—rifles, pistols, and machine guns.

Lucy stepped closer to her hostage, pressing the gun against his back. "If you come any closer, he dies!"

The left side of the crowd parted, letting two men and a woman march through. These three were all Chinese. The man in the center was short, with thinning hair. His uniform was crisp and brimming with shiny medals. The man on his left towered over the shorter man. His neck was thick, and from his bulging biceps, he must do steroids. The woman walked two steps behind the men. She had delicate features but something about the sharpness of the angles in her face set Lucy on edge.

The hostage stopped.

Lucy did, too. "It looks like you're the man in charge. You must be, Tianzi. Listen, I don't want any trouble. I just want my daughter."

Tianzi smiled and nodded slightly. "Of course. Those feelings are understandable. But I cannot let you take the boy."

"Keep the boy," Lucy said without a pang of guilt. "I only want my little girl. Let me take her, and we'll leave."

"Your answer raises many questions in my mind, Lucy Green. Ones we will discuss shortly."

"Sorry, but I don't have time to talk."

Tianzi nodded.

The woman next to Tianzi drew her pistol and shot Lucy's hostage in the head.

Tianzi smiled. "On the contrary. You have all the time that I am willing to give you."

6

THE MUD SUCKER

Cain Haight

I follow Angel, Bob, and H down a long hallway. Angel is wearing one of those puck lights clipped to her uniform. The further we go, what's wrong with this situation keeps making my brain itch.

"I'm confused about something, H," I whisper, knowing the others can probably hear me, too. Aren't you three like the commanders of this outfit? Why aren't you delegating? It makes as much sense as the original Star Trek when the entire senior staff goes to explore the hostile planet."

"That's not my call." H grumbles.

"We're not an army," Angel says. "Besides H, we have less than a dozen soldiers, and all of them are recovering from wounds, physical and mental, that preclude me from sending them back into a potential combat situation. Bureaucrats are replaceable. People with fighting experience are scarce."

"And this isn't a combat mission," Bob adds.

We reach a loading dock, and Angel stops. There are three

closed bays where 18-wheelers can back in to unload. All three sit empty except for half a dozen carts with long poles attached.

"Exactly," Angel says. "Cain and I will recon while Bob and H go on a snatch-and-grab."

"What are they snatching and grabbing?" I ask, miffed that my goal is being tacked onto another plan.

"I have over a hundred people to feed," Angel says. "Anytime we go out, it turns into a supply run."

I nod. What else can I do? They've got kids and elderly to feed. That I get. I point at the carts. "Is that what the redneck rickshaws are for?"

"Grab a cart. I'm taking the Red Wagon." H smiles. "She's got mountain bike tires."

"The Blue Bomber is mine," Bob says, dropping off the dock and onto the tar. I built her for speed, and she's quiet as a mouse."

"What is it with boys and their toys?" Angel rolls her eyes as she grabs the chain for the door. "The rules are simple out there, Cain. Follow my lead and keep your mouth shut. We're following my combat rules—you break an order and risk the lives of my men, and I put you down. Understood?"

The light she's holding shows Angel's expression. There isn't a hint of bluffing, and she's not saying it as a boast to act tough. There's a coldness there that makes my stomach tighten. Even though she just promised to kill me if I step out of line, and I believe she will, I feel bad for her.

I give a flippant salute and nod.

"Cain, grab a cart, too. We'll leave ours when we split up so H and Bob can fill them."

I drop down and walk over to the poorly camouflaged cart that's more brown than green. "I'll take the mud sucker." I can't help but crack a smile. "My daughter, Bri, calls everyone she's mad at a mud sucker. And right now, I hate this cart because I know if I take it, I'm going to fill it up. And that means I'm coming back here instead of getting my little girl."

"Recon first." H lays a big hand on my shoulder. "Then we'll figure something out about getting your girl."

As Angel pulls on the chain to raise the door, I notice that Bob doesn't say anything and doesn't look at me. I get why. He's an honest guy. He knows what I'm up against and doesn't think I have a chance of getting Bri back.

I intend to prove him wrong.

7

YOU WANT TO DIE?

Mercy Yoder

Mercy Yoder stirred in the back of the creaking wagon, her eyes still shut as she fought to hold onto the fading fragments of her dream. It hadn't been a nightmare, but it had left a lingering unease in her mind. She strained to recall the details, knowing something important was hidden within the hazy images. But like trying to catch a butterfly with her bare hands, the dream slipped through her fingers and vanished.

A gentle breeze carried the warm, floral scent of fresh wild roses across her face. She closed her eyes and inhaled deeply, savoring the sweet, intoxicating fragrance that enveloped her. The wagon shuddered and bounced along the uneven trail, stirring up dust. Where was she being taken?

A flood of memories rushed back, overwhelming Mercy. She could almost feel the rumble of the motorcycle beneath her as she rode on the back of Sadie's bike, with Lucy leading the way on another. A pack of vicious bone rats ambushed them. A sharp bone spike pierced Lucy's engine, causing black smoke to billow out and the engine to sputter and die. Sadie stopped as well. Panic set in as they realized there was no way one motorcycle could safely carry all three women. Mercy knew who had to go on—Lucy had a better chance of rescuing the children, and if Lucy died, Mercy couldn't bear to think of the horrors that would await the woman who so openly rejected the Lord's salvation. Without hesitation, Mercy jumped from the bike and sprinted off the road, luring the monsters away from her friends. Terrified, she ran toward a chain-linked fence, hoping it would protect her from the beasts quickly gaining on her. But she was too slow, and they caught her.

The cart hit a large bump, and Mercy's body rocked violently, but she forced herself to remain still and continue unraveling the events that had led her to this moment. The wolves' snarls echoed in her ears. Their hot breaths tickled the back of her neck as they circled her. She knelt on the rough ground. She clasped her hands tightly as she prayed and waited for the inevitable attack.

She should be dead.

Was she?

Mercy opened one eye, the bright sunlight forcing her to squint. She found herself in the back of a wagon, traveling across a vast open field. On either side of her sat several large canvas sacks, brimming with an unknown cargo. The sun was at its peak in the sky, casting a warm golden glow over the emerald-green grass stretching before them. The blades of grass swayed gently in the breeze, creating a mesmerizing dance of light and shadow. Mercy couldn't help but be captivated by the beauty of it all.

Maybe this is Heaven?

She glanced to her left.

A massive, bone-white wolf trotted alongside the wagon, its powerful muscles rippling beneath its thick fur. Its head was bigger than a horse's, and it turned to look at Mercy with black eyes that reflected the sun. She couldn't believe what she saw—this couldn't be real. She squeezed her eyes shut, trying to will away the terrifying creature. But when she opened them again, it was still there, keeping pace with the wagon. The sound of its heavy paws hitting the ground echoed in her ears. This wasn't Heaven or a dream—it was a nightmare that came to life before her very eyes. Mercy tried to control her breathing, but panic threatened to overwhelm her.

Calm down and think!

Her thoughts scattered like leaves in a storm as she tried to focus. She moved her arms and legs. She wasn't bound in any way, but a bone wolf followed next to the wagon. She may have been free, but there was nowhere she could go. Still, maybe there was a river nearby. If there was, she could make a run for it.

"Don't even think about it."

The woman's voice made Mercy jump.

"You can stop pretending you're asleep. I know you're awake."

Mercy opened her eyes and sat up. As she glanced around, she wondered if she was having a nightmare. What she saw couldn't be real. It just couldn't be. The old farm wagon Mercy rode in wasn't pulled by horses—two giant bone wolves were yoked together and attached to the wagon. A third bone wolf trotted on her left and slightly behind. And on Mercy's right ambled a massive bone white grizzly bear.

Sitting on its back was a woman. She wore all black and had ashen skin. She stared at Mercy with blue eyes. A scar ran from her jaw, parallel to her nose, through her eyebrow, and along the right side of her head, which was shaved bald. The left side of her hair was streaked black and grey and hung around her shoulders. She searched Mercy's eyes, saying nothing as the wagon continued on its way.

"Hello," was all Mercy could think to say.

The woman laughed. It was a rapid sound like a red-beaked woodpecker at dawn.

The great bear turned its head to gaze up at the woman laughing on its back.

The woman leaned forward, patted its thick neck, and stared at Mercy. "Your friends left you to die."

Mercy glanced around as if she could still see Lucy and Sadie riding off. But that was last night, and hopefully, they were long gone. "Did they get away?" She asked hopefully.

The woman's black eyebrows pulled together. "You care?"

"They're my friends."

"They left you to die."

Mercy's lips pressed together. "I don't mean any disrespect, but that's not correct. I chose to stay. One of the motorcycles broke down, and all three of us couldn't ride on one."

"I saw. Why you get off?"

"I didn't want Lucy to die."

The woman scowled. "So *you* want to die?"

"No. I'd like to live, please." The wagon jostled over a bump, and she grabbed the side to avoid falling.

The woman laughed so hard that all the animals turned to stare at her. Although her voice was deep for a woman, her laugh was light and high. "You so polite about it."

"Thank you... What is your name?"

The woman's eyes hardened. "I don't have one anymore."

"Oh," Mercy swallowed, puzzled how to respond. "Well, then. I thank you, miss."

"You have name. What is it?"

"Mercy Yoder."

"Mercy." The woman repeated her name and bit her lip. "You should have stayed on motorcycle, Mercy Yoder."

The woman's words were like a punch in her gut, and the muscles in her stomach tightened. Pushing her fears aside, Mercy lifted her chin, "Are you going to kill me?"

"No, Mercy. I not kill you." The woman's blue eyes locked with Mercy's. "If me choose, I let you go. You would die soon out here. You make stupid choices."

Mercy exhaled. She sat there blinking in disbelief. This woman wasn't going to kill her. "Thank you, miss." Mercy inclined her head and grabbed the side of the wagon. "I'll let myself out."

"No. Not up to me. Choice not mine. He chooses if you live or die."

Mercy swallowed. The hope she had faded. "Who decides if I die?"

"Malik. I bring you to him."

8

BLACKIE

Cain Haight

In under five minutes, sweat is plastering my shirt to my back and dripping down my face. The four of us are jogging down the street, winding our way around torched or abandoned cars and piles of clothes.

It takes me a minute to figure out what the deal is with the clothes. There aren't any bodies, so I can't understand why there would be so many. Then I notice the other items in the piles. Glasses, earrings, and other jewelry. Then I see the hair. Every pile was a person. The monsters got the bones.

I've seen a lot of death, but this is something different. The piles are everywhere. I try to stop picturing the victims, but I can't. I see one pile in a wheelchair, and then three sets of kids' clothes, and it's all I can do not to start bawling.

My cart bangs off some junk in the street.

Angel glares back like she's about to draw and shoot me.

H slows down and moves beside me. "Stay frosty." He whispers and speeds back up to his spot in the convoy.

Stay frosty.

Soldiers have probably said something like that to each other since my namesake picked up that rock. But this was a war on a level I never imagined.

Angel turns and heads to a four-story building. Except for one store on the first floor, the building has been ransacked. Thick, roll-down security doors and barred gates had prevented it from being destroyed.

Bob parks his cart and rushes over to the door. He slides off his backpack and removes a small bag in a fluid motion. After selecting two metal tools, he crouches and works on the lock.

Despite still wanting to throw up, I crack a smile, wink at H, and whisper, "Go figure. A cop who can pick locks."

H grins back.

Angel snaps her fingers. She points at H and Bob and then at the ground. Then she taps her chest, points at me, and down the street. I'm still miffed that H and Bob will collect supplies while Angel and I go on recon. I would have preferred four sets of eyes, but since we're finally moving toward Bri, I start jogging.

Angel takes point, and I follow close. She's fast, quiet, and sticks to the shadows. There's something almost cat-like about her motions.

At the thought of a cat, my gaze starts darting around. Sure enough, I catch a glance of that black cat following us. I don't know how it got out of the building without us seeing it. Why didn't it stay in the shelter where all the kids showered it with attention? They named her Blackie. It lacks originality, but it fits.

The cat is watching me as it darts along to my right. I try not to look at it because I don't want to let Angel know it followed us. The cat suddenly rushes ahead. It must have caught sight of something to eat because it's moving like a rocket. It dashes under a truck, races along the curb, disappears beneath a car, and appears a moment later triumphantly holding a rat in her jaws.

My smile is short-lived.

The cat's head jerks toward the building behind her, and the rat drops from her mouth. Blackie races by me, staring me right in the face as she goes. I swear it's trying to warn me about whatever is in that building. She doesn't stick around and disappears into the shadows.

I click my tongue and dart for the cover of a burned-out doorway.

Angel ducks low and hides behind a pickup.

My shotgun is out, and I force myself to breathe easily and listen. Something is in the building on the right. I glance out. It was a corner grocery store. I stare at Angel, but her focus is on the store, too.

A Chinese soldier appears carrying a duffle bag. He hurries around the corner to the side street and I lose sight of him. Two more similar-looking men hurry out of the store and go after him. A minute later, a fourth Chinese soldier appears, but he stops in the middle of the sidewalk. He, too, is holding a duffle bag, but he's nervously scanning the street. He glances the way the others went, drops the bag and starts running straight in my direction.

I press my back against the wall.

The soldier's boots thud off the concrete as he races down the sidewalk. Each step brings him closer to me. I have no clue why he's running, but this could be my big chance to gain intel. This guy would have all the information that I'm looking for. I crouch, ready to spring up and grab him.

He slides to a stop, just out of my reach. He's peering around, looking at which way to go.

I lunge forward, grab his shirt, and yank him behind the corner where I'm hiding.

His eyes go wide, and his mouth drops open.

I point my shotgun barrel at his face.

He looks at me and breaks into a grin. "Thank you!"

My eyebrows press together. Why is it that I always end up with the crazy ones?

9

HOW BAD COULD IT BE?

Evan Green

Evan was seated in his father's 1961 Chevy C10, the back of the truck packed to the brim with all his camping gear and spare gas. Lucy and the others had taken the river, but he'd never been a fan of water-based activities. His tall frame made canoes feel like a tight squeeze, and he'd had a couple of embarrassing tipping incidents. So, he'd opted for the more straightforward approach, a direct highway route into Lieper's Forge.

Lucy had a significant head start on him, and if he were to have any chance of catching up to her, he'd have to go overland.

He put the transmission into gear and pulled out of the garage. Everyone in town was getting ready for the monsters, so no one paid him much attention. He preferred that. His heart was pounding in his chest, and it was hard to breathe. If he stopped to talk to someone, he might change his mind and chicken out.

Everywhere he looked, men, women, and even the kids were busy following Goose's instructions and setting up a perimeter defense of the town's center. In a way, he felt guilty for not helping them, but the sense of guilt he felt for letting his wife head off to face the danger lurking outside the town was worse. Besides, everyone in Ridgecrest was helping with that task. Lucy only had two women and Cain with her. She needed him.

Evan glanced at his reflection, rolling its eyes in the rearview mirror, and flipped the lever up. He was lying to himself, and he knew it. Lucy didn't need him. She never had and probably never would. The worst part was, he could understand why—he was inept.

He grew up wanting to be cool and brave. He towered over his peers, but instead of looking up to him, they called him Barney behind his back. The nickname fit him. He was like Barney Fife, the bumbling deputy. Uncoordinated and scared of his shadow, who knows how he would have turned out without his father?

Evan slowed down at the stop sign at the end of Main Street and put his blinker on. Muttering how stupid he was for obeying traffic laws when there wasn't another car on the road during the apocalypse, he hit the gas and cut the wheel.

The speedometer slowly ticked up as he headed for the highway. Enough was enough. He'd be Barney no more. He was a grown man, and this was his time to turn his life around. He wouldn't let the past hold him back. Today was the first day of his future. Today, he was strong and confident, and nothing would phase him.

Something thumped on the roof of the cab.

Evan glanced at the ceiling, wondering if a large black walnut had fallen off a tree.

A small shadow appeared on the windshield.

Evan slowed and gasped as a squirrel slid down the glass onto the hood.

The little creature chittered and shook like a dog drying

itself off. It raised a thin tail that didn't look like a squirrel's at all and turned around. It stared at Evan with huge black eyes.

Evan smiled.

The creature opened its mouth and revealed dozens of pointed teeth.

Evan shrieked and mashed the gas pedal to the floor.

The truck skidded sideways. The bone rat bashed into the windshield, rolled up the glass, and disappeared. The front end shook as the truck crossed off the tar. Evan swerved back onto the road. He gripped the steering wheel tighter, trying to stop his shaking hands. He'd heard about the bone rats but hadn't ever seen one. It was like a demon rat with teeth!

He grinned. That was his first monster encounter. Besides screaming, he'd dealt with the problem relatively quickly. Who knows, maybe the rest of the way out of town would be clear.

Something pierced the metal on the cab's roof, sounding like nails on a chalkboard. A quarter-sized hole appeared, and sunlight streamed in.

Evan shrieked.

The bone rat must be holding on to the top of the roof. Again and again, it thrust its spiked tail through the metal.

Evan slammed on the brakes.

The rat sailed off the truck and into the road.

Evan mashed the gas pedal to the floor and aimed at the monster. The truck shuddered slightly as the tires squashed the creature. He pulled down the rearview mirror and exhaled when he saw the flattened beast.

He glanced at the ceiling and the half-dozen holes. His father was going to be furious. He loved the truck. He even had a model of it on his desk at town hall.

Turning onto the on-ramp for the highway, Evan relaxed as the wind cooled his face. That was twice now that he'd defeated a monster. Even though it was only one, he'd still count it as two victories. He glanced down at the radio. There was no reason to turn it on. No stations were left to transmit, but he would have loved to hear some rock and roll.

The truck reached the crest of the ramp, and Evan's eyes widened. Dozens of bone rats were crossing the highway. Startled, they stopped and turned toward him.

Cranking up his window as fast as he could, Evan jammed the gas down so hard he hurt his ankle. The truck's engine roared, and the chassis rocked as he crushed fleeing bone rats beneath his tires. That horrible noise was drowned out by shrieking metal and thumps.

A bone-white spike shattered the back window and stuck into the dashboard. A hole appeared in the windshield, quickly followed by four more. A spike tore through the passenger door and struck his seatbelt holder. The driver's side window shattered.

Evan ducked low and held his arms rigid as he pressed his foot to the floor. The crunching and breaking and thumping trailed off. He glanced up, but the rearview mirror was so spiderwebbed he couldn't see. He looked toward the side mirrors, but the driver's mirror was broken, and the passenger one was gone. Spikes peppered the hood, but the truck was still running, and miraculously, Evan hadn't been hit.

He chuckled as he gave himself a once-over. Somehow, through a hail of spikes, he escaped unscathed. His chuckle built into a full-blown laugh.

"Woo! Yeah!" Evan cheered and raised his fist out the broken window.

Brushing bits of broken glass from the door, the dash, and his lap, he blinked back tears as the wind smacked him in the face. It felt wonderful to be alive.

He could do this. He could make it to Lieper's Forge, find Lucy, and bring her home. Things were terrible out here but if he kept his nerve and wits about him, how bad could it be?

10

IS IT TRUE?

Matt Browner

Matt Browner walked down the steps of the doctor's office and stopped next to Amos Yoder's wagon. The Amish man knelt on the grass beside the back wheel, silently praying while the church bell rang out its warning. People were flooding into town, and Matt needed to know as much as he could about what the heck was going on before getting the mayor.

"I'm sorry to interrupt, Amos. But I need to talk to you."

Amos glanced up, lowered his head, shut his eyes, and said, "In Jesus' name, Amen. I was praying for Lonnie and Camila."

Matt handed him a water bottle. "The doc doesn't know if either of them are going to make it." He stared at his shaking fingers and took a deep breath, trying to steady his nerves. "You've got to tell me what's going on, Amos. You owe me that."

Amos stood up and straightened his shoulders. "I do. For starters, my name isn't Amos Yoder. It's Shawn Morgan. I'm a deserter from the Army. I was in the Core of Engineers and worked on a series of tunnels and bunkers that run from Fort

Burgess to here. That's where I was hiding Jesse Pickett and Ani."

"Is she the woman that Cain found? The one out at the Dixon place?"

"Yes. She's Jacob's mother."

Matt turned his head and glared at the sky. He was mad enough to spit. "I thought he was your grandson. You lied about that, too?"

"I've lied about a lot of things, but no more. I'm sorry. Jacob showed up on my porch one night. I came into town to find out who he was. That's when we learned the Dark happened."

"And you said nothing?"

"I prayed about it. Jacob was so frightened, and everyone in town was terrified. I didn't know how people would react, so I decided to wait and figure it out."

"What about Jesse? Why didn't you tell us about him?"

"I found Jesse washed up on the creek. Whatever he'd seen in Lieper's Forge snapped his mind. He'd suffered a breakdown and was terrified. He begged me not to tell his father.

"Jesse could have told us what happened to the others."

Amos shook his head. "Jesse was incoherent. He didn't say anything that made sense for months besides begging to be left alone to die."

"Where is the bunker? Are there more? Do you have supplies? Can we go there?"

Amos held up his hand. "My bunker has been breached. The monsters tunneled in. We got out just in time. On the way here, we ran into Paul Longhorn's sons and sent them out to warn the other families."

"The border has fallen." Matt ran his hand along the back of his neck. "People are coming in from all around saying the same thing. We're setting up the barricades."

"Barricades aren't going to stop these monsters. Ani said an army was on its way."

"We don't have another choice. We need to trust Goose's plan."

"We need to trust God," Amos said.

"I am, Amos. Believe me, I am. You were in all the meetings, too. You didn't give any objections then."

Amos nodded. "I didn't realize what we were dealing with. I hadn't seen the monsters up close. We can't hold off an army of them."

"We got no choice but to try!" Matt shouted, his frustration getting the better of him.

A horn blared, and an old flatbed rolled into view. Mayor Green stood in the back with a blowhorn. "I need everyone to listen. Pay attention, people, and we'll get through this. We need everyone to head to the community center. We're all going to gather there."

Matt grabbed Amos by the arm and started walking. "Come with me."

"Everyone settle down!" Martin's voice boomed across the square. "Head over to the community center, and I'll answer your questions. I need—" The blowhorn snapped off, and Martin pointed at Matt. "Where the heck have you been?"

"I've kinda had my hands full, Martin."

"Look around, Sheriff!" Martin banged on the truck's roof three times, and it lurched to a stop. "Who knows how long we have before those creatures get here? We're getting reports from all over." Martin glared at Amos as he climbed down from the truck. "And I'm hearing things about you, Amos, that I simply can't believe. My son said you showed up with that woman Cain claimed to have found, as well as Jesse Pickett. Is there any truth to either of those stories?"

"Yes, Mayor. There is." Amos said. "I haven't been entirely truthful with you."

Martin's mouth moved, but no words came out. His eyes narrowed, and he looked about ready to pop out of his head.

"Not entirely truthful? Are you serious? You're a bald-faced liar, Amos Yoder."

Amos cleared his throat. "I am. But if you give me a minute—"

"We don't have a minute." Martin snapped. "We need to get everyone heading to the community center. Matt, I need you to select every able man, woman, and child over twelve to take positions at the barricades."

The roar of a motorcycle racing down the street made people step aside, and everyone stopped to look. Billy Pickett kept the throttle pinned back until he caught sight of the mayor and skidded to a stop. He leaped off the bike, letting it crash onto the grass, and marched over.

"Is it true? Is it?" Billy headed straight at Amos.

Martin stepped in front of him, cutting him off. "Hold on there, Billy."

Billy's eyes were wild, and he got into Martin's face. "Shut up, Mayor. We heard Jesse is here and Amos kept him hid. It's my kin we're talking about." Billy shoved Martin aside and reached for his gun.

Matt punched Billy in the jaw.

Billy's head rocked to the side, and he staggered a step to the left.

Matt grabbed Billy's pistol out of the holster and stepped back, aiming the weapon at Billy's chest. "You need to calm down, Billy."

Billy wiped the back of his mouth with his hand, leaving a long red streak on his skin. "You know what, Sheriff? I reckon I do." He spit. "My uncle Frank is on the way, and he's bringing everyone with him. When he gets here, he's gonna burn this town to the ground."

11

STEP ASIDE, CAIN

Cain Haight

"Please, help me." The soldier pleads and steps forward.

I grab him by the shirt, spin him around, and push him into the destroyed store. It had been some salon or nail place but was gutted by fire. I steer the soldier to the back and behind the counter. "Hide. Make a sound, and you're dead."

He nods rapidly and squats down against the wall, curling his arms around his legs.

I keep my shotgun aimed at him while I wait. There's a hole beneath where the cash register used to sit, and it gives me a good view while I can stay hidden.

Footsteps sound on the sidewalk outside. A lone soldier comes into view. He shines a light around the store and says something in Chinese. I don't have to speak the language to guess he's swearing.

I'm trying to determine what he's got for a weapon, but he isn't holding any. He doesn't even have a holster.

As my questions continue to grow, he runs back the way he came.

I turn my attention back to my new prisoner. I hold my finger against my mouth, but from the grin on the man's gaunt face, he's not going to try anything. It looks like he's as happy as a kid on his birthday that he got away from those guys and was caught by me.

Outside, I hear an engine rumble to life. Soon, it fades into the distance.

Keeping my shotgun trained on my captive, I motion for him to stand and face the wall. I pat him down. Besides a package of peanut butter cookies in the bottom pocket of his cargo pants, he has nothing on him.

"My name is Bolin Qiáo. I surrender."

"You're from Fort Burgess?"

"Yes. But I am not an American soldier."

"I get that from your uniform. You're Chinese?"

"Yes. But I'm not a soldier. I'm a technician. Please help me. I can't go back there."

"I'm not going to hurt you. But you are going to help me."

The sound of boots crunching debris makes me spin, my shotgun sweeping the room.

Angel sneaks inside, her pistol drawn and aimed at Bolin. She glares at me with her lips drawn back so far her teeth gleam white.

"Easy Commander." I lower my shotgun. "All of the recon we need just fell in our lap."

Angel stares at me like I'm the stupidest man on the planet. "We can't stay here, and he can't come with us. Turn around." She orders Bolin.

From the cold steel in her eyes and the determined set of her jaw, I realize that she plans on shooting him in the back of the head. I move between her and Bolin.

"Take it down a notch. He surrendered."

"He's the enemy, and we can't bring him back."

"I'm not the enemy," Bolin begs. "Please. I mean no one harm."

"If they find out we exist, they will wipe us out," Angel says.

"If we take Bolin with us, they won't find out."

"I can't risk that. Step aside, Cain."

"Please don't," Bolin begs.

The scent of ammonia fills the room, and something drips onto the floor.

"You made him wet himself." I scowl. "If you think he's that much of a threat, blindfold him and lock him up when we get back."

"I surrender. Please don't shoot me."

Angel shakes her head and keeps her pistol pointed at Bolin. "This is on you, Cain. You had to go get a prisoner."

"I didn't go get him. He ran into me. I'd call it an answer to prayer. Now, I'm no murderer, and I'm not going to stand by when someone else gets killed. So put down your pistol. I'm not asking." I glance at my shotgun, which is aimed at Angel's chest.

Angel doesn't move.

Bolin slowly turns around. His hands shake, and tears roll down his thin cheeks. The front of his pants is wet. His mouth moves, but no sound comes out. He's not looking at me. He's staring at Angel.

Angel blinks.

"Please," Bolin sobs.

Angel holsters her gun, and she stares at me with pure venom in her eyes. "Tie his hands behind his back. If he gets away, I'm killing you, Cain."

12

ASK ME A QUESTION

Lucy Green

Lucy sat in the large empty room bound securely to a heavy metal chair bolted to the floor. The twenty-by-twenty room had no windows, and the twelve-foot ceiling was nearly invisible in the light cast by the four oil lamps. There was only one door which she faced. The walls were white, besides the stains left by the soot of the lamps, which cast a red and yellow glow throughout the room. The cement floor was painted white except for the large dark stain beneath her feet.

Like a prisoner in an electric chair, she had been strapped down with leather bindings. Her hands were bound to the arms of the chair, a strap cinched around her chest, and each ankle was held firm against the legs.

Maybe she deserved to die. She'd gotten that soldier killed. She hadn't pulled the trigger, but he wouldn't have been in that situation if it hadn't been for her.

Lucy hung her head. It seemed all she did was bring misery into people's lives. She was the opposite of Midas. He turned everything to gold as she changed it to ash. Look what she'd done to Cain. Did he drown hating her? Probably. She couldn't blame him. She hated herself, too. And what about her mother? Where had they taken Sadie? She was hurt, but... Lucy closed her eyes and tried to drive the image of the last time she looked at her mother out of her mind. Sadie had stared at Lucy in disgust. The disappointment in her daughter was etched across her mother's face.

And what about Mercy? She'd thrown her life away, and for what? A failed attempt to rescue the children. Did the stupid Amish woman or any of them expect that she planned on staying at the base once they got there?

That was until she saw what the base was like. She'd thought Ridgecrest was a hell hole until she got here. Now, it seemed like paradise. But it was too late. There was no getting out of this.

The door across from her slowly swung open, and the creepy woman who'd shot Lucy's hostage backed into the room. The woman pulled a cart covered with a towel.

Lucy sat up straight. She'd seen every horror movie ever made, and surprisingly, the list of possible items on the cart was limited.

The door closed behind the woman with a loud click.

"We are jumping the gun here," Lucy said. "I don't know if you've done this before, but this is the part where you ask me questions. Let me tell you, I'll answer them all. You don't need anything on that cart. You ask, and I'll answer."

The woman stopped the cart next to Lucy and smiled down at her. "Yes. Yes, you will." She lifted the towel, revealing a car battery and wires attached to a rod with a leather grip. Next to them sat a bottle of water. She folded the towel and carefully placed it in the corner of the cart.

"My name is Lucy Green. I'm the daughter-in-law of the

Mayor of Ridgecrest. That's the town up on the plateau. What do you want to know?"

The woman grinned, picked up the rod, and pressed it against Lucy's side.

Lucy screamed and thrashed against her bonds. "Ask me a question!"

The woman pressed the wires against Lucy's legs.

Over and over, Lucy would scream, and the woman would wait and then shock her again. Lucy begged and pleaded, but the woman said nothing.

Losing count of how many times she'd been abused, Lucy sat there shaking, bathed in sweat, with tears rolling down her cheeks. Her throat was raw from screaming.

The door opened again.

Tianzi, the giant who'd been with him earlier, and Fen entered the room. Fen moved to stand several feet away while Tianzi approached, the giant walking two steps behind him.

Lucy took a shaky breath. "Why aren't you asking me anything?"

"Because you were not ready for the questions, my dear." Tianzi snapped his fingers.

The woman picked the water bottle off the cart and opened it. She carried it over to Lucy.

Lucy's mouth was so dry she'd kill for a drink. "Thank you."

The woman poured the water over Lucy's head.

Lucy didn't care. She raised her mouth and licked at the water like a dog—until she tasted it. She spit. It was salt water.

Tianzi snapped, and the woman lifted the rod attached to the battery.

Lucy's eyes widened in fear. The shocks had grown steadily more painful. Now that she was covered in salt water which conducted electricity, who knew how bad the next shock would be? "Ask me what you want to know!" Lucy screamed and pulled vainly against her bonds. "Just ask!"

Tianzi smiled. "Perhaps you are ready. I want to know about the boy's mother. Tell me about her."

"Jacob's mother? I don't know her. She's Mercy Yoder's sister. An Amish girl."

"That's a lie." Tianzi shook his head.

"I'm not lying. Ask Fen." Lucy gazed pleadingly at Fen, standing at attention in the corner.

"Look at me, Lucy," Tianzi said. "I'm referring to the woman who came to Ridgecrest before Fen and Nicholi arrived."

"That one? She's Jacob's mother? I don't know anything about her either. My husband claimed he found her. I didn't believe him."

"You didn't believe your husband?"

"He's my ex. And he was drunk."

"And what is his name?"

"Cain Haight."

Tianzi snapped his fingers.

The woman stuck the rod against Lucy's ribs.

Electricity crackled. Lucy shrieked.

"What is his real name?" Tianzi said.

Fen stepped forward. "She's telling the truth. There was a man named Cain Haight in Ridgecrest. He was a soldier."

"Really?" Tianzi cocked an eyebrow. "I thought she was making that name up."

"Even dead, he's getting back at me," Lucy muttered.

"Repeat that," Tianzi said.

"He's dead. Cain died on the way here. Drowned."

Lucy continued to explain everything that happened on the way there but left off the part about D and his gang.

Tianzi listened attentively but let her talk. He didn't ask any questions until she reached the part about Mercy getting off the motorcycle.

"You expect me to believe that this woman who came all the

way to rescue the boy simply chose to value your life over hers?"

Lucy shook her head. "I'm telling the truth. She's one of the nutty Christian types. She thinks I'm heading to hell and probably has some savior complex. She's a full-on believer if you know what I mean."

"What happened to her?"

"What do you think? She took off running without a gun, and a pack of wolves chased her. The only way she's breathing is if that God of hers granted her a miracle."

"I don't believe in miracles," Tianzi said. "And neither should you. Now, I have no further use of you."

"What?" Lucy gasped. So far, Tianzi hadn't bluffed about anything. And if he didn't need her, that could only mean he would get rid of her. "You're a man, right? If I were in your shoes, I could think of many uses for me. I clean up nice. If you let me live, I'll put the biggest smile on your face that you've ever had."

The woman's face twisted in disgust. She raised the rod like she was about to smash it over Lucy's head.

"Tianzi, forgive my interruption." Fen bowed low and waited.

"What is it?"

"I am not telling you anything you do not already know, but the girl often spoke of her mother and grandmother on the trip. Until you get what you desire from her, they could be of use to control the girl."

Tianzi pressed his lips together as he studied Lucy. "You raised a feral beast. Your little brat bit a guard and almost blinded another."

Lucy tucked her chin to her chest to hide her smile. "I'm sorry. I can talk to her. She'll listen to me. She'll listen to her momma."

Tianzi took the rod out of the woman's hands. He stuck it under Lucy's chin, the wires inches from her skin. He forced Lucy's head up, and she stared into his black eyes. "Perhaps Fen is correct, and it would be better if I kept you for a while." He grinned. "After all, who doesn't like to smile?"

13

APEX SERVICE

Evan Green

Evan barreled down the highway, but without the windshield, the wind and bugs pelted him in the face. And that wasn't the worst part—a bone spike had torn off the visor, and the sun blinded him. He thought about pulling over and getting his sunglasses out of one of the bags in the back. But that would mean he'd have to get out of the truck, and he wasn't keen on that idea at all.

The highway slowly curled around, and Evan's mouth dropped open. The road, which he had expected to be clear, was now a sea of vehicles all heading toward Ridgecrest. The usually empty breakdown lane and the grass strip on either side were now occupied by cars.

Why did they stop? Where did they go?

Even from this distance, he could see that most vehicles had open doors or were heavily damaged. An exit sign pointed to his right. He braked hard and cut the wheel. There was no getting past that traffic jam. He'd have to take the back roads.

Slowing down, he blinked rapidly and wiped his eyes with his hand.

Piles of clothes and shoes sat along the road and in the grass. At first, he thought a Goodwill truck must have dumped its load, but there were dozens and dozens of outfits lying on the ground.

He slowed even more and leaned out the broken window. A pair of man's boots lay behind a pair of blue jeans and a red t-shirt. The jeans even had a belt. A blue and white cap was in front of that with a wig stuck to it.

Evan stopped and stared.

A pair of glasses and a set of dentures sat in front of the cap. Pieces of dried leather clung...

Evan gagged and threw up.

That was no wig, and it wasn't leather—it was skin. That pile had been a person. He vomited again when he remembered how Lucy said she found Gunner Pickett. She said the monster had eaten all his bones, leaving behind a skin suit.

He mashed the gas pedal to the floor, and the engine revved high. Tears sprang to his eyes as he drove over the remains of the people whose cars had gotten stuck on the highway.

"Sorry. I'm sorry." Evan cried as his tires crunched and crushed over the open-air graveyard.

Soon, the piles of clothes ended, and the road became clear again. He rinsed out his mouth with the bottle of water. But a sickly-sweet scent clung to the truck. It made him gag, but there was nothing left to throw up.

A sign on the left announced White Pine RV Park. He could see many different RVs through the trees but wasn't about to pull in. His plan was not to stop until he reached Lieper's forge or found Lucy and the others.

Because he'd exited the highway, the river was now on his left. He caught glimpses of it now and again but didn't see any boats. Houses dotted either side of the road, but no sign of people living there. Some were boarded up, others had burned down, but none appeared occupied.

The truck lurched to the right and became harder to steer. He glanced back. The passenger side tire must have blown.

He swore. A flat was bad, and changing the rear tire would be a pain with all the gear in the back weighing it down. His eyes widened. He hadn't checked the spare. Did it have one? Did the spare have air?

Evan opened his mouth to swear again when he rounded a sharp turn, and a building on his left came into view—Apex Service.

"Sweet!" He slowed down. It was a service station. If he needed air, they were sure to have a tire pump.

The truck shuddered and pulled hard to the right.

Evan stopped. He reached for the door handle but didn't open it. He peered up and down the deserted road and licked his dry lips.

"Man up." He muttered and shoved the door open.

At least he knew how to fix a tire.

He dropped out of the truck, his boots sounding like a cannon going off in the quiet. He decided not to shut the door. Making his way around the front of the truck, he glared at the front tire. It, too, was going flat.

What had he hit?

Bending over, he ran his hand along the tread and noticed four nails sticking out of the rubber. He walked to the back of the truck, and several nails had punctured that tire, too.

On the side of the road, something moved.

He ducked down behind the truck. His breath caught in his throat.

Boots sounded on the tar. More than one person approached.

"Get your hands up and come out." A man yelled in a thick New York accent.

Evan eyed the closed passenger-side door. His pistol lay on the front seat in its holster. He hated the way it dug into his side when he drove so he'd taken it off. That was a bad idea.

"Move!" Another man ordered.

Evan raised his arms. His hands shook so hard he grimaced at how fearful he must look. Gritting his teeth, he flexed his fingers to stop them from trembling and marched around the truck.

Three men stood on the side of the road near the garage. They all held pistols, but their lecherous grins made his heart sink. They were in their mid-thirties. All were thin, had bushy, unkept beards, and one had only one arm.

"Where you headed?" New York asked.

"Lieper's Forge," Evan said, his voice surprisingly steady.

"Where you coming from?"

"Ridgecrest."

"Really," New York smiled at the others. "How are they doing up there?"

"Not so well now," Evan admitted. "The monsters are attacking. They crossed the border."

"Border? Did you guys make a wall or something to keep them out?"

"They've left us alone for a year. But now they're coming into town."

The one-armed man scowled at the others. "I told you that guy was telling the truth."

Evan raised an eyebrow. He wanted to ask who was telling the truth about what, but the growing knot in his stomach tightened his throat.

"Doesn't matter now if the monsters have moved on to that town. We'll have to wait until they're done with it" New York said to the men, before looking at Evan. "Is that why you left? Because the monsters came?"

"No. I'm looking for my wife. She left a few days ago with two women and a man."

The one-armed man looked like a dog as he bared his teeth. "They were in canoes, right? One of them was an Amish woman?"

Evan hesitated. "I, ah…"

"Your wife and her friends cost us a lot." New York eyed the truck. "Looks like you're gonna have to pay it back."

Evan's hands started shaking. He flexed his fingers, but it didn't work this time, and they started trembling even more. "I don't know what they did, but I don't mean you any harm. I'll split my supplies with you."

The one-armed man laughed. "The thing you've got to understand is that your friends killed some of our friends. How are you going to repay that?"

Evan lifted his chin. These men were going to kill him. He was sure of that. At least he died trying to right his cowardice, even if no one would ever know.

The one-armed man lifted his gun.

The wind blew across the right side of Evan's face. It was strong enough to fling the pollen into his eyes. He closed his right eye as he stared at the barrel of the gun pointed at his chest.

A car engine roared down the road toward them. A light blue 1962 Chevy Impala raced down the center line and swerved toward the three men.

It struck the men so hard and so fast it sounded like one large thump. The men's bodies sailed through the air and over the car, landing on the tar with sickening wet smacks.

The Impala skidded to a stop.

Evan stood there, shocked, unable to move. His would-be murderers lay on the road.

"Hurry!" A man in the Impala shouted as the car's reverse lights came on.

Evan lowered his arms, but his legs felt like his feet were stuck to the cement.

The door to the garage burst open.

"RUN!" The driver screamed as he shoved open the passenger door.

A gunshot rang out.

Evan sprinted to the car. He jumped in, and the tires spun before he could close the door.

More gunshots sounded behind them.

The fifty-something-year-old man driving swerved right. Momentum slammed the door into Evan's back. The man jerked the wheel to the left, and Evan bashed his head off the door frame.

"Did I kill them? I didn't mean to kill them. I thought they'd drop their guns and jump out of the way. Were they breathing?" The man spoke rapidly, brushing his thinning hair with a shaking hand. "I knew they were going kill you. They're no good. They came around my place and shot at me. That's why I was circling around to get to Ridgecrest. You're not heading to Lieper's Forge, are you? No need to do that. The whole city is gone."

"Calm down," Evan said, fighting back his own fear.

"Calm down? How? I've never raised my hand to anyone before, let alone killed three men. But they were going to shoot you. I'm sure of it. Maybe they're not dead. How can you be so calm? Are you a soldier? You must be. You're not even shaking. Me? I'm shaking like a cat after a rainstorm."

"A soldier?" Evan grinned. "No, I'm—ow!" He turned to face the man and winced as pain raced up his right side. He reached back and grimaced as he touched his sweat-soaked shirt.

"You all right?" The driver asked.

"Fine. I hit my back on the door getting in," Evan stared at his wet hand. His palm was covered in blood.

"You, you, you..." The driver stuttered. "You've been shot!"

14

HE KILLS ME

Cain Haight

I'm standing in the old break room with Angel, H, and Bob. We got back to the camp without incident. Angel still looks ready to shoot me. She's pacing the floor and muttering beneath her breath. Her arms are crossed, and she's gripping her sides so tightly that her knuckles turn white. I think it's to keep herself from exploding.

I'm leaning against the counter, waiting for her permission to talk to Bolin. We've got him tied up to a chair in the bathroom after letting him wash and giving him a change of pants. My foot is falling asleep, so I shift my weight.

Angel glares at me like I've awakened a sleeping dragon. Her arms thrust out wide, and she lets fly a tirade of Spanish. The veins on her neck stand out as she yells at me rapid-fire.

With all of the hand gestures and her tone, I'm sure she's not complimenting me. But it certainly makes it easier getting chewed out in a language I don't understand. I nod sympathetically and add a couple of shrugs in for good measure.

After a couple of minutes, Angel winds down. She wipes

her mouth with the back of her hand and fixes me with a stare. "I didn't know you speak Spanish."

"I don't, but—"

That was obviously the wrong thing to say.

Angel lunges at me, and it takes both Bob and H to hold her back. She almost gets me with a kick, so I move a little closer to the door.

"I didn't want to interrupt you," I say.

Angel straightens up. "Let me go." Her voice is tight but in control. "You have jeopardized the lives of every man, woman, and child here with your actions."

"Technically, so have you."

Bob and H are standing slightly behind Angel. They shake their heads. Bob makes a slashing motion in front of his throat, and H holds his index finger against his lips. They're the universal signs to shut up, but I don't.

"Every time you go out scavenging, you risk their lives because you could get caught or lead the soldiers back here. But it's a calculated risk. And no offense, ma'am, but the information Bolin has is valuable to you, too."

Angel's brown eyes smolder, but she lets me keep talking.

"If his army is out scavenging for supplies, too," I continue, "Something's gone south at the base. That means you should be worried. If they keep looking for food, they will eventually find you."

Bob clears his throat. "From the condition of the prisoner and the facts of the situation, I'd have to agree with Cain's assessment."

Angel glances at H.

H shakes his head. "It doesn't make sense why they're out looking for food. The supplies at the base would last for years. Maybe Bolin is a spy."

"I have too many questions about him to leave them

unasked," Angel says. "Like, why did they only have one gun between them?"

I grin. "Great. Let's go ask him."

Angel points at the floor. "You're staying here, Cain."

"Not a chance. But you ask him all the questions you want first, and then I get my turn. I need to know the layout of the base and where they have my daughter."

"You still plan on going through with your suicide mission?" Angel asks.

"The way I see it, if they're starving, my chances just improved."

Angel shakes her head, then marches over and opens the door. Bob and H follow her into the hallway with me bringing up the rear.

Angel didn't agree to my coming but it doesn't matter. Nothing is stopping me from speaking with Bolin.

As we get closer to the bathroom where they're holding Bolin, I hear voices. They're low at first, but one of them gasps and shouts, "Stop. Please. You're killing me!"

Angel rips out her pistol and kicks the door.

Bob and H enter like a breach team—Bob heads left, and H goes right.

I cover the rear with my shotgun.

Bolin is still tied to the chair in the middle of the floor, staring wide-eyed at the four of us. Tears stream down his face.

Standing beside him, holding a bowl and spoon, is Jerry Pace, the comedian. The man's black hair is hidden beneath a towel wrapped around his head. He flashes a lopsided grin and gives a one-shouldered shrug. "Sorry. I can't resist a captive audience."

Bolin laughs so hard that he starts coughing. "He's killing me! I can't take it. He's pretending to be a mother feeding a bratty kid. Make him stop."

"Can you believe I'm a huge hit in China?" Jerry beams. "Bolin's a comedy fan! What are the odds?"

"What are you doing in here, Jerry?" Angel holsters her pistol and stomps forward. "I gave specific orders for no one to come in here."

Jerry swallows and steps back. "I got that memo, but someone of a higher rank thought the prisoner might be hungry. They ordered me to bring him some oatmeal."

"Higher rank?" Angel's neck flushes red. "How many times have I told you my mother doesn't have a rank!"

"Technically not, but since she's in charge of the kitchen, that's a higher rank to me." Jerry sets the bowl and spoon on the counter next to one of the sinks. "I think I'll go now." Holding the towel on his head, he hurries out of the room.

Bob, H and I try to hide our smiles as Angel glares after him.

Bolin is still grinning. "I've seen all of his specials. He's so funny. He slays me when he does the helicopter mom routine. I can't believe—"

"Stop talking," Angel says, grabbing a folding chair and setting it in front of him. "I need you to understand something. I'm going to ask you questions. If you don't answer them honestly..." Angel cracks her neck. "We'll banish you."

From the way he pales and starts shaking, Angel might as well have threatened to set him on fire, castrate, and then disembowel him. "No! Ask. Ask, and I'll tell you whatever you want to know."

"Start at the beginning. Why did the Chinese soldiers come to Fort Burgess?"

Bolin attempts to shrug, but the ropes tying him to the chair prevent his shoulders from rising far. "I was ordered to come. They never tell us much. They say go, I go. Being an electrician, I assumed I would be installing or fixing something, but I never found out what. The city was attacked before we got started. Then, most of the American forces responded."

"Why didn't you help defend the city?"

"We wanted to help, but our commander said no."

"You left us out there to die." The low rumble in H's voice echoes off the tiles.

"Not me!" Bolin says. "Tianzi ordered us to stand down. And then he gave the order to close the base."

"Tianzi gave that order?" Angel asks, and Bolin nods. "What did Commander Gibson say about that?"

Bolin looks down.

Angel waits.

"Commander Gibson died. Tianzi said Gibson killed himself."

H's hands ball into fists. "Commander Gibson wouldn't have killed himself when his men needed him most."

"I only know what Tianzi told us. Most of the Americans reacted the way you did. They didn't believe it. But Tianzi took command and shut the base. Many Americans went to stop him, and a fight broke out."

"What were the Russians doing during this?" I ask.

"They were trying to calm everyone down. I found that very surprising because I thought they hated... I mean, I thought Russians didn't particularly care for Americans. But they tried to get Tianzi to change his mind and let the people into the base. But then everything happened all at once." Bolin stares back down at the floor.

The room goes quiet as everyone waits to hear what happened.

"The machine guns blocking the road opened fire on the people fleeing the city. The American soldiers tried to stop them, and Tianzi ordered his men to kill them. Everyone began shooting at each other. It was horrible. My friend Li Jie and I hid, but the earthquake happened. After that, the monsters came."

"What are you talking about?" Angel raised an eyebrow. "There wasn't an earthquake."

"I don't know the right word for it. A sinkhole? But it was long. It split the base in two. Right after the city was attacked, the ground shook. Then, the supply depot Li Jie and I were hiding behind disappeared into the ground. Gone! It was the diggers. The monster with the long snouts."

"I've seen them," I say. "They're like giant moles."

"More monsters came out of the hole, and the soldiers fought them and each other. Tianzi ordered them to open the spillway and flood the channel running down the middle of the base. That flooded the hole and drove the monsters back, but now the base was cut in two. The Russians were on one side, and Tianzi controlled the East."

"What about the remaining Americans?" H asks. "What side did they end up on?"

"Everyone was scattered to both sides. Tianzi said that we're all that's left. We're the new world order and need to pull together because the monsters keep attacking. He then gave everyone the option of giving him their allegiance."

"What did he mean by you're all that's left?" Angel asks.

"Tianzi said China was gone. Nukes obliterated it. So were Russia, Europe, and the rest of America. He said destiny saved him to bring about a better world."

"What happened to the soldiers who didn't surrender to Tianzi?" H asks.

"Some escaped to the Russian side of the base. The others were killed."

"How many men do the Russians have?"

Bolin shrugs. "I have no idea. The Russian in charge is named Andreeva. He's a big man. He refused to join Tianzi, and they wasted no time setting up barriers."

"So the West side of the base is being controlled by Russians?"

"Andreeva is in control, but Americans and Chinese soldiers are working with him now. He offered sanctuary to anyone wanting to come to his side. Tianzi posted guards to kill all deserters. If you tried, he also ordered the death of your friend."

"This Tianzi sounds like a real nut job. You said he used the spillway to flood the hole the monsters made. What spillway are you talking about?" I ask.

"The one connected to the moat around the base," Bolin says.

I looked at Bob, confused. "Fort Burgess doesn't have a moat."

"It does now," Bob explains. "They built a huge flood channel around the perimeter of the base five years back."

I open my mouth, but Bob motions for me to wait to ask questions. I'm about to let him know how I feel about him telling me to shut up, but I imagine that, being a cop, he'd rather be the one asking the interview questions. If he can keep his mouth shut, so can I.

"Why were you outside of the base?" Angel asked. "What was your mission?"

"To search for food. When the monsters attacked, they destroyed both the ammunition depot and our food supplies."

H whispers, "It's like they knew where to strike to cause the most damage."

The hairs on the back of my neck rise. "I thought those ghouls had some control over the monsters, but I didn't think they could give them specific orders like that."

Angel presses her hands together, her right thumb pushing hard against the back of her left hand. "I suspected as much, too. But if that is true, it means someone ordered those creatures to attack. Why would these ghouls want to destroy the city and then the base?"

"Maybe the city wasn't their main target," I say. "The base could have been their target all along. That's where they came from."

Everyone in the room turns to stare at me in disbelief.

"Think about it." I cross my arms. "This is where the monsters first showed up. The army also built a moat around the base five years ago. They knew that water is a natural barrier for these creatures. Only the Army wasn't keeping them out then. They were trying to keep them in."

"Are you saying that the Army made the bone beasts?" H says. "That's crazy."

"I don't know if they made them, but the facts are that they showed up here after the Dark started."

Angel turns back to Bolin. "What was your *real* role in the army?"

"An electrician. I swear."

"Where were you last stationed? What was the purpose of your assignment?"

"It was a re-educational facility in Ma Ding."

"A jail," Angel says. "And what work did you do—specifically?"

"We wired the fences and cells."

Angel's eyes narrow. "You electrified the fences and cells."

Bolin hangs his head. "I had to follow my orders."

"Is that why they sent you to Fort Burgess?" Angel's voice loses its hard edge. "If we are going to survive this, we need to know the truth, Bolin."

Bolin won't look her in the eye. He goes from staring at the floor to the ceiling and then the door. "You'll banish me."

Angel shakes her head. "Not for telling the truth, I won't."

"I didn't lie." Bolin's breathing speeds up, and he starts sweating. "When we were installing the facility in Ma Ding, I heard rumors. And the cells weren't the right size. They said they were for solitary confinement, but they were big. Too big for people. One of the engineers got drunk one night. He talked about monsters. We all thought he was just drunk. He was disappeared the next day. A dozen men came and took him. That is the government's way of sending us a message to remain silent."

"You never saw these creatures?"

"No, but the base was in Ma Ding Valley."

Angel pales, and Bob nods in understanding.

"What am I missing here?" I ask.

"A year and a half ago, the Ma Ding Dam ruptured. The Chinese military base and town in the valley beneath it were annihilated." Angel says. "We thought it was a terrorist attack."

"It wasn't," Bolin says. "My father was an engineer there. He never admitted what he did, but they were ordered to scuttle the dam."

"He told you that?" Angel asks.

"In a note. He left it for me before he hung himself. He knew the flood would kill everything in the valley. The government did too, but they said what was happening there would be worse if it spread. My father thought he was preventing the spread of a virus. Now I'm not sure."

A silence descends on the room as the gravity of his words sinks in. Things make a lot more sense now that all the crazy is coming out.

"Hold on." H starts pacing. "You want me to believe that America was carrying out the same type of research here? On U.S. soil?"

"I don't know. I don't know." Bolin closes his eyes.

Angel motions H to back up. "Why didn't you have a gun?"

"The monsters destroyed the ammunition depot. We have to conserve ammunition. Only those with the brand of Tianzi are allowed to get any."

That news makes me grin. "My odds keep getting better."

Angel frowns. "Not now, Cain."

"Odds for what?" Bolin asks.

"Forget him," Angel snaps her fingers. "Look at me. How many soldiers are left in the base?"

"I only know our side. Two hundred or less."

H gasps. "It can't be that few."

"Between the monsters and the fighting, most died. And there have been several purges. Tianzi trusts no one. He believes he has been selected to lead the world into a new beginning."

"A little girl and boy were brought into the base. Where are they keeping them?" Angel asks.

My heart is ready to explode as I hold my breath.

"The Den."

"What's that?" My voice rumbles out in a low growl.

"It's a building in the center of the compound. There's a bunker underneath it."

"Why do they call it the Den?" Angel asks.

"They keep a monster in there. We hear it once in a while. I don't know what it is."

H places a restraining hand on my shoulder. I feel like running out of the room and attacking the base now. "They put my little girl into a place with a monster?"

"They keep the creature isolated in a special room on the lowest floor. It can't get out."

"Easy, Cain." H pulls me back a step.

"What about the women who were brought to the base?" Angel says.

"One was hurt, so they took her to the infirmary. The other they brought to Tianzi's bunker for questioning."

Angel leans back in her chair. "Do you know if they're being treated fairly?"

"For now. All Tianzi wants is the boy. How long he lets the

others live is anyone's guess." Bolin shrugs. "If someone is useless, he doesn't let them live long."

I stomp forward. "That little girl is my daughter. You're going to tell me everything I want to know about the layout of that base."

Bolin's eyes widen in horror. "You're not thinking about going there? You're crazy. Even if you make it past the mine-field, Tianzi will kill you!"

H groans. "They mined around the base?"

Bolin nods. "We did it to keep the monsters out. They patrol on the other side of the moat."

"Would you listen to him, Cain?" H says. "There's no way to get inside that base. You'd have to make it across the moat and then the minefield. After that, there is a barbed wire fence, and then there are guards. If you try to do this, you will die."

I meet H's hard stare. "There are some things worse than dying. Doing nothing while my little girl is trapped with a monster is one of them."

Bolin lifts his chin. "You saved my life by bringing me here. I am sorry to tell you, but your friend is right. That place is a living hell. If you go there, there will be no coming back."

I cross my arms and, despite my fears, flash a cocky smile. "I've been to Hell and back before. Besides, I plan on being long gone before the Devil knows I'm there."

15

LIES

Bri Haight

Bri Haight sat on the bed, huddled in the corner with her back pressed against the wall. Her legs were pulled to her chest, and she wrapped her arms around her knees. She hadn't seen Jacob since they locked her in this room. There were no windows, so she didn't know if it was day or night. She was starving. After scratching one of the soldiers and biting another one's hand, she doubted they'd give her something to eat soon.

Bri rested her chin on her knees. Normally, she'd cry, but that wasn't what she felt like at all. She was mad—really, really, mad. Jumping off the bed, she glared around the room. Besides the bed, there was a stool, a toilet, and a sink with a metal cup on it.

She marched over to the sink and turned on the faucet. Nothing came out. She tried the other side. Not even a drop of water. Picking up the cup, she flung it at the door. It bounced off and pinged as it danced across the tiled floor.

"You can't do this to me!" Bri screamed as she picked up the cup and stomped to the door. "I'm a kid! There are still laws!"

She banged the cup against the door. It rang loudly, so she shouted even more. "Let me out of here—you rat-faced, mud-sucking boogers!" Over and over, she slammed the cup off the door, slowly bending the bottom of the cup inward.

The door handle turned, and Bri jumped back. She dropped the cup and picked up the stool.

Fen walked through the door and shut it behind her. "I suggest you shut up and put the stool down." Fen's face was bruised, and she moved stiffly.

"Let me go, or I'll put it down on your head."

Fen laughed. "You are your mother's daughter."

"You don't know anything about my momma."

Fen's smile vanished. "I met her in Ridgecrest, and unfortunately, she is now here. Along with your grandmother."

All the strength vanished from Bri's arm, and the stool banged off the floor when she dropped it. It rolled in a half circle.

Fen set it upright and sat down. "Sit on the bed. We need to talk, and there isn't much time."

"You're a skunk-faced liar. My Mawmaw and Momma aren't here. Daddy would have come for me."

"Your mother told me who your father really is. And he's dead. At least according to your mother. And if you don't want to wind up like him and get the rest of your family killed, you'll listen to me."

Bri's eyes filled with tears. She clutched her chest. Her heart hurt.

"I can get you and your family out of here, but you must listen. Ask yourself, what would your father want?"

"Give me your gun, and I'll show you."

"If you still feel like that afterward, so be it. But for now, sit."

Bri stood there with her hands balled into fists and shaking. Was her Daddy dead? No. Not her Daddy. Momma must be lying to fool them. That's what she'd do. She always said the quickest way out of a problem was to lie, so she'd go along with Momma's lie. She moved to the edge of the bed and sat down.

"A man is coming here to speak with you. You can't tell him what happened to Nicholi."

Bri's eyes widened. "You're scared of what they'd do to you. I'm going to tell them."

"And then you, your mother, and grandmother will die. And Jacob will be alone with these monsters."

Bri blinked rapidly. Who were the monsters he was talking about?

"You are to tell them the story about the bone bear attacking our canoes. But it was Nicholi's canoe that was struck by a rock and sank. Jacob wore his life vest, and we pulled him in. Nicholi never surfaced. Understood?"

"Why should I help you?"

Fen glanced back at the door. When her eyes met Bri's again, there was fear inside them. "We don't have much time. Repeat the story back to me."

Bri crossed her arms. The roles were now reversed, and she wouldn't keep her mouth shut unless Fen gave her a good reason. "You brought me here. None of this would have happened if it weren't for you."

Fen leaned closer and spoke rapid-fire, her voice a whisper. "I had no choice. They have my husband. I didn't want you to come or your family to follow. I never thought they would, and I am sorry." Her black eyes lost their hard edge and watered.

A lie was a lie, and that made Fen a liar, but Bri believed her now. "A bone bear broke through the brush and started throwing rocks. One hit Nicholi's canoe. Jacob bobbed up downstream because of his life vest, but Nicholi never came back up."

Fen exhaled. "Be patient. I promise I will get you out."

Bri leaned forward. "Just you remember. I can always

change my mind and tell them the truth. Then—" she dragged her thumb across her throat.

Fen rolled her eyes and hurried out of the room.

The door locked, and Bri was left alone once more.

Tears poured down her cheeks, and she burst into tears. Collapsing on the bed, she curled into a ball and wept. It wasn't true. It wasn't. Momma lied. Daddy promised if something bad ever happened, he'd come for her. Besides, Daddy always said he was too mean to die.

16

A LIVE COWARD

Evan Green

Evan kept his hand pressed against his wound as the man raced down the road. For a car built in 1962, the Impala was a rocket. "I don't think it's that bad," Evan said, holding onto the dashboard with his free hand as the car skidded into a curve.

"Not that bad?" The man's voice rose high. "You've been shot. That's never good. Keep pressure on it. We're almost there. I'm Sam, by the way."

"Evan Green. Nice meeting you."

"You've got to be a local, right? The locals were all real nice. Of course, none of them stuck around after the power went out. At least none of my neighbors did. I'm not blaming them. Most people in town probably didn't know I was there. I only moved in a month before." Sam pointed to a house on the left. The big two-story farmhouse sat high on the bank, set far off the road. An American and Tennessee State flag flapped in the breeze on poles in the front yard.

"It's way bigger than I need, but I got it for a steal. I'm from Chicago. You couldn't buy a shed in Chicago for what I paid.

My ex and I split the cash from the sale of our house. Besides that, the divorce was easy because we didn't have any kids. Am I talking too much? I've got a habit of doing that when I'm nervous."

Sam slowed, but the tires screeched as he pulled into the driveway and raced up the hill. An F150 pickup truck and a 1972 Ford Cortina were parked in the driveway, and a 1969 Volkswagen Bug was in the second bay of the open garage.

"I take it you collect antique cars?" Evan said as Sam parked in the empty spot in the garage.

"They're not mine. Right before the world exploded, my neighbor asked if he could keep them here while he redid his garage. It was only supposed to be for a couple of days, but that was over a year ago, so I thought it would be alright to take one."

Evan opened his door.

"Hold on. Let me help you." Sam hurried around the car and helped Evan toward the house. Sam glanced at Evan's side and quickly looked away. "It's bad. I knew it. Come inside. I've got a first aid kit." He held open the door as Evan walked in.

The kitchen was large, with an island in the center and a breakfast nook in front of tall windows overlooking the backyard. He even had a view of the river. Every cabinet door sat open, and all the drawers had been pulled out.

"Did you get robbed?" Evan asked as Sam helped him over to the table.

"Don't sit down. Lie on the table. The light is good here. I'll be right back. I've got a med kit." Sam rushed out of the room.

Evan looked at the wide table. It had stout legs and should be able to bear his weight. Groaning, he set his stomach against the side and leaned forward. Pain raced up his side, and fresh blood seeped between his fingers.

Sam returned to the room with a large duffle bag with a red circle and white cross. "It was stupid not to bring this with me when I left. And no, I didn't get robbed. I ran out of food. I ate the last crumb and decided to go instead of sitting here and dying. I'm not like you. I'm scared of my own shadow. It took starvation to make me leave my nest."

Evan shook his head. "I'm not as brave as you think."

"Don't try to make me feel better. I'm a live coward. No shame in that." Sam reached into the bag and began removing items and placing them on the table.

"You saved my life. That was a pretty brave thing to do."

"There wasn't anything brave about it. I shut my eyes and stomped on the gas." Sam grimaced. "I'm going to need to look at your wound."

Evan pulled his bloody hand away. "Are you a doctor?"

As Sam lifted Evan's shirt, his complexion paled. "No. I studied to be an EMT before college. I passed all the classes and then dropped out."

"Why was that?"

Sam gagged. "I'm not good with blood. Real blood." He grabbed a bottle of alcohol off the table.

"Wait," Evan said. "Do you have anything for the pain?"

"Here." Sam reached into his bag and put a bottle of pills on the table. "Only take one."

"Do you have anything that will work faster? Booze?"

"I don't drink. That's what ended my marriage." Sam poured the alcohol on Evan's back.

Evan swore and slammed his hand down on the table.

"Sorry. It's going to sting. But that's a humdinger of a pain pill. You won't be feeling anything soon."

Evan inhaled sharply and realized it didn't hurt as much as he thought. Squeezing his hands into fists, he glanced around the kitchen at the cabinets. "So you hid out here for a year?"

"I didn't have a choice. After a few days without power, I tried to go to my neighbors' and saw the nightmare squirrels. I barely made it back to the house. After that, I took one of the cars, and those guys at the garage shot at me. That's why I took the back road around the place. But when I saw you pulling over, I figured it was a trap, and I couldn't let you walk into it, so I came to see if I could warn you."

"You saved my life. Thank you."

Sam grinned. "I still don't think it was brave. But I had to try. A little girl saved my life a few days ago. If a kid can do that—"

"A little girl?" Evan asked through clenched teeth as Sam continued to clean the wound. "Where did you see her? Who was she with?"

"Out in the river." Sam pointed out the window. "I've got some good news. The bullet only clipped your love handle. There are two holes, but they're not deep. As Forrest Gump would say, that's a million-dollar wound."

"On the river? Were they in a canoe? Who was the girl with?"

"Two boats. The girl was in one with a lady, and a big fella was in the other canoe. I ran down to try to get them to stop. The little girl warned me, so I ducked before they shot at me. If it weren't for her, I'd be dead." Sam's hands started to shake. "Are you friends with them?"

"No. But that girl is my wife's daughter."

"Wouldn't that make her your daughter, too?"

Evan ran his hand over his face as Sam prodded the bullet wound with some metal instrument. "We just got married. The girl's real father doesn't like me at all."

"But she's still your stepdaughter, right?"

Evan nodded as he pressed his lips together to keep from screaming. "She is. Her name is Bri. Those people kidnapped her and a little boy. Did you see the boy?"

"What is wrong with people? Don't we have enough real monsters in this world with those nightmare squirrels? You'd think people would stop attacking each other, but no. People have gotten worse. Even more evil if that's—"

"What about the boy?" Evan shouted through gritted teeth but quickly added. "Sorry."

"No need to apologize. I tend to go on." Sam thought for a moment and shook his head. "I can't say. I didn't get the best look at them because of me running down the hill and them shooting at me."

"What about three women and a man? Did you see them? They would have been following the first group."

Sam nodded. "I'm putting in some stitches, so don't move. This is going to pinch."

Evan closed his eyes and pounded the table as Sam held his skin together and stabbed him with the needle.

"They paddled past a little while after. I can't tell you how long it was. After the woman shot at me, I ran back to the house and fell asleep. I didn't know if they were with the first group and was too scared to call out."

Evan hung his head. Sweat rolled into his eyes, he breathed heavily, and his eyelids drooped.

"I'm almost done."

"Good. I'm going to need one of those cars."

"You can't go now. It's getting dark. The squirrels come out then. Other things, too. I hear them. Besides, once that pill kicks in, you'll be asleep. Get a good night's rest, and in the morning, I'll go to Ridgecrest with you. I'll drive."

"I'm not going back. I have to go to get my wife. She's headed to Fort Burgess."

Sam stared Evan in the eyes. "Why did I bother stitching you up? If you go there, you'll be dead by this time tomorrow."

17

RATS?

Cain Haight

I load my backpack, check my ammo and guns, and head for the escalators.

H is waiting for me with his arms crossed. "You're not leaving right now? It's getting dark."

"I'm not afraid of the dark."

"Neither am I. It's what's *in* the dark that I'm afraid of." H chuckles.

So do I. "You heard what Bolin said. I don't have time to wait around."

"At least figure out a plan. What are you going to do about the minefield? How are you going to get across it?"

"Then I'll go straight down the road. I'll take out the first guards before they know what's going on."

"So you plan on making a frontal assault with a troop strength of one. I think they teach that in Military Tactics Sure to Fail."

"Surprise is on my side."

Bob comes jogging up with a short guy with a bushy beard running beside him. "Hold on, Cain. Atticus here has a plan."

My eyes narrow. "You're the guy who tased me."

Atticus shrugs. "Nothin' personal. Just followin' orders is all." He looks to Bob. "Which plan do you want me to tell him? The one with the hopper or the rats?"

"Did he say rats?" H asks.

"Stick to the plan about the hopper," Bob says.

"Right. That one is simpler. All you need is a hopper." Atticus's hands are moving all over the place as he speaks. "I know where we can get one. With it, you float up and over the minefield and fence like a dandelion in the wind."

I shake my head. "I take it this hopper thing is some kind of hot air balloon? That'll never work. Because of the fire, I'll glow like a lightning bug at night. When they see that glow, everyone with a gun will start shooting."

Atticus grins and taps the side of his head. "I figured that part out already. The hopper isn't hot air. It's helium. The US Army used to use hoppers to work on the blimps. They're a big ole bag attached by ropes to a wooden bench. They even tried to get a sport goin'. They called it balloon jumpin', but the fella that started it jumped right into some power lines and got barbequed."

H shakes his head. "What's the plan with the rats?"

Atticus's face lights up. "Ya see, there's lots of rats in the city. If we catch them, we can use them to clear the minefield by—"

Bob holds up his hand, cutting Atticus off. "Don't bring up the rat plan again." Bob stares at me. "I know there's no talking you out of going, but the hopper plan makes sense. Atticus knows where to get one, too."

"Right before the Dark, the Museum had one on display, but it works," Atticus explains. "They even had a demonstration because it was the anniversary of the base. All the gear should still be there, and the Museum is right close to Fort Burgess."

"I think we should hear more about the rats," H says.

Atticus opens his mouth, but Bob cuts him off again. "Do you have a better plan, Cain?"

H laughs. "No! Cain's plan should be called the last charge of the crazy man."

I feel like smacking H, but he's right. So is Bob. But Atticus' plan doesn't sound much safer than storming the front gate. "I'm willing to try it, but how does this hopper thing work?"

"There's nothing to it." Atticus scratches his beard. "There's no way to steer and no ballast. But the wind is always blowin' east off the plateau. All I've gots to do is calculate how much helium to use. Too little, and you'll end up in the minefield. But as my daddy would say, that would be the lesser of two evils."

Thinking about landing in a minefield makes my stomach tighten up. "How is ending up in a minefield the lesser evil?"

"Because you can jump, and you'll float right back up! But if I put too much helium in the balloon...."

"He'll fly off into space?" H's eyes widen.

Atticus shakes his head and smiles. "Nope. He'll float up until the atmosphere pops the balloon, and then he'll fall back to Earth."

"Fantastic," I mutter.

"Don't you worry none." Atticus nods reassuringly. "I wasn't good in any class in school 'cept math." He taps his head again. "And I got a way with figures."

I turn to look at Bob.

Bob grins crookedly. "I never said it was a surefire plan. But I think it's the only one with a chance."

"There's one other problem," I say. "How is Atticus going to make these calculations without seeing the balloon?"

"Don't worry about that," Bob says. "The three of us are going with you."

18

SCOURGE

Mercy Yoder

Mercy sat in the back of the wagon as they crossed over old farms. The grass had grown tall, but the wolves had no issues pulling the wagon. The woman riding the bear looked back at Mercy every once in a while. Her head tipped to the side like she was studying Mercy. It reminded Mercy of how people stared at a painting in the museum.

After another hour of rolling hills, Mercy faced a different problem: she needed to relieve herself. "Miss?" She finally gained the courage to call out.

All of the animals turned their heads.

The woman turned back, her piercing blue eyes commanding the animals' attention. They immediately stopped. "Get out."

Mercy climbed over the side of the wagon.

The massive wolf beside her emitted a low, menacing growl, sending shivers down Mercy's spine. Mercy held up her hands, but the beast suddenly trotted around to the other side. Mercy hurriedly finished her business and climbed back into the wagon. "Thank you, Miss."

The woman's lip curled. "I don't like that name."

Mercy cringed. "Sorry. Ma'am?"

"That's worse." The woman shifted on the back of the bear. The sun peeking out behind her made Mercy squint. "What is the first name you think of?"

"The first woman's name? Eve."

"Eve. That works. We ride."

As one, the animals started moving at the same time.

Mercy exhaled as she leaned her back against the side of the wagon. This was a nightmare, but she wasn't dreaming. She placed her trembling hands on her lap and prayed silently, thanking God that Eve liked the name she'd blurted out.

They climbed a gentle slope and continued along the ridge. Down below, a white farmhouse gleamed in the sun. A red barn sat off to the left. Clothes hung on a line blowing in the wind. The barn door opened a crack, and a child ran out. She raced toward the house with her little arms and legs, a blur, brown hair streaming out behind her.

The wolf beside the wagon raised its head and howled.

Eve nodded, and the wolf started running.

The door of the house clanged open, and a woman appeared. She scooped the girl up in her arms and slammed the door.

Eve slid off the bear and marched to the front of the wagon. The wolves pranced and pulled against their bindings. Eve unbuckled one of the wolves, and it raced toward the house.

The wagon jerked forward as the other wolf tried to run, too.

Eve punched the wolf in the nose.

The wolf snapped and glared at her.

Eve growled.

The wolf lowered its head.

"Call them back!" Mercy pleaded. "It's a child and mother!"

"They are scourge," Eve said, grabbing the leather buckle securing the other wolf.

Mercy grabbed the buckboard. She had no idea what Eve meant; except she viewed them as enemies. "They are still helpless."

"They must die." Eve freed the other wolf.

The monster moved so quickly that it made Mercy gasp. With its ears pinned back on its head, it joined the hunt.

"They've done nothing." Mercy pleaded.

"They've done everything." Eve raised her hand and motioned forward.

The bear reared up on its hind legs. It was monstrous—standing over 13 feet. It landed on its front paws, and the wagon shook. With surprising speed, it charged down the hill and toward the farm.

Eve smiled.

A helplessness Mercy had never known swept over her. Those poor people below were going to be ripped apart, and all she could do was watch. Her hands shook. Her stomach tightened into an angry ball. Anger grew into frustration and exploded into rage.

"NO!" Mercy leaped over the wagon's side and jumped onto Eve. She crashed into the woman and grabbed around her shoulders. They rolled in the tall grass, and Mercy ended up sitting on Eve's stomach, pinning her to the ground. "Call them back!"

Eve's fist struck Mercy at the base of her jaw.

Mercy's vision blurred as her head jerked back. Another punch on the opposite side of her head knocked her sideways and to the ground.

Eve scrambled to her feet.

Mercy did, too. "Please!"

Eve shifted forward, and her right hand hit Mercy in the stomach.

All of the breath shot out of Mercy's lungs. She doubled forward.

Eve's fist came down on Mercy's face.

Mercy crashed to the ground. Her face slammed into the dirt.

The wolves howled. They had reached the farmhouse.

Eve kicked Mercy in the stomach.

Mercy curled into a fetal position. She gasped for breath, but none came.

"Stupid scourge." Eve turned her back on Mercy and walked forward to watch the monsters attack the house.

Mercy wheezed. Blood dripped from her nose onto the ground next to her hand. She pictured her poor, sweet horse, Susanna, getting killed by the same kind of monsters. That little girl and her mother were about to meet a similar fate.

Mercy's hands clawed the ground as she pushed herself to her feet. She charged forward and jumped on Eve's back. Wrapping one arm around Eve's neck and the other around her waist, they crashed to the ground.

Eve landed on top of Mercy, but Mercy didn't let go.

"Please call them off! Please! I don't want to hurt you."

Eve's elbow slammed into Mercy's stomach.

Mercy groaned in pain but held on.

Eve's elbow slammed into her again.

Mercy's hands opened, and Eve slipped free.

Eve rolled to her feet. She reached down, seized Mercy's dress collar, and lifted her onto her knees. With her right fist, Eve repeatedly punched Mercy in the face.

Mercy's vision blurred, and she couldn't think straight. She grabbed hold of Eve's belt. Another blow struck Mercy's jaw. Mercy clutched Eve's belt tighter, but whatever she held onto jerked free.

Eve raised her right fist. Her left was twisted around the fabric of Mercy's dress.

Mercy stared down at whatever she had taken off Eve's belt. She had pulled a knife out of its scabbard. The blade was seven inches long and gleamed. Mercy's fingers tightened around the handle.

Eve gasped. Her blue eyes widened as she noticed the knife.

Mercy stared up at the woman who seemed determined to kill her. Blood ran down her chin and dripped on her hand. Her head felt like someone was squeezing it. Her teeth clenched. A voice inside her shrieked, *'KILL HER!'*

Mercy pulled back her arm. A softer voice whispered, *'Mercy.'* Mercy dropped the knife. "Please call them back."

Eve's fist slammed into Mercy's jaw, and everything went black.

19

SOMETHIN' DIED

Cain Haight

The four of us jog through the city in the dead of the night. The moon is faint behind some clouds and provides just enough light that I don't run into an abandoned car or telephone pole. I'm following behind Atticus while Bob takes point with H after him.

My brain is having a really hard time with these guys helping me. Or maybe it's my heart that's struggling with it. These guys are risking their lives for me. How can I ever thank them for that?

We occasionally stop to catch our breath or if Bob hears something. Mostly, what he hears or sees is a rat. Atticus doesn't say anything, but he holds up his hands each time to display how many there've been. He's already over twenty. I'm convinced that he'd like to go ahead with his rat plan, and the thought of flying off into space is making me regret at least not listening to him about it.

Bob starts jogging again, and we follow. The Military Museum sits between the Art and Science Museum. Half of the

Art building is gone. Bri would be crying if she were here. I took her a couple of times, and she'd taken field trips there for school. It was her favorite.

We hurry up the steps, and Bob opens the door. We file silently inside, and Bob flicks on his flashlight. As we each snap on our lights, the museum appears before us. It looks like you could dust, vacuum, and open it in the morning. Everything is neat, and nothing is smashed or gutted.

"The hopper should be in the aeronautics wing," Atticus says to Bob, who shrugs.

I shine my flashlight on the counter and pick up a brochure. On the back is a map. I point to the right, and we set off.

Four sets of boots echo loudly off the tiles. Even though we're all moving as quietly as possible, it sounds like a platoon on a military parade.

We pass a WWI tank and head toward the large opening on the other side. In the glow of our flashlights, I see our prize. Like a kid's balloon a day after the birthday party, the hopper droops; limply tethered to a wooden bench, but still floating.

"Don't that beat all!" Atticus hurries over to it. "It's still got a lot of helium in it. That'll speed things up."

"Where would they keep the helium containers?" Bob asks.

Atticus shrugs.

I check the map on the brochure. "There's a maintenance area through those doors." I point to the far right corner of the room. "But there's a big room through the doors on the left that's not labeled."

"H and I will take the left," Bob says. "You and Atticus head right."

I nod, and everyone starts moving.

Atticus falls in behind me. He's keeping close, but like a little kid, he's shining his flashlight all around, peering at the displays as we go.

I open the double doors, which lead to a hallway. We pass a

couple of small offices and, at the end, reach another set of double doors. I open one, and a rancid smell burns my nose.

"Somethin' died in there." Atticus covers his nose so fast that he catches his beard in his hand. It looks like he's using his beard as a mask, and despite my fear of the cause of the odor, I smile.

"Hold up." I prop the door open with my boot and shine the light around the room. It's a loading area, and the large roll-up door is open.

"Somethin' must have come in and died," Atticus whispers.

I motion to try to get him to shut up and he holds a finger over his lips. Left to right, I shine my flashlight around the room. It glints off a dozen grey cylinders.

Before I can stop him, Atticus rushes past me. He stops and pulls out a pair of reading glasses.

My head is on a swivel as I finish clearing the room and move to cover him.

"Jackpot! Helium!" Atticus pats me on the back.

"Shhh. How many canisters do we need?"

"Right now, guessin' mind ya, I figure..." Atticus tugs on his beard. "A canister holds 244 cubic feet. That hopper is at least two-thirds full and needs 3,000 cubic feet, so five tanks should do us. Seven, to be sure."

The thought of floating to the moon makes me want to say six, but I keep my mouth shut. I shine my light around the room until it lands on a utility cart. "I can load that up and take it out the loading dock."

"That hopper won't fit down the hallway. But we should be able to get it out the front of the museum," Atticus says.

I walk over to the cart. Half a pallet of office paper is stacked on it. "Before we do this, let's get Bob and H."

Atticus' attention is fixed on the corner of the room. He whistles low and strides over to whatever he's found. "I've discovered the source of the smell. One of those bone bears came in and died. It's huge." He picks up a broom.

"Don't!"

Atticus spins the broom in his hand, and he taps the handle against the top of the bone bear's head with a loud rap. "Don't go gettin' your knickers in a bunch. It's dead as a doornail."

My flashlight lands on the beast. "That's way bigger than a black bear or even a grizzly. Back away from it."

Atticus holds the broom like a spear and pokes the thing in the head twice more. "Hey! Can you please tell my friend that you are dead?"

The bone bear opens its eyes.

The broom falls out of Atticus' hands, but he doesn't move.

I leap forward. With my left hand, I grab the collar of Atticus' shirt and yank him back. My shotgun swings up in my right, and I fire.

The blast is loud, but the bone bear's roar is deafening.

I keep firing as I shove Atticus towards the doors.

The little guy runs as fast as he can down the hallway, but I'm catching up to him even though I'm looking back at the bear and shooting as I go.

I'm dumping every round of my shotgun into that bear's head, and it's only slowing him down a bit. It fills the corridor as it charges. Smoke, gunpowder, and pieces of bone being blasted off fill the air.

I only have two rounds left when we reach the double doors. I slam them shut behind us. There's no lock, but I doubt that bear knows how to turn the handle to get them open.

The bear slams into the doors with the force of a dump truck. The right door bursts open, but the one on the left is ripped off its hinges and smashes into me.

The wind is knocked out of my lungs first by the impact of the door and again when I hit the floor. I slide several feet across the tile with the door on top of my legs. My shotgun bounces across the floor and disappears beneath a display counter.

The bear roars and ambles toward me.

I reach for my pistol, but the door is pinning me to the floor. My holster is wedged against my leg, and I can't get a grip on my gun.

A gunshot rings out, and pieces of bone fly off the bear's head. It turns to glare at this new threat.

Bob is standing in the middle of the room in a shooter's stance, firing.

The bear charges.

Bob looks as calm as if he's at the range, taking his time, making each shot count.

Claws rake the tile. The beast is gaining speed as he bears down on the cop.

Bob drops his magazine and slams the next one in place in a fluid motion practiced a thousand times. He racks the slide and keeps firing.

The bear lowers his head and rams into Bob.

Man and beast slam together and crash to the floor. They both slide to a stop, but neither gets up.

20

FORGIVE THEM

Amos Yoder

Amos waited with Ani and Jesse Pickett in the doctor's office living room. Ani sat on his left, her grip on his hand tightening with each passing moment, while Jesse sat on the floor, his eyes darting nervously around the room, hiding behind a high-backed chair in the corner. The room was filled with an unsettling silence, broken only by Amos' hollow words, "Everything is going to be okay."

Occasionally, he'd hear a noise and glance at the door, hoping it was Sarah. She was helping Betsy Weber and Doc Harmon. A bone wolf had bitten off Lonnie's arm. They managed to stop the bleeding, but the boy was in bad shape. Camila Moreno was worse. She'd just given birth, but during their escape to town, had been stabbed by a bone spike in her side.

Amos bowed his head and tried to pray, but the words wouldn't come. He wanted to help, but with Frank Pickett coming to town, Matt and the Mayor wanted him to stay with Jesse and let them deal with Frank.

Jesse rocked in the corner, furiously sketching in his book.

Amos didn't need to see what he was drawing. Jesse always sketched the same thing. Jesse sketched Ridgecrest as if you were looking at it from a hot-air balloon. On all sides of Ridgecrest, huge, dark waves reared up, poised to crash over the town. Emerging through the water were creatures with claws, tusks, and horns. In the center of the beasts, wrapped in a swirl of shadows, stood a man with his hand outstretched.

Whatever Jesse saw in his broken mind, Amos had seen it too. Since Jacob had shown up on his doorstep, God had been trying to show Amos something. He didn't know what, but every night, he'd dreamt of a storm like none other, and he was standing in the center. Cain was always with him.

The dream ended the same way each time. The two of them stood in the eye, staring at the destruction. Circling them, caught up in the maelstrom, were the people Amos loved most —Sarah, Mercy, and Jacob. There were others as well—people from the town. Everyone was screaming in fear and calling out to Cain and Amos for help.

The dream always ended the same. Cain rushed forward, and Amos woke up. He didn't know if Cain lived or died or what happened next.

Amos hung his head. Where were Cain and Mercy now? Had they found Jacob? Were they even alive?

The sound of many engines grew louder outside. There were so many families coming into town, but this was different. Amos rose and crossed to the windows.

Dozens of trucks filled the street.

The Picketts had arrived. The unruly mob was shouting and screaming at the people backing away from their caravan of vehicles. Above all the noise, one question rose—"Where is Amos Yoder?"

Someone pointed to the doctor's office.

Amos gasped. "Ani, Jesse, you stay here. Don't come out." He rushed over to the door, locked it, and closed it. The front door bashed open as he walked down the hallway lined with family photographs.

Billy Pickett stood there with a shotgun in his left hand. "I gots him!"

Five men rushed into the house behind Billy.

"Hold on a minute," Amos said, walking forward. "Let me talk to Frank."

Cole Pickett punched Amos in the face.

Amos stumbled sideways. He grabbed the wall as his vision blurred.

Someone grabbed his beard and yanked him forward. Another punch slammed into his right eye.

"Bring him out!" Billy yelled.

Hands seized Amos from all sides. He tripped as they pulled him forward and dragged him down the hallway.

The door broke off its top hinge as the men pushed and shoved each other to get outside. They pulled him onto the porch, and the crowd cheered.

"He kidnapped Jesse!" Billy shouted.

The men on either side of him jerked Amos to his feet, keeping a tight grip on his arms.

"I didn't kidnap him," Amos said. "I found him down—"

Daisy Pickett ran forward and flung a rock.

The stone struck Amos in the shoulder. He flinched backward, but the men held him in place.

Several more stones arced through the air. Most struck Amos, but one hit Cole in the face.

"Stop throwing junk, you idiots!" Billy shouted.

A coiled-up rope landed at Amos' feet.

Silence descended on the crowd.

Billy grinned. "Looks like we're gonna have a hangin'."

The crowd cheered.

"Billy, stop!" Amos struggled, but his arms were jerked behind his back.

Cole ripped off Amos' belt and used it to tie Amos' hands.

"Good thing you've got suspenders to keep your pants up." Colt laughed as he wiped the blood dripping down the side of his face caused by the wayward rock.

"I didn't hurt Jesse. I took care of him." Amos shouted.

"String him up!" The crowd yelled louder.

"Where's Frank? Let me speak to Frank." Amos pleaded.

Billy jerked his thumb toward the tree in the front yard.

Four men lifted Amos into the air and carried him off the porch. Daisy slapped Amos in the face as they paraded him by. A truck engine roared as it backed up, stopping when it was beneath a thick branch.

Someone tossed the rope into the tree.

They hoisted Amos into the air and stood him up in the back of the pickup.

Billy and Cole grabbed the tailgate and scrambled up to stand beside him. Billy placed the noose over Amos' head. He jerked the rope tight, and the coarse material cut into Amos' skin.

"You folks don't understand," Amos called out. "I was helping Jesse. I was doing what God wanted me to do."

Cole jumped down.

The truck's engine revved. The truck bed shook, sending vibrations racing up Amos' legs.

Amos stared in horror at the crowd. He knew them, and they knew him, but he barely recognized them now. Their faces were twisted in hate and rage. Their lips pulled back as they screamed and swore and spit. With raised fists and voices, they all cried—"Hang him!"

Billy jumped to the ground. He reached out and pounded the side of the truck three times.

The engine roared. The tires spun on the grass until they caught traction, and the truck surged forward.

For a moment, Amos felt like he was floating. He looked at the star-filled sky and said, "Forgive them."

The rope jerked tight around his neck, and everything went black.

21

THE EXAMINER

Lucy Green

Lucy's legs felt like they weighed a hundred pounds apiece as Fen and the woman who'd tortured her marched her across the darkened base. "How is my mother?"

The woman spun, her fist slamming into Lucy's stomach and knocking the wind out of her lungs.

Lucy dropped to her knees.

The woman raised her arm, her fist ready to slam into Lucy's face.

Fen stepped between them. "Tianzi wants her unharmed, Pi."

Pi shifted her stance so she stood nose-to-nose with Fen. "You dare tell me what Tianzi wants?"

To Lucy's surprise, Fen bowed her head. "I did not mean any disrespect."

Pi inclined her head away from Fen and then glared at Lucy. She grabbed Lucy's hair and yanked her up.

Pain shot down Lucy's scalp as she struggled to stand.

"Move!" Pi pushed Lucy toward a one-story, white cement building with a solitary guard standing in front.

"I can see why you didn't tell me your name," Lucy muttered.

"Do not speak," Pi ordered.

Lucy couldn't be sure, but she thought Fen smiled.

The three marched up the stairs and through two double glass doors. The room was dark, but a single oil lamp sat burning on a wide counter in the back. There were no windows and only a door behind the counter.

Fen took the lamp and opened the door.

Pi shoved Lucy forward.

Lucy ground her teeth and pressed her palms against her stomach to keep her hands from balling into fists. Now wasn't the time to make a break for it. But she'd be sure to stick it to Pi when it was.

A white, tiled hallway led straight to two Chinese guards standing before a steel door. An oil lamp hung on the wall. The guards snapped to attention and stared straight ahead as the three women approached.

When they reached the end, Pi stopped and glared at the guards. From the smug expression on Pi's face, Lucy knew the twisted woman drew satisfaction from making other people fear her.

The guards continued to stare forward. The one on the left broke out in a sweat and swallowed.

Pi nodded.

The guard on the right spun on his heels, unlocked the door, and held it open.

Light from the oil lamps spilled into a foyer beyond and a staircase leading down.

Fen nudged Lucy forward. As they walked through the door, Fen stepped to her right and flicked a light switch.

Lucy blinked as electrical lights blazed overhead and down the stairs. She peered over the railing to the bottom far below. Closed elevator doors on her right gave hope to her aching legs. The lights on the panel were off, but maybe it worked?

"Please tell me we're taking the elevator down?"

Pi slammed Lucy against the railing. She grabbed the back of Lucy's neck and forced her upper body over the side.

Lucy gasped as she stared down at the long drop.

"I ordered you not to speak. Perhaps I should close your mouth more permanently."

Lucy clung onto the metal bar of the railing, but Pi was pushing her forward and tipping her out over the abyss. Lucy debated pleading for her life or simply begging Pi to stop.

"You know what?" Lucy turned her head to stare Pi in the face. "If you think Tianzi will be okay with you disobeying his orders, do it. You and I know he won't. But you know something he will believe? It's when I let it slip that you think you can do a better job running things than him."

Pi's fist slammed into Lucy's kidney.

Lucy gasped. Her legs buckled, and she sank to her knees.

Pi drew her pistol and aimed it at Lucy's face. Her black eyes were wild, and her hand shook. Her chest rose and fell with each ragged breath.

"Or you can stop beating me, and I'll keep my mouth shut." Lucy bowed her head. The action made her stomach churn. Even fake submission made her want to throw up.

"Take her to the room," Pi said as she holstered her pistol. "The examiner will be down shortly."

Fen snapped to attention and saluted.

Pi turned and marched back to the hallway, the door closing behind her with a foreboding click.

Fen leaned down and whispered, "You play a dangerous game. Do not speak." She helped Lucy to her feet and turned her around, so she noticed a camera mounted above the elevator.

Lucy nodded and kept her mouth closed. It seemed Fen had no love for Pi either.

Fen led Lucy over to the stairs.

Holding the railing and dreading each step, Lucy started down. The muscles in her legs trembled, sending pain coursing up her spine. It seemed to take forever, but they finally reached the bottom. Lucy glanced up and gasped.

She had been walking with her head down, staring at her feet to make sure she didn't fall, so she hadn't paid attention to her surroundings. At the bottom of the staircase, a long hallway began. The floor was tiled white and covered with a red and gold carpet. Photographs of the Tennessee countryside hung on the walls with dark, wooden tables underneath them. It wasn't at all what she expected.

They passed two closed doors, and Fen stopped. She glanced at the camera mounted above the door and then turned the handle.

The space was the size of a large hotel room and furnished as such. A king-sized bed sat opposite a large-screen TV mounted on the wall. A door on the far wall was closed, and a kitchenette sat to the left. Lights blazed, and electricity hummed.

Lucy stood in the doorway, blinking. For a moment, it felt like everything that happened had been a nightmare, and she was waking up.

Fen roughly grabbed her and yanked her into the room.

Lucy stumbled and crashed into Fen's chest.

"Don't talk—cameras," Fen whispered. "Stupid, clumsy fool!" She raised her arm as if to strike but pushed Lucy toward the kitchenette and the small table with two chairs instead.

Lucy collapsed onto the wooden chair and stared at the

floor. On the one hand, she wanted to kill Fen for taking Bri. But why would Fen tell her about the cameras?

Fen glared at her and stood at attention next to the closed door.

The minutes ticked by. Lucy shifted uncomfortably on the hard seat and glanced at the bed. What she wouldn't do to lie down and close her eyes. But she had other, more pressing needs. Pushing aside the humiliation of having to ask, Lucy said, "I need to use the bathroom."

"Wait," Fen said.

"For what?"

"You are to be examined first." Fen stared straight ahead. The muscles in her jaw flexed.

"Examined?"

A knock on the door made her jump.

Fen opened it.

A Chinese man in a white lab coat stood in the doorway. He saw Fen, took half a step forward, and snapped to attention. A myriad of expressions passed over his face. Obviously, he knew Fen, but Lucy couldn't tell if he liked or hated her. In his right hand, he held a black bag. His left arm ended in a stump six inches below the elbow.

"You are to examine her immediately and report your findings to Tianzi. Understood?" Fen said.

The man opened his mouth as if to say something, closed it, and nodded.

Fen marched past him, disappearing from sight.

As her footsteps faded down the hallway, the man looked after her. His shoulders slumped. Walking back into the room, he awkwardly closed the door while holding the bag. Crossing to the kitchenette, he set his bag on the counter and opened it. "My name is Dr. Kim. I have been ordered to conduct a full examination of your person." He removed a cloth gown and a specimen cup from the bag. "Please change in the restroom and provide a urine sample."

Lucy grabbed the items and hurried through the door. The bathroom was larger than she expected, with a tub and shower. Walking in the rain was the closest she'd come to a shower in a year. The thought of taking a long, hot one made her want to tell the doctor to wait for the exam—until she remembered his stump.

For some reason, she doubted it was an accident. Maybe it was the way the doctor had said he'd been ordered, or the memory of Tianzi having the soldier killed, but Lucy hurried to get undressed.

The sound of the flushing toilet and the running water from the faucet was so familiar that she washed her hands in amazement. Oh, the life she'd taken for granted. For a moment, everything seemed normal.

Someone knocked on the door. "We need to hurry." Dr. Kim said.

Lucy dried her hands and came out, giving Dr. Kim the specimen vial. "What's that for?"

"Tests." Dr. Kim said, setting it down on the table and leading Lucy over to the table.

He asked her many questions as he gave her a complete medical examination. Dr. Kim kept reaching out with his missing left hand, the stump pressing against her skin and making her cringe.

"I apologize." Dr. Kim said.

Lucy shook her head. "No. I do. There's always been something about...missing parts that freaks me out. Maybe it's because my uncle lost three fingers in a hay baler and always tried to tickle me with the stumps."

Dr. Kim smiled but didn't look into her eyes. "It's difficult to get used to."

"What happened?"

Dr. Kim shook his head. "Nothing."

"That certainly doesn't look like nothing."

Dr. Kim stared at her, his brown eyes wide. "I don't know why you are here, but you are. You must learn to stay quiet. For your safety."

Lucy nodded. If a bone monster had taken off his hand, he wouldn't be reacting how he is. A different kind of monster must have been responsible. "What's the deal with this Tianzi?"

"Shhh." Dr. Kim's gaze darted all over the room. His hand trembled as he paced a stethoscope against Lucy's chest. "He's the new Emperor." He whispered. "You must be careful and do what he says."

"I'll do whatever he wants if he gives me my daughter back."

"Bri?"

Lucy gasped. "Have you seen her?"

"Shhh. Yes. And your mother. For now, they live. You should not have come."

"I didn't have a choice. Fen took Bri."

Lucy cringed as something dripped on her skin. She stared at Dr. Kim as he wiped away a tear.

"You know Fen?"

He sniffed and nodded. "What she did, she did against her will."

"Bull."

"No." Dr. Kim straightened up. "That is why I lost my hand. They cut it off to encourage Fen to go and complete the mission."

"That's sick. How would that encourage her?"

"Because if she had not returned with the boy, they would have started cutting off the rest of me. I hoped she would have let me die." Dr. Kim looked away.

Lucy placed a gentle hand on the man's shaking arm. She wanted to say something, but when she noticed the camera in the corner near the ceiling, she closed her mouth and simply nodded.

Dr. Kim stepped away. "We are done. You are to shower and dress with an outfit from the closet." He gathered everything up and left, leaving Lucy alone and staring at the door.

Lucy hung her head. Not only were there monsters outside, but now she was locked in here with one.

22

MORE THAN TRY

Bri Haight

Bri sat on the bed, staring at the wall, when she heard footsteps out in the hallway. She thought about hiding underneath the bed, but they'd find her. Keys jingled, and the door swung open.

Two men and a woman marched through. They were all Chinese. The man in the front was short, with thinning hair. His nose was sharp and pointy, and his eyes were beady like a rat's. Shiny medals covered his chest. The man behind him was as big as a wrestler on TV. He filled up the doorway as he walked through and then stood in the corner. A woman came in last. She stared at Bri in a way that made Bri want to hide underneath the covers.

"Didn't your parents teach you manners, little girl?" The short man asked. "Stand when I come into the room."

Bri wanted to say something bad back, but the way the woman creepily smiled at her changed her mind. Bri slid off the bed and stared at the man.

"You are Bri Green?"

Bri nodded.

The short man snapped his fingers, and the giant man walked to stand behind Bri.

"I taught my dog that trick," Bri said. "But after I give him a cookie."

The short man chuckled. "You are a brave little girl. And funny. I like that. But right now I need honesty from you. Understand?"

Bri nodded.

"I don't think you do. Chao." He pointed at the wall to her right.

It was made of cement blocks that looked like Legos. Chao punched the block, and it cracked.

"One lie." The man held up his hand. "And Chao will do that to you. Now, do you understand?"

Bri nodded quickly. "Yes, sir."

"I am, Tianzi. Explain to me the night you were taken from your home."

Bri blinked. She rehearsed the story Fen wanted her to tell about Nicholi and the bone bear but Fen hadn't said anything about other stuff. Bri inhaled and decided to tell the truth. She explained how Fen and Nicholi kidnapped her and Jacob. She explained they drugged Jacob and took them in the canoes.

"How do you know the boy?"

"He's my friend."

"What do you know about him?"

"His name's Jacob. He's five. He likes pie. Apple pie."

"What about his parents? What do you know about them?"

Bri shrugged. "Nothing. I don't think he's got none. Mercy Yoder is his aunt."

"His antt?" Tianzi scowled. "What are you saying?"

"Aunt." Bri stretched the vowel out. "I think."

Tianzi stepped forward. He was very short, so he didn't

need to lean far to stare directly into Bri's eyes. His breath stunk like old people food. "What happened to Nicholi?"

Bri made a face like she was confused. Her momma always said if you were gonna lie, lie slow. "That's the big blonde one?"

Tianzi nodded.

"A bone bear broke through the brush and started throwing rocks. One hit Nicholi's canoe. A really big rock. The canoe tipped over. Jacob bobbed up downstream. He was wearing his life vest. But Nicholi never came back up."

"Did the woman search for him?"

"A little."

Tianzi looked over his shoulder at the creepy woman standing behind him.

Her eyes narrowed. "What do you mean a little?"

Bri swallowed. The woman's voice sounded even creepier than she looked. Each word cracked like a whip at the end.

"Answer her, Bri." Tianzi's stinking breath made Bri's nose itch.

"There was a crazy monster bear throwing rocks at us. Would you stick around?"

Tianzi straightened up. "A few more questions. Who came looking for you?"

Bri opened her mouth and closed it.

"Ha! You were going to lie!" Tianzi raised his hand.

"NO!" Bri shouted. "I was going to say, how am I supposed to know, Brainiac? But I thought that would get you mad."

Tianzi opened his fist and lightly patted Bri's cheek with the palm of his hand.

She cringed and tried not to make a face.

"What is your mother's name?"

"Lucy Green."

"And your grandmother?"

"Mawmaw Sadie."

"Who is your father?"

Bri's fingernails dug into the palms of her hands. "I've got two. My momma married Evan Green."

"And your real father?"

"Cain Haight." Bri stretched out the last name and stared defiantly back into Tianzi's eyes.

"Very good, child. One last question. Who do you want to die—your mother or Mawmaw?"

Bri shook her head. "What? Neither of them!" She raised back her fist.

Chao grabbed her by the back of the neck and yanked her off the floor.

Pain shot up her back. She kicked at the large man, but he was too far away for her legs to reach.

"Enough," Tianzi said.

Chao dropped Bri, and she landed hard on her butt. Tears filled her eyes. She glared up at Tianzi.

Tianzi lifted his chin and stared down his nose at her. "I will permit both of them to live if you do everything I say."

Bri sniffed and wiped her nose with the back of her hand. "What do you want me to do?"

"You are to take care of Jacob. Convince him that we are his friends, too."

Bri tried to stop herself from making a face but couldn't. She rolled her eyes. "I'll try!" She quickly added.

"You need to do more than try. If Jacob doesn't believe that we are his friends, then I will ask you that question again, and Chao will make you give me an answer. Do you understand?"

"Yes."

"Good, child." Tianzi smiled. "Now come with us."

23

WIND AND PRAYER

Cain Haight

I shove the door off me, rip my pistol from its holster, and rush over to the bear. One of Bob's rounds hit it in the eye. I put four more rounds into it to ensure it's dead, then turn to Bob.

He's lying on his back on the tile. He's not moving, but he's breathing.

Atticus rushes up beside me. There's a nasty gash on his forehead. "Is he dead?"

"No." I drop down on my knees beside Bob.

The far left doors bang open, and H races into the room with his pistol drawn. He runs over to us, his eyes rounding in concern. "Is he dead?"

Bob opens his eyes. "I must look pretty bad if everybody keeps asking that question. Did I get it?"

H grins. "Bearly. Get it?"

Bob winces, "Don't make me laugh."

"Why? Is the pain unbearable?" H keeps it up.

Bob chuckles and groans. "You're a jerk. Stop. I think I broke a rib."

"You know what they say," H kneels down. "Grin and bear it."

"He's going to shoot you if you don't stop," I say. "H, you check him out. There's a cart in the storage area we found. The helium tanks are there, too. After I unload the tanks, you can use the cart to bring Bob back to the camp."

"I think I can walk." Bob tries to sit up, but H holds him down.

"Wait until I see how busted up you are," H says.

Atticus points at the balloon. "I can take the hopper out the front. Meet me there with the helium."

I stare at Bob. "Nice shooting. Thanks for saving my life."

"I was just worried about my own," Bob says through gritted teeth as H helps him sit up.

I nod, then jog over to retrieve my shotgun. I reload while I trot down the hallway. Bob's a good man, and they tend to deflect credit given. He could have easily run the other way while the bear ate me. In fact, Bob didn't even have to be here in the first place.

My debts keep piling up.

I quickly unload the paper on the cart and start laying the helium tanks on top of it. Picturing myself floating up to the moon, I'm tempted to take only six tanks, but Atticus said we should take seven, so I load the cart full. The idea of landing in the middle of a minefield isn't any more appealing than flying away.

The new cart is made for moving heavy objects in a museum, and it handles the roughly 700 pounds surprisingly easily. I push it out the open loading dock door and head outside. The sky is overcast and there's a good breeze blowing. At first, the wind on my face feels good until I remember what I'm going to do.

I steer the cart down the side road to the front of the museum.

Atticus and the hopper are waiting for me. He's tethered the balloon to the light post. He grins, licks his finger, and holds it up to the sky. "The wind is perfect. You've got nothing to worry about there. Of course, we still gots to make sure you don't fly off or come down and blow up or overshoot the base."

I park the cart close to the hopper and remove the first tank. "I'm glad you brought that up. You said there's no way of steering this thing, but is there some way of lowering it down? Is there like a baffle or something?"

"Not in the original design. The hopper was filled up and tethered. The ground crew would pull it down. But I thought about that and came up with a solution, I think." Atticus taps his head and points at the side of the balloon. "The Atticus helium release system."

My heart starts pounding. Taped to the side of the hopper is a long strip of duct tape connected to a thick fishing line.

"I've poked a series of holes in the side of the balloon and covered them up with a long strip of duct tape. The tape is connected to the fishing line. When you wants to come down, pull on the fishing line, and as the tape comes off, more and more holes will be revealed, and the lower you'll go!"

"How do I know it's not going to pop?"

Atticus strokes his beard. "I don't figure it would. I suppose that's possible. Sure hope it don't."

While he fills the balloon, I unload the rest of the helium canisters.

H and Bob come out the front door. Bob is moving slowly, but he's walking on his own power.

"I have a new cart for you," I say as Bob takes the ramp instead of the stairs.

"I don't need it. I'm going to try to walk it off." Bob says.

H rolls his eyes.

"You should still take this cart, H," I say. "With its big tires, it's perfect for scavenging."

"You're right. We can use it." H grins at Bob. "Can you bear-lieve it?"

Bob groans. I don't know if he's hurting since he's moving or because the joke was that bad.

"Almost finished!" Atticus calls out. "Cain, I need you to sit on the bench."

Puzzled, I stare at the hopper, now fully inflated and tugging on its tether. Two ropes hang down from the balloon and Atticus has attached a wooden bench between them.

"That's the seat?" My mouth drops open. "There's no basket or even a chair?"

H chuckles. "Don't let that get you *deflated*. Hop-per to it, buddy."

I rest my hand on my pistol as I stomp over to the balloon. "I'm not as nice as Bob, H. I will shoot you if you say one more joke."

Bob laughs.

I sit on a three-foot-long and two-foot-wide plank, and the Hopper starts sinking.

"Don't move around," Attics says as he turns the lever on the helium tank. "The trick is gonna be fillin' it enough so you'll make it over the minefield."

"How's he going to come back down?" Bob asks.

"I made a quick-release system," Attics beams.

"Is that the fishing line and duct tape?" H points and then whispers something to Bob.

Bob swallows. "Are you sure about that, Atticus? That balloon is under a lot of pressure."

"I'm sure. Mostly. Sixty-seventy percent at least."

I brush my hair back. "I'm going all in on this plan, and you're only sixty-seventy percent sure?"

"Take it easy." Atticus puts his hand back on the helium lever as I rise up. "Worst-case scenario is it doesn't work at all and the fishing line snaps. If I were you, I'd shoot the balloon then."

"Everyone within a mile will hear a gun fired in the air!"

"True, but it beats flyin' to France." Atticus strokes his beard. "Wait, I'm wrong. Worser case is if I didn't put enough air in and you come down in the minefield."

With my feet dangling in the air, the hopper starts rotating slowly, and I've got to turn to glare at Atticus.

"Nope. Nope." Atticus shuts off the helium. "That's wrong too. The worsest case is you pull on the tape, and the hopper pops. Then you'll just fall to the ground."

"That's wrong, too." A smart-aleck grin crosses H's face. "What if the balloon pops when he's over the minefield?"

I'm about ready to go for my gun when Bob shakes his head.

"You're both wrong," Bob says. "If Cain pulls the tape and the hopper pops, he could land on a mine and *then* get blown into the barbed wire fence!"

"I hate you all," I say as I force myself to laugh.

These guys are risking their lives for me. I know they care what happens, but since there's nothing they can do, they break out the gallows humor.

"Thanks for those uplifting jokes," I say. "They really lightened my spirit."

H laughs so hard I know it's forced.

"If I don't see you again, thanks," I say.

"When you do make it out, make sure you stop by and get us."

"And what? Take you all back to Ridgecrest?"

"You don't think we came just because we like you, did ya?" H winks.

"How are you going to move all those survivors?"

"Leave that to us," Bob says.

Atticus lifts his chin. "The wind is shifting. We better cast him off."

"Wait!" H says, his face serious. "How are you going to make sure that Cain lands on the east side of the base?"

Atticus licks his finger and holds it up. "Wind and prayer."

I look at Atticus and nod.

The old man bows his head for a moment and unclicks the tether.

24

TOMORROW YOU DIE

Mercy Yoder

Mercy opened her left eye and moaned. Something was wrong. Her right eye wouldn't open. She reached up, and her fingers touched the bandages wrapped around her throbbing head.

The wagon jostled as the wheels struck a bump. Pain shuddered through her body. Her stomach ached. Her ribs were tender, and it hurt to open her mouth. She peered around. The sky was darkening. How long had she been unconscious? She gasped, and the pain as her stomach clenched made her nauseous. Grabbing the end of the wagon, she pulled herself up so her head was over the side and threw up—right in the face of the giant wolf trotting behind them.

The beast skidded sideways and shook its head.

Eve laughed.

The wolf growled and glared at Mercy.

Mercy slid back, pressing against the sideboard. She hung her throbbing head and wiped her mouth.

"Look in the sack on your right," Eve said. "The one with red."

Mercy glanced down. Four canvas sacks sat on her right. The smallest had a red grain label on it. It was held closed with a man's belt.

"Open it," Eve said.

Mercy's fingers shook as she undid the belt and peered into the sack. Inside were supplies and several water bottles.

"Drink. Eat."

"Thank you." Mercy removed one of the water bottles and a pack of peanut butter crackers. "Would you like some?"

Eve scowled.

Mercy bowed her head. "Dear Lord, thank you for the food and water you have provided. Please help that family—"

"NO!" Eve jammed her thumb against her chest. "I gave you water. I am Eve. Not Lord."

Puzzled, Mercy shook her head and then nodded. "Yes, you did. I meant no disrespect. I was praying. I do that out loud sometimes. I was saying thank you for the water and food."

"You were thanking this man named Lord?" Eve glanced around.

"I was praying. Talking to God."

Eve's back stiffened, raising her higher in the saddle. "First, you say you are speaking to a man called Lord. Now, his name is God? Where is he?"

Mercy's head throbbed. "You've never heard of God?"

"Has he ever heard of me?" Eve seemed quite agitated as she defiantly glared in all directions.

The bear raised his head and sniffed but kept moving forward.

"I'm sure He has—"

Eve cut her off. "Then tell him to come out or go away. And stop talking to him. Besides, he can't help that family now. I killed them."

"No. Why?" Mercy's voice broke, and so did she. Tears poured down her cheeks, and sobs wracked her frame. The more she cried, the more her stomach hurt. She threw up again and collapsed onto the floor of the wagon. She gasped for breath between sobs.

"Stupid scourge," Eve said and then urged the bear forward. The bear charged until it reached the wolves pulling the wagon. It slowed and matched their pace.

Mercy sucked in air in rapid, shallow breaths. She was hyperventilating, but as she tried to calm down, all she could picture was the mother, clutching the little girl in terror as the wolves broke through the door.

Mercy wheezed, and her world spun into darkness once again.

***

The tailboard of the wagon bashed off the back wheels. Mercy groaned as Eve grabbed her by her ankles and dragged her out. Mercy tumbled out of the wagon and fell to the ground. The water bottle and crackers landed beside her.

"You didn't eat or drink?" Eve glared down at her.

"I'm sorry," Mercy said, picking up the items. "I think I passed out again." Mercy glanced around. A small fire blazed a few yards away. The wolves and bear were gone.

"They needed to eat. So do you. Go." Eve pushed Mercy toward the fire.

Mercy stumbled forward. The fire glowed brightly, and she squinted her one functioning eye. Four small birds and a fish roasted on a spit above the flames.

"Sit." Eve pointed at a log.

Mercy trudged over and sat down. She opened the water bottle and bowed her head. "Lord—"

"Not again!" Eve shouted. "STOP!"

Mercy clamped her mouth closed and continued to pray silently.

Dear Lord, thank you for the food. Please help Eve to—

Eve marched over and glared down at her. She drew her knife and pointed the blade toward Mercy. "I told you to stop! Eve gave you the water. Eve gave you the food. Not this Lord."

"I stopped."

"No, you didn't. And I don't need anyone's help."

Mercy gasped.

Eve's eyes sparkled blue. They were brighter than just reflecting the light from the fire. They were softly glowing.

"You heard what I was thinking?" Mercy said.

Eve grabbed a stick off the fire and handed it to Mercy. Two roasted small birds and a fish were skewered on it. "Eve caught them. Eve cooked them. You thank Eve!"

"I do. Thank you very much. But I had to thank God, too."

Eve lifted her skewer off the fire and kicked the log. Sparks rose high into the night sky. "What did this God do?" The veins in her neck stuck out as she screamed.

"They were His birds." Mercy said.

Eve's eyebrows pinched together. She looked down at the birds. "I caught them in the field. And the fish in a pond we passed. Does God own the land?"

"Yes. In a way."

Eve sat on a log opposite Mercy. She bit down on the fish, eating the head. As she chewed loudly, the bones crunched in her mouth.

Mercy looked at the ground.

"Was this God hiding in the farm?"

Mercy shook her head. How could she explain that God was invisible?

"Ha!" Eve laughed and took a bite out of the fish. "If he is invisible, then God is not real."

Mercy swallowed. This woman could read her mind. How was that possible?

Eve shook her head and ate the tail of the fish. "You think you're so smart, but you don't know me. You can't hear me."

"You know what I'm thinking?"

Eve thrust a greasy finger out. "Eat!"

Mercy took a bite of the bird. It tasted like chicken but was too small. She shut her eyes as she pictured the little girl running out of the barn. Tears rolled down her cheeks.

"Stop crying!" Eve bit into one of the birds on her skewer. Bones snapped as she chewed loudly.

She eats the bone?

"You don't?"

Mercy shook her head. It was so strange not speaking and having her thoughts read. "I'm sorry." Mercy took a sip of water and sniffed, but more tears sprang from her eyes and clung to her lashes.

"Enough! I didn't kill them. Neither did the wolves."

Mercy's eyes widened.

"Or the bear. I'm not tricking you. I called them back."

"Thank you! Oh, thank you!" Mercy sobbed.

"Now, why are you bawling? Stop. Let me eat in peace."

Mercy nodded and took another bite of the bird. Relief washed over her, and the knot in her stomach relaxed as it did. She was starving. After finishing the birds, she ate the fish, carefully picking out the tiny bones. "This was very good. Thank you."

Eve nodded.

Mercy opened her mouth and closed it. She was going to ask Eve why she didn't kill the family, but she didn't want to anger her again.

Eve's eyes narrowed. "You."

"Me what?" Mercy shrugged as she used a little of the bottled water to rinse her fingers. "Did I think something?"

"You asked why I let the scourge live. Because you asked. Now, I ask the questions. Why did you drop the knife?"

Mercy stared at Eve. Her greyish skin shimmered in the firelight. The flames highlighted the scars on the side of her shaved head.

Eve stood, her hands balled into fists at her side. "Do not pity me. Pity yourself. Tomorrow I take you to him. He knows nothing about mercy. Tomorrow, you will die."

25

THINGS ARE LOOKING UP

Cain Haight

I'm sitting on a wooden bench strapped to a giant balloon, slowly floating over a destroyed city. I'm trying to cross a moat, a minefield, and barbed-wire fences. After that, all I've got to do is take on an Army to rescue my daughter, my ex-wife and her mother, and a little boy. But somehow, I'm not freaked out.

The wind is gently moving me toward the base, and I'm feeling this really odd sense of peace. Every once in a while, I catch a glimpse of stars through the clouds, and it takes my breath away.

I can see a couple of lights on in the base. They're dim, so I figure they come from inside a building. I'm holding onto the two ropes like a little kid on a swing. My legs dangle, and I gaze at the darkness around me.

Far off to my left, a small fire burns. It's back along the highway. I can't tell much about it, but it puzzles me. Anyone lighting a fire at night was asking for trouble. I'd reckon anybody so foolish wouldn't have made it a year into the Dark, though.

A gust of wind rocks the balloon, and my grip tightens on the ropes. The swaying doesn't bother me, but how fast I'm rising does. I focus on the two dim lights in the army base, and one of them blinks out.

My heart is pounding. If that other light shuts off, I'll have no reference to how high I am or where the base is. I can't see the ground with the clouds blocking the moon and stars.

The hopper creaks and continues to rise. I'm also moving forward at a pretty good clip. I can't tell exactly how fast, but I think I would beat someone running on the ground.

I take hold of the fishing line. Slowly, I pull, steadily building pressure until the line starts digging into my skin. It's so taut I'm worried it's going to snap. I let out a little slack and tug.

My breath catches in my throat. I think I hear the tape pulling free a little. I give another tug and nothing. I pull harder. The fishing line snaps and floats down until it's streaming behind me, one end still gripped in my hand.

I swear.

The last thing I want to do is fire my pistol. Not only will the muzzle flash look like a flare, but the shot will echo for miles. Maybe there's another way?

Gritting my teeth, I grab the ropes and pull myself up so I'm standing on the bench. Stretching my arm up, I'm four feet away from the bottom of the hopper. Maybe I can shimmy up the rope and make a small cut?

I reach down for my knife when something flies by close to me. From the shadow and sound of its wings, it had to be a huge bird. I'm glad it didn't crash into the balloon.

Something smacks into the bench next to my right boot. I stare at a four-inch, bone-white spike embedded in the wood next to my boot.

There are flying monsters, too?

Five whooshing sounds break the silence as more spikes

sail past me. I catch a glimpse of the bird as it makes a pass like a fighter jet.

I reach for my pistol when I realize that the hopper is hissing above me. Suddenly, I'm descending. Whatever that demon in the dark is, it solved the problem of my flying away to the moon. But now I'm descending too quickly!

"Thanks, stupid," I whisper as I lower myself down and sit on the bench.

I pull out the spike. It's similar to bone rats but much thinner and lighter. Still, it sunk into the wood. Getting hit by one of them might not kill you, but it wouldn't be fun.

Wings flutter, and a few more bone spikes whizz by me.

The hopper rocks, and I start going down a lot faster.

I check for my light in the base. It's still on and drawing closer, but I'm too far away. The clouds part a little, and the moon glints off the barbed-wire fence. I'm still a hundred yards short.

I'm screwed. I'm going to land in the minefield!

Holding onto the ropes, I slide off the bench. It tips up and presses against my back. My legs dangle as the ground slowly rises to meet me.

"Please don't step on a mine! Please don't step on a mine!" I repeat over and over. My right boot hits the ground. I go into a deep squat and push up as hard as possible with one leg. Like an astronaut on the moon, I jump like Superman. I almost start laughing as I sail back into the air until I realize I will only float about thirty feet before coming back down.

Bracing myself to repeat the process, I see a crater ahead. Something must have set off one of the mines. That means that spot is clear! Twisting my body and pulling the ropes, I aim for the crater. The hopper cooperates, and I float just enough to the right.

I put both feet down, run along the bottom of the crater, and jump as high as I can when I reach the top. I soar into the air. I float higher than the fence but won't make it, judging from my trajectory. At the rate the hopper is losing lift, I will never clear the top of the fence.

Unless....

I rip my knife out of my sheath.

The hopper continues upward but starts to slow down.

I slice through one of the ropes, holding the bench, and groan as I hang onto the other rope with one arm.

I'm starting to descend.

I slice the rope, still holding the bench, but my blade doesn't cut all the way through.

Bracing for impact, I have no choice but to land with both feet down. I push so hard that my head hits the bottom of the balloon. I'm hanging onto the one rope as I shoot upward. The bench swings back and bashes into my legs. It slides down the rope and falls free.

I watch as it tumbles toward the ground.

My eyes widen, and I hold my breath.

The bench hits the ground with a loud thump and bounces into the air.

Nothing goes boom. I exhale. I'm almost to the fence and high enough to get over. I'm going to make it.

The board hits the ground again. The brilliant light beneath my feet blinds me, and a millisecond later, a deafening boom makes me want to cover my ears, but I can't because I'm hanging onto a rope. Chunks of dirt and rock smack into me and tear into the hopper.

The balloon hisses loudly and plummets. I can't see or hear anything but know I'm falling quickly. I'm not dropping, but I'm coming down fast enough that it's going to hurt a lot if I hit something.

The fence appears right in front of me. I lift my legs, but my right boot catches on the barbed wire. The rope pulls out of my hand. With my boot stuck on top of the fence, my body pivots forward and bashes off the fence. All the air is knocked from my lungs.

I'm hanging upside down, feeling like a bug that just got swatted out of the sky. I slip out of my boot and drop head-first to the ground. My shoulders take most of the impact, but it still feels like someone hit me with a hammer upside the head.

I blink rapidly, trying to clear my head. A thunk beside me makes me roll onto my knees and look. My boot fell off the fence and landed in the dirt beside me. I pick it up and smile. I've made it alive into the camp in one piece with all my gear. Things are looking up.

I pull my boot back on and stand up.

The whole world shifts sideways as the blood rushes to my head. Bright sparkles fill my vision. I'm falling forward. I try to tell myself to raise my arms, but my body isn't cooperating. Maybe I landed on my head harder than I tho—

26

LISTEN

Bri Haight

Bri walked beside Tianzi down a long hallway to a metal door. The mean woman followed on Tianzi's right. Chao marched behind them, holding up an oil lamp.

At the end of the hallway, a lamp flickered on the wall. Two men stood guard in front of a metal door. When they saw Tianzi, they snapped to attention.

One of the soldiers turned, unlocked the door, and held it open until they passed.

Bri expected to walk into a room, but it was a stairwell. The light from the lamp Chao held reflected off the wall, but the stairs disappeared into the darkness. Bri swallowed. She didn't like this at all.

The door closed behind them and locked.

Chao blew out the light, plunging them into darkness.

"Stupid goofus!" Bri said.

Something clicked, and ceiling lights flickered on. She peered over the railing. A metal staircase led down, and lights glowed all the way to the bottom far below.

"If you are afraid of the dark," Tianzi said, placing a cold hand on Bri's shoulder. "Do not wander off. There are things down there that you should be terrified of."

Bri swallowed and grasped the railing with a shaking hand. To the right, there was an elevator. The doors were closed, and the lights were off. She'd much rather ride down in the elevator, but Tainzi nudged her forward.

They made their way down the stairs. The air cooled, and the hum of a motor echoed off the walls.

"How do you have lights?" Bri asked.

"This place is special. So is Jacob. That's why we need you to be nice to him."

"I am nice to him. He's my friend."

"I want to be his friend too. Remember that. Do you remember what I promised if that doesn't happen?"

How could Bri forget the horrible man's words? He said he'd make her pick if her momma or Mawmaw died. She thought about pushing him down the stairs, but Chao was close behind them, and he'd probably stop her. And what would she do after? She couldn't outrun a giant.

Down and down they went until they reached a large hallway. The floor was tiled white, but there was a red and gold carpet on the floor. Pictures hung on the walls and there were dark, wooden tables underneath them. It reminded Bri of a fancy hotel she'd seen in a movie. It wasn't at all what she expected.

They passed several closed doors until they reached a four-way intersection. The hallway continued off in every direction. Tianzi prodded her to the right. She walked by two more doors, and he stopped and grabbed her shoulder.

Leaning forward so he was staring into her eyes, he gave her a creepy smile.

Her eyes widened. "Chitty Chitty Bang Bang," The words tumbled out of her mouth.

Tianzi gazed at the woman beside them and raised an eyebrow. "Pi, is that a Southern colloquialism?"

Bri giggled when the woman reached into her pocket. "Your name is Pi?"

Pi scowled and took out a phone.

"You have a phone?" Bri's mouth fell open. "Does it work? Who can you call?"

Pi said something in Chinese into the phone, followed by the words, "Chitty Chitty Bang Bang." She read the screen and shook her head. "It is an old American movie."

"Why did you say Chitty Chitty Bang Bang?" Tianzi asked.

Bri opened her mouth. She couldn't say he reminded her of the creepy child catcher, so she shrugged. "I'm a kid. We say stupid stuff."

Tianzi scowled. "Not anymore. Do not forget why I brought you here. You are to talk to Jacob. Convince him that we are his friends. Do you understand?"

Bri nodded.

"Good. Now smile. Smile at me like I am your friend."

Bri stared at his beady eyes and her stomach didn't feel good. She forced her lips to curl up.

"Bigger!" Tianzi's grin widened, and he looked like a psycho.

Bri smiled so big her cheeks hurt.

"Good." Tianzi nodded.

Pi opened the door.

The room was cheery and bright. In the corner, a huge TV played "The Flintstones". Bean bags and toys littered the floor.

"Jacob?" Tianzi called out in a tone that made Bri want to run the other way. "I've brought someone you want to see."

A pile of beanbags in the corner shook.

Bri walked forward. "Jacob? It's me. Can I talk to you?"

He didn't answer.

Tianzi said something to Pi and Chao, then stepped into the room after Bri.

The bags shook again.

"Maybe you should come back?" Bri said to Tianzi. "Why don't you let me play with Jacob a bit, got it?"

Tianzi glared at her.

Bri rolled her eyes. "Where am I going to go? We'll watch some TV."

Tianzi grabbed her arm, leaned forward, and whispered, "Make him understand, or it will not go well for you."

His stinky breath made her want to turn away, but she stared back at him. "I got it."

"I'll have Auntie Pi bring you two lunch," Tianzi said in a sing-song voice.

Bri couldn't help but make a face.

Out from the beanbag pile came a little giggle.

"Oh, good!" Tianzi grinned. "Peanut butter and jelly. Your favorite. Auntie will come right back with it."

Footsteps sounded behind them as Pi hurried out of the room.

Bri motioned Tianzi to leave.

He kept smiling with his mouth, but his eyes narrowed. "See you soon, you two huggy buddies."

Bri turned to the beanbag and made a face that consisted of rolling her eyes to the ceiling and sticking out her tongue.

Jacob giggled again.

Tianzi clapped his hands together, nodded at Bri, and left.

Bri exhaled.

The bean bag tower tumbled outward as Jacob raced from under his hiding place. He wrapped his arms around Bri as tears poured down his cheeks. He was sobbing and crying so much she couldn't understand what he was saying.

"It's okay, Jacob. It's okay. We're going to get out of here. My daddy's coming for us."

Jacob sniffed, wiped his nose, and nodded.

"See?" Bri rubbed his back like her mawmaw rubbed hers when she was sad. "We're going to be okay."

Jacob started crying again. He said something, but she couldn't understand him.

"Stop blubbering like a baby. What are you saying?"

He held her hand and led her to the corner of the room and the TV. He grabbed the power cord and pulled it out of the wall, plunging the room into silence.

Bri pointed at the TV remote lying on the ground. "You know that has a mute button, right?"

Jacob placed his finger over her mouth and knelt. He put his head close to the outlet and motioned for her to do the same.

Bri got down on her knees and scooted as close to the wall as she could. Her Daddy always told her to respect something that could kill you quickly, so she didn't touch the electrical outlet but placed her ear close.

All she heard was her heart thumping inside her chest. She listened harder and was about to stop when she heard the scraping. It sounded like Mawmaw pulling rocks out of the garden. Her eyebrows knit together. "What is it?"

Jacob's lip trembled. "He's coming to get us."

27

FRANK PICKETT

Amos Yoder

Amos coughed, and his eyes fluttered open. He tried to swallow, but his mouth was dry and tasted like blood. He lay on the ground, surrounded by people all shouting. Sarah was kneeling beside him. Tears ran down her cheeks as she loosened the noose and took it off his head.

"I guess I'm not dead," Amos said.

Sarah handed him a bottle of water and helped him sit up.

"You broke my nose." Billy Pickett sat on the ground five feet away, holding his shirt to his bloody face.

"I told you to leave Amos Yoder to me." Frank Pickett screamed.

Amos glanced up.

Frank Pickett loomed over Billy with a pistol in each hand. He stared down the crowd, slowly fixing each man with a cold glare and pointing a gun at their chest. "Anyone else want to argue?"

Frank's brother Boone strode out the broken front door to

the doctor's office. "Jesse's inside, Frank. He says he won't come out."

"Tell him his father's out here."

"I did."

"Well, what did he say?"

Boone took a deep breath. "He said he was scared."

Frank stepped back. His brows knit together, and he grimaced like he'd been punched. He glared down at Amos.

"You stay away from him, Frank Pickett." Sarah stood up as she helped Amos struggle to his feet, too. "You don't know why—"

"I don't care why!" Frank screamed, the veins rising along his temples like snakes moving beneath the skin. "Move aside. I don't particularly care for shootin' women."

Amos reached for Sarah, but she knocked his hand away.

"Move aside, Sarah. You see what your yellow dog of a husband hidin' behind his wife did to my son? He made him a coward. Just like himself."

Amos moved forward, but two men behind him seized his arms.

"You are a fool, Frank Pickett. Amos isn't a coward, and neither is your boy. Everyone else that left town is dead. But Jesse made it back. He was hurt and almost dead but was strong enough to get home, and you don't see that."

"Then why don't he have the guts to come out and say it to my face?" Frank shouted.

"Because he's more terrified of his father than the monsters that killed his friends. You've already lost one boy. You almost lost another. Is this any way to welcome him home?"

Frank jammed the pistol in his right hand into the holster. He raised his arm. His palm was open, and his fingers shook with rage.

"DON'T!"

Everyone turned to stare at the house.

Jesse Pickett stood on the porch, holding his sketch pad, with Ani at his side. "Leave her be, Dad. Mrs. Yoder was a friend of Momma's."

Frank holstered his other gun. The crowd parted to let him pass as he walked toward the porch. He stopped at the bottom step and stared at Jesse like he hadn't seen him before.

Billy pushed through the crowd and moved to stand next to Frank. "Why are you alive? I bet it's 'cause you ran."

A rock sailed out from the group and struck Billy in the head. He stumbled forward, his hand covering his fresh wound. "Who threw that?"

"I did." Daisy marched over and got in his face. "Who are you to call someone a coward for running away from those monsters? You stayed here. Jesse volunteered to go. Everyone tried to talk him out of it, but he wanted to help. So shut your mouth." Daisy's hands balled into fists.

"Don't hit him, Daisy," Jesse said. "I did run. We all did—after the bullets ran out. But as night came, I was the only one left." He turned to stare at his father. "But I remembered what you taught me when you'd take me hunting about covering my scent. I made it to the river and went slow. And I did what Momma always said. I prayed. I didn't know what to say except Momma's prayer."

As he spoke, Frank repeated Psalm 23 with his son.

"The Lord is my shepherd; I shall not want. He makes me lie down in green pastures. He leads me beside still waters. He restores my soul. He leads me in paths of righteousness for his name's sake. Even though I walk through the valley of the shadow of death, I will fear no evil, for you are with me; your rod and your staff, they comfort me. You prepare a table before me in the presence of my enemies; you anoint my head with oil; my cup overflows. Surely goodness and mercy shall follow me all the days of my life, and I shall dwell in the house of the Lord forever."

Frank burst into tears. He thundered up the stairs and embraced his son.

Jesse wept.

The crowd cheered.

Amos' attention shifted to Ani. She stiffened up. Her arms were rigid at her side. She lifted her chin and tilted her head like she was listening to something far away. Her eyes were closed. When she opened them, Amos gasped.

Her blue eyes glowed. She stared at Amos in horror. "They're here!"

All around the town, the sound of gunfire erupted.

The battle for Ridgecrest had begun.

28

ABOVE MY PAY GRADE

Cain Haight

I came to, bound to a chair in a pitch-black room. I try to move, but it's useless. I can feel the rope tied around my wrists, so I'm guessing that's what they used to bind each ankle and wrap around my chest, too. There's no breaking the ropes. I pull, push, and wriggle, but whoever cinched these ropes knew their knots.

Is this what Bolin felt like? Trapped and wondering what his captors were going to do to him?

I'm not waxing patriotic, but I'd much rather be captured by Americans. I've seen enough movies to know getting caught by the Chinese or Russians doesn't end well. Still, I'm getting bored, and I'm ticked off. I made it all the way into the base only to get caught. Seeing how I can't break or untie my bonds, I settle on another idea to get free.

I start shaking and groaning. I'm no actor but I was in a school play once. It was only because I wanted to get close to Lucy, and she was playing Glenda. I played the Wizard until I got fired for upping the special effects with a little lighter fluid.

Still, I think I had what they call natural talent.

I groan louder. I keep at it, building in volume, until I hear a noise outside and see the light underneath a door. Then I really pour it on. I moan and rock back and forth, pushing the chair off the floor with my toes. The chair tips to the left, and I fall sideways. I bash off a tile floor. The arm of the chair takes most of the impact, so it doesn't hurt much.

Two big soldiers shove open the door and shine a light on me.

I shake like a paint can on a mixer. My head twitches, and I let some spit fly for good measure.

The guards say something to each other in Russian. One drops down to his knees and tries to roll me onto my back. Since I'm tied to a chair, when he does, my head is lying at a downward angle with my feet higher than my head.

I start gagging like I'm choking. Spit is flying out of my mouth, and I start gasping for air.

The other guard kneels down. They yell at each other in Russian, debating what to do.

I add this trick I learned as a kid from my Uncle Mark. I roll my eyes up in my head and open the lids wide. It used to freak everyone out and it still works.

The guards gasp. They start untying the ropes.

My legs are free, and they're working on the rope around my chest.

I gasp three times, go stiff, and then slump back down, holding my breath.

One of the guards swears in English but with a thick Russian accent. He snaps open a knife.

"Stop!" A man shouts from the doorway, followed by the sound of a shotgun racking a round into the chamber.

The guards stop.

My lungs are burning from playing dead. So I gulp in air and start twitching and shaking again.

The man in the doorway says something in Russian.

The guards stand and hurry away from me.

My hands and chest are still tied to the chair, but my legs are free. Lot of good that will do me against a shotgun.

The man says something else, and the new guards march over to me. They grab the chair and pull me back into a sitting position.

I hang my head and start wheezing.

The man in the doorway claps. "Very good. Very convincing. I would have believed you, but you made a little mistake. If you were really having a seizure, your fingers would have been stiff. But your hands were relaxed, ready to make your move."

I take a deep breath, and when I raise my head, I look him in the eye.

The man is a bear of a Russian. He's in his fifties, but his bushy grey and white beard makes him look older. Wide-shouldered with a pot belly, he strolls into the room, and the guards come to attention. One grabs a metal folding chair against the wall and opens it for the man.

The big man sits down. "What was your mission? Why did Tianzi send you?"

Tianzi is the man Bolin said was in charge of the Eastern half of the army base. Did the wind blow me off course and I landed on the wrong side?

"I cannot understand him or you," the Russian says. "The world has gone into the toilet. We don't want to fight Tianzi. We just want to be left alone. If you tell me the truth, you can stay, or I will send you back."

I can't help but cock an eyebrow. There's no way this guy would let me go if I were his enemy.

One of the guards says something in Russian.

The big guy shakes his head. "Are you another assassin sent to kill me? Why? If you kill me, someone else will only take my place. But again, we don't want to fight you."

Running footsteps sound in the hallway. Two men appear in the doorway and snap to attention. One is dressed in Russian blue camouflage, and the other is an American.

The American stares at me and shakes his head. "I've never seen him. And that isn't a real uniform."

"I never said it was," I say.

"He speaks!" The big Russian grins and glances over his shoulder at the American. "Are you certain?"

"Positive."

"Sorry to make you come all this way, Steven. Thank you."

Steven nods, and both the men head back down the hall the way they came.

"Who are you?" The big Russian asks. "I am Luka."

I eye the insignia on his shoulder and guess as to his rank. "Colonel Luka Andreeva?"

"I was only Captain Andreeva." Luka shrugs. "But no more. Mother Russia is gone. So too, is America, no? We are all equal now."

"Then why do you still wear the uniform?"

"It bothers the others when I walk around naked."

I laugh.

Luka joins in. "What is your name?"

"Cain Haight."

Luka rubs his hand down his face. "Why do you want to make things so difficult?"

"That's really my name."

"From your accent, you were clearly born here in the Bible Belt. And you expect me to believe that a Christian American woman named her son Cain, especially with a last name like Haight?"

I sit there blinking for a minute as I realize something. "You know, I always just blamed my father. But you're right. My mother should have said no."

Luka crosses his beefy arms. "Why has Tianzi sent you here? What was your mission?"

"Didn't you hear Steven? I'm not working for Tianzi."

"Just because you're not wearing a uniform doesn't prove that. And it was a large base. Steven couldn't know everyone."

"If I was working for this Tianzi, why did I cross the minefield from the city on a balloon?"

One of the guards punched the other guard in the arm. "Balloon!"

Luka's eyes widen. "It was a balloon? Then you are crazy."

"That depends on who you ask. But I don't work for Tianzi and I've got nothing against you." I take a deep breath. If Tianzi is Luka's enemy, he may look favorably on my plan. "I need to reach the east side of the base. Tianzi captured my daughter and friends."

Luka and the guards exchange glances. "Continue."

"A Chinese soldier kidnapped my daughter and her friend. Three women and I came after them." I leave off Nickoli's involvement just in case these guys know him.

"Where did you come from?"

"A little town South of here." I lie.

Luka spends the next hour grilling me about where I came from and what it was like there. The only thing I lie about is the location of Ridgecrest. Other than that, I tell the truth. Whether or not he believes me, I don't know.

When he finishes asking questions, Luka's lips press into a thin line and disappear behind his beard. "Why do the creatures stay out of Ridgecrest? Is it surrounded by water? Do none of the birds attack? What about the ghouls and rats?"

"The town doesn't have a moat. We call it the boundary, but it's just an area you don't cross. The monsters never attacked the town."

"Why do they leave you alone?" Luka's voice is pleading.

All I can do is shrug. "Do they attack the base?"

"Relentlessly. Tianzi drives them back, but we are losing the war of attrition. We are not many. Mostly Russians. Some Americans, like Steven, and a few Chinese."

"I heard that Tianzi is low on ammo. Is that true?"

Luka nods. "We all are. The monsters targeted that and the food. The ammunition building sits at the bottom of a pit."

"Without guns, how does Tianzi drive the monsters away then?"

"He still has some traditional weapons, but I think he has a special machine. The Chinese brought lots of equipment with them. All we know is something makes the creatures flee. I was hoping that this Ridgecrest had one, too."

I shake my head. "No. I didn't even know about the creatures until recently."

"You are fortunate. The little I know about them, I wish I did not. These experiments were...what is the term? Above my pay grade?"

"But you're sure the monsters were created?"

Luka chuckles bitterly. "Why do you look so surprised? Men have always dabbled in what they don't know. Here, it is no different."

I try to lean forward but can't because of the ropes. "This is different. I never thought the American Army would work on something like that with China and Russia."

"The project started over twenty years ago as a joint program between universities. As I said, it was well above my pay grade. I only know enough to make me feel so guilty that I didn't try to stop it. I can't sleep at night anymore. The experiments began innocently enough. The goal was to communicate with animals. The universities had good intentions."

"My mother used to say the road to Hell is paved with good intentions."

"Your mother was right. Whatever they did, it morphed the

test subjects. They had research facilities in all three countries. When some of the subjects escaped, the military stepped in."

"They didn't shut it down?"

"The fools should have. They didn't see the danger. They only saw the military possibilities."

I cock an eyebrow. "And you want me to believe they decided to cooperate with each other?"

"Believe it or not, it is the truth. These changes in the animals and the test subjects frightened the governments enough to work together—at least on this."

Goosebumps rise along my arms. My chest tightens, and it's hard for me to get the words out. "You said animals and test subjects? Are you saying they experimented on humans?"

"At first, the professors experimented on students or even themselves. They wanted to communicate with animals and communication is a two-way road. But there were unforeseen side effects. That's when they turned to soldiers and others as test subjects."

"What others?"

"They collected different people from all over the globe— men, women, even children. From every race, they brought them in. But the test subjects did not want to be contained. There was a breach in China."

"Ma Ding."

"Yes. The government tried to contain the breach."

"By killing everyone in the valley. Are you saying flooding the valley didn't kill the monsters?"

"Some survived. My unit joined American and Chinese forces and performed clean-up. That's why we were called here. It turns out that some of the monsters escaped years ago under-neath Fort Burgess. But they stayed hidden, and they bred. I think they were waiting for the right time to attack. When the EMP hit, the cages lost power, and the monsters attacked. They freed all the test subjects along with the creatures."

"So it was a jailbreak? But who fired the EMP?"

"We don't know. No country or terrorist group claimed responsibility. It could have been a solar flare."

I let my head roll back on my shoulders and stare at the ceiling in disbelief. "So the Dark didn't make these creatures—we did?"

Luka nods. "And we cannot hold out much longer. This Ridgecrest, you said it has a Mayor. Is he a fair man?"

"The Mayor is a man, so fair is open for interpretation. What do you want?"

"Sanctuary. We will abide by their laws if Ridgecrest is safe from these monsters. We can help them too. We're skilled."

"Then maybe we can help each other. You help me get my girl, and I'll talk to the Mayor."

Luka shakes his head. "I want you to know I am a father, too. I understand what you are going through. But I have a responsibility to the men who put their faith in me. Our numbers are too small to take on Tianzi and win."

"I don't need many men."

"If we help you, Tianzi will never forgive or forget. It will be constant war with both him and the monsters. I cannot help you, and there is no way you can do it alone. When we saw them arrive with the little girl and boy, my heart broke for the children. But there was nothing I could do then or now. I am sorry."

My throat tightens. The chair scrapes against the floor as I strain against the ropes.

The guards shift forward warily.

"You saw them?"

"They brought them in a few days ago. A little later, a truck arrived with the two captured women."

"Only two?"

He describes Lucy and Sadie. "Tianzi has no respect for life

—anyone's. If a person is deemed useless, they will be disposed of."

"Untie me. Please." Begging has always been the hardest thing for me to do. But I'm doing it now. "I just want to get my daughter back. I swear if I get caught, I won't say anything to Tianzi. He won't know I even talked to you. The Chinese woman would have told him about me. He'll know I came from Ridgecrest to get my daughter."

"Do you expect me to hand you back your guns?"

The rope cuts into my skin as I push forward. "Don't give them back then. I'll get a weapon on the other side of the fence."

Luka roars with laughter. He glances at the guards, who are laughing too. "You are going to take on Tianzi unarmed and single-handedly?"

"What would you do for your daughter?" I scream.

Luka stops laughing. His stare bores into me.

I've hit a nerve.

His hands ball into fists. "My family was in Moscow. Moscow is gone, and so is my family. It was America who fired the bombs that killed them." Luka stands and pulls out a knife.

"I'm sorry they're dead, but I didn't push the button."

Luka steps forward, the blade gleaming in the light. He holds the knife out to a guard. "Cut him free and take him to the fence. They have taken the children to the Den. Point out where it is, give him his weapons, and let him go."

I exhale.

Luka stomps to the door as the guard with the knife crosses behind me. "You will die, Cain Haight. You do not have a chance."

I meet his cold stare with one of my own. "I still have to try."

29

THE BEAST

Lucy Green

As the warm water cascading over her body washed all of the grime and filth away, Lucy took no pleasure in the shower. How could she? Tianzi would soon be there. Then what would happen?

Guilt washed over her. During her life, she used many different men. To her, they were simply a means to an end. She did it without giving their feelings a second thought. She pictured Cain, but the image in her mind wasn't of the steely-eyed man; it was of a young boy with a bouquet of wildflowers clutched in his hand so tightly he was breaking most of the stems. He had offered her his love. In return, she played with his heart.

Now, it was her time to be used.

The water went cold, and she shut it off. A steady stream dripped off her hair and pinged against the tub. She shook her head, but there was no denying it. She wasn't using Tianzi—he was using her.

She toweled off and headed to the closet. She expected to

find something soft and sexy, but the rack was filled with different sizes of tan military coveralls. She couldn't tell if they were made for a man or a woman.

Lucy's eyes narrowed. Was this some communist thing? Did Tianzi want to make her feel she was just one of the masses? She didn't know what his game was, but she could play games, too.

After ransacking the bureau, she found underwear that fit. She didn't look for a bra but wasn't about to go commando in that scratchy getup. She put on the coveralls, leaving the zipper slightly higher than her belly button.

Lucy examined herself in the mirror. Even with leaving more skin exposed than a starlet on the red carpet, the coveralls hung straight down, leaving her looking as sexy as an empty toilet paper tube. Marching back to the closet, she grabbed one of the belts dangling from a hanger and cinched it around her waist. Another glance in the mirror proved what Lucy already knew—she didn't look like some generic-looking schmuck anymore.

The door to the room opened.

Pi entered, her hand resting on the pistol on her hip. She scanned the room and then snapped to attention. Tianzi followed, strolling through the door as one of the two guards in the hallway pulled the door shut.

Lucy tried to meet Tianzi's gaze, but his eyes were busy traveling all over her body.

When he had finished ogling her, he glanced at Pi.

Pi shot forward, her fist slamming into Lucy's midsection.

The air exploded out of Lucy's mouth, and she doubled up.

Pi grabbed Lucy's hair and pulled her head lower than her waist. "When he enters the room, bow."

Lucy gasped in air through clenched teeth. Her body trembled—not from fear but from rage. She pressed her lips together. She wouldn't say a word. Not now. Not until she got

Bri. But before leaving here, she'd make sure Pi regretted mistreating her.

Pi let go of Lucy's hair.

Lucy stayed looking at the floor, unsure what to do.

Tianzi turned his right-hand palm up and bent his fingers. "Rise." He smiled at Lucy. "I am fond of what you did with your outfit." He crossed over to the chairs and sat. "Leave us, Pi."

Pi's lips parted. She bowed quickly, her head almost level with her knees, then exited the room.

Lucy lifted her chin and tried to breathe normally despite the fresh pain in her gut. "Are you ready for that smile?"

Tianzi scowled. "Do not speak unless I permit it."

Lucy nodded as fresh fantasies of how she would get back at him played through her mind.

"Lie on the bed."

Lucy reached for the zipper of her coveralls, but Tianzi shook his head.

"Leave your clothes on. Your lab results are not back. For now, I want to ask you questions."

Lucy forced herself not to respond as she climbed onto the bed, lay on her side, and stared at the man calmly sitting at the table.

The minutes ticked by, and all Tianzi did was stare at her. It was creepy. She was used to men staring at her, but he wasn't looking at her like a normal man would gaze at a woman lying on a bed. He studied her with an aloofness that made her mouth go dry. It was as if he were looking at a specimen in a cage.

How long transpired, she didn't know, but she was starting to crack. She needed this to end. Just when she was about to scream, someone said her name—"Lucy."

But it wasn't Tianzi. His mouth hadn't moved.

Lucy glanced around the room. She'd heard it, hadn't she?

"Lucy." It was louder now but so odd. Deep and muffled,

like someone calling up from down in a well. "I know you now."

The hairs rose on the back of Lucy's neck. The voice wasn't coming from someone in the room. It was coming from inside her head.

Tianzi grinned. "You hear it."

Fear gripped Lucy's throat. She couldn't speak. She wanted to run. Even knowing the guards were standing outside the door, she thought of breaking free and dashing away from whatever it was that spoke inside her head.

Tianzi raised his hand. In his palm was a controller of some kind. He pressed a button.

Lucy exhaled. The raised hair on the back of her neck fell down. Her hands had balled the sheet in her grip, and her arms shook. "What was that?" She clamped her mouth shut and bowed her head. "Forgive me."

"You are forgiven for that transgression," Tianzi said. "Look at me. What did the beast say?"

"Beast? It spoke in a man's voice." Lucy's eyebrows knit together. "It knew my name. He said he knows me."

"Did it say anything else?"

Lucy shook her head. "His voice was strange. Who is he?"

"Nian is not a who. It is my tool to remake the world. And it is almost ready. Now that the boy is here, we are about to proceed. You are familiar with the people in Ridgecrest, are you not?"

"Sure, I know them. I was born and bred there."

"Bred." Tianzi smiles. "A prophetic choice of words. Let me ask you this, Lucy Green, are the people of Ridgecrest as willing to comply as you, for their survival?"

Lucy tried unsuccessfully not to make a face. She covered her frown with a smile and a sugary response dripping with Southern charm. "They sure are. You've heard of Southern hospitality. Ridgecrest is that saying's hometown."

Tianzi crossed his legs and folded his hands in his lap. "You must be a fabulous gambler, but I thought I made it clear about trying to lie to me."

Lucy's mind raced. Fen would have already told Tianzi all about Ridgecrest. Lucy would be dense if she tried lying about the town now. "Some of them will go along with you. Most will listen to what you have to say. If you go in there ordering them to follow you, you've got another thing coming. America may not exist anymore, but you're not gonna convince any of them of that. Their logic is that since they're Americans, as long as they're alive, so is the U.S. of A."

Tianzi grinned. "Excellent. I was hoping that would be the case. Good ole Southern independent fighting spirit. That's exactly what I am hoping for."

"You want them to fight back?"

"It will not be a fight. They will comply. I can guarantee that."

Lucy felt all of the warmth drain out of her body. She was used to men's empty boasts. That was another trait that seemed to unite them all. From the drunk at the end of the bar to politicians, they all bragged and inflated what they could do. But there was a cold confidence in Tianzi's eyes. He wasn't puffing himself up. "How?" The thought escaped her lips with a puff of breath.

"Everything in due time." Tianzi stared at her and inhaled deeply. A familiar gleam shined in his eyes, but he swallowed down his arousal and stood. "I will return later." He glanced at a spot on the floor next to the side of the bed.

Lucy slid out of bed. Unsure if she should speak, Lucy bowed low but straightened up on her own without waiting to be commanded to do so.

The corner of Tianzi's mouth ticked up. "I will have something more appropriate for you to wear sent down."

It seemed that Tianzi shared a weakness with powerful

men. On the outside, they demanded obedience. But her slight act of defiance aroused him. She was sure of it. And if there was something that she was very good at, it was exploiting a man's weakness.

Lucy lowered her chin and fixed him with a seductive stare.

"Soon," Tianzi said before leaving.

Lucy walked over to the bed, careful not to let the camera see her expression. Tianzi was playing a game, and while Lucy didn't know what he was after, it didn't matter. She was playing her own game now. And in the game of manipulating men, she was a grand master.

30

DADDY'S ON HIS WAY

Cain Haight

One guard cuts me free, and the other hands me my boots. As I put them on, the guard with the knife crosses to the corner of the room and picks up my backpack. I nod, stand, and take out my water bottle.

Both guard's hands move toward their guns then they relax.

"Do you speak English?" I ask the one with the knife.

"A little. He does not. I am Konstantin."

"Cain." I finish my water bottle.

Konstantin points to a bucket in the corner. "There is more water there. It is fresh."

"Thank you." I fill up my thermos, take another long drink, and fill it up again.

"This town you spoke of," Konstantin presses his hands together tightly. "Is it true? Is there a place where the monsters leave you alone?"

I nod. "Yeah."

Konstantin touches his chest. "We're not your enemies.

When your government asked us to come, we came—not to fight, but to help the Americans. But now we need help. We're trapped here. There is no communication and no planes. We're stuck between the monsters and Tianzi's army. We would surrender to you. Will you take us to this Ridgecrest?"

I look between Konstantin and the other guard. "I have to get my daughter first."

Konstantin says something in Russian.

The other guard rolls his eyes and shakes his head.

"To attack Tianzi is crazy. You will die."

"I have to try."

"Then tell us where this town is. We will go there and beg them to take us in."

My eyes narrow. "I can't. But I'll tell you what. Do you have a truck?"

"I can get one that runs."

"Good. You get the truck, and when I get my daughter, we'll all go."

Konstantin's shoulders slump. "Then we are trapped. You have no chance."

"I think you're counting me out a little too early. I made it this far, didn't I?"

Konstantin smiles and repeats what I said. The other guard nods.

"Take me to the fence and show me this place they call the Den."

Konstantin leads the way down the hall, with his buddy following me.

The buddy keeps speaking in Russian, and his voice gets louder and more intense. He grabs my shoulder, and I spin around, ready to block a punch, but he's not swinging.

"Wait!" Konstantin gets between us. "Gleb's got a good idea."

I cock an eyebrow. "I'm kind of in a glass house regarding names, but did you say Gleb or Glen?"

"Glen?" Konstantin and Gleb make a face and laugh. "Who names someone Glen?"

Gleb takes off his shirt and hat and hands them to me. He clears his throat and motions to Konstantin.

"It's for a disguise. Some Russians went with Tianzi. You would blend in better."

Gleb widens his eyes and stares at his friend.

"He wants to know if he can come too. If you make it back."

"Sure. Why not." I say as I pull Gleb's shirt over my head.

Gleb suddenly reaches out and grabs the patch on the shoulder of the shirt. A knife appears in his other hand, and he slices the Russian flag off and then carefully puts it into his pants pocket.

"Tianzi makes all of his soldiers wear no insignia."

"Got it. Do you have any idea how many guards they have over there? Or what the layout is?"

Konstantin translates for Gleb, and they have a brief, animated conversation. It sounds like they're arguing, but how they look at each other is friendly enough. "We will show you outside. Come."

I follow them outdoors. It's still dark, but I don't know how long it will last. It would be better to wait, but I can't risk Luka changing his mind. Or, if Tianzi is as impatient as they say, I can't risk delaying.

Konstantin leads me to a staircase attached to a damaged two-story building. Most of the top story is gone, but we climb high enough so I can see the other side of the base.

The clouds have thinned, and I can make out the outline of several buildings past the fence dividing the base. A dark gap separates one side of the base from the other.

"Getting under the fence is no problem," Konstantin says.

"The spot between the barrels and the burned-out car lifts up. After that is the channel, it is filled with water. Can you swim?"

I nod.

"Good. Do you see the squarish building past the two long ones? The long ones are barracks. Twenty men each. There are more on the other side of the base. Most of the buildings on this side were destroyed. Past them is the square building. That is the Den. Your daughter and the boy are there."

"Guards?"

"Five."

"What else is in there? Why do they call it the Den?"

Konstantin and Gleb speak in Russian. Gleb nods. "There is something in there," Konstantin says. "Something secret even before the Dark. Gleb heard it. He said it wasn't human. We all laughed. That was before we saw the monsters."

"Did he see it?" I point at my eyes.

Gleb shakes his head.

"It spoke to him," Konstantin touches the side of his head. "But Gleb didn't hear it with his ears. It spoke *inside* his head."

A burning rage sweeps through my body. The muscles in my back tighten, and if I weren't about to sneak into an enemy army base, I'd scream at the sky. My little angel is trapped in a building with a demon. I turn and march down the stairs, with them following after me.

"This is where we part company," I whisper as I check my pistol and shotgun, which are still loaded and chambered.

"We will get the truck," Konstantin says. "Will you keep your promise?"

"Get it. Because I'm coming back with my little girl." I keep to the shadows cast by the second floor as I head to the fence. Crouching low, I move silently and fast. I reach the burned-out car and squat down.

The sounds of a summer night in the south echo around me—clicking bugs, the wind rustling leaves, and flowing water.

It's so quiet that it's hard to imagine this was once a busy army base. But the Dark has changed everything it's touched. I'm not letting it take my girl.

As I approach the fence, I see the hole scooped out in the dirt beneath it. It's big enough that if I lie down, I can slip under. I drop to my belly and push my backpack through first. I crawl under and stay on my stomach.

The chasm ahead is visible, but I can't see the water. I hear it. It's moving and louder than I expected.

Scurrying forward, I reach the edge. The cement is broken in two, and the other side is at least twenty yards out. I peer over the side. There's about a six-foot drop to the water below, but that isn't the problem—the current is. It's moving at a fast clip. There's no way I can simply lower myself in.

Swearing under my breath, I slip my backpack over my shoulders and cinch it tight. I crawl back several feet and crouch. I try to swallow, but my mouth is bone dry. I dread doing this more than floating over a minefield using 100-year-old technology, but I don't have any other choice.

I run as fast and as quietly as I can and dive into the darkness. I keep my hands out in front of me and pray I'm not going to hit an unseen rock with my face. It's a gamble, but so is this whole mission.

My hands splash into the water, and I slice beneath the surface. The current grabs me and starts trying to roll me over, but I'm going full-on Superman with my arms straight out. As soon as I begin to slow, I swim harder than I ever have. Maybe it's the memory of almost dying in the Devil's washing machine that's making me panic, but I'm kicking like a drowning man until my fingers hit the dirt on the other side.

The current slams into me and drags me along the bank. I grab a piece of rebar sticking out of the cracked cement. The water pulls me sideways, but there's no way I'm letting go.

Hand over hand, I hoist myself up and climb over the ledge.

I crawl to a burned-out, tipped-over truck and stop to catch my breath. Water streams down my cheeks and drips on the ground.

A smile crosses my face. I'm getting closer.

Hang on, Bri. Daddy's on his way.

31

RING OF FIRE

Matt Browner

Matt Browner raced across the town square toward an old pickup with sheet metal welded against the sides as the Church bell rang. Several men were busy setting up a hunting stand while Goose shouted instructions to them from the back of the truck.

"Hurry up, Fellas! You all are movin' in slow motion. Those dang gum beasts ain't gonna be goin' so slow. You still gotta turn on the ring."

"Goose!" Matt stopped and tried to catch his breath. "How's it going? Why aren't you set up?"

"We're almost there." Goose grinned. He was sitting in the back of the truck, his broken leg propped up on a box. A blue tarp covered something taking up half the truck bed. "This is the last section needin' to git closed."

The sound of gunfire to the north made them all turn.

"You better hurry it up." Matt swallowed down his rising fears.

The men finished with the hunting stand and looked to Goose.

"Barry and Dan, get to the house and wait for my signal. Lou and Hector, you take this stand. The rest of you head over to the Martin's place and see if they need help."

Matt fixed Goose with a stare as the men ran in all directions. "Are you sure this is going to work?"

"A hundred percent. Between the ring and our firepower, we can hold off an army." He angled his head toward the object covered by the blue tarp in the back. "I can't use it properly because of my leg." He knocked on his cast, and it sounded like rock.

Matt walked down to the trunk and stared at the gray cast. "That's not plaster."

"We didn't have none, so I made do. Cement and rebar."

"That's got to weigh twenty pounds."

"Feels like it does. It's only temporary 'til I see the Doc. Check this out." Goose grabbed the tarp and pulled it off. Sitting in the back of the truck bed, welded to the floor, was a Gatling Gun and a huge box of belt-fed ammo.

"I can help feed it, but you gots to shoot." Goose said. "Do you mind?"

Matt laughed. "Mind? I'd love to."

From out of the darkness, a wolf howled. A dozen more answered its call.

"They're close." Goose pulled himself up to sit on the truck's extended wheel bump out. "Get ready."

Matt scrambled into the back.

"Light it up, boys!" Goose yelled.

Matt looked toward the house.

Nothing happened.

In the distance, a hundred yards away at the tree line, all the bushes started moving.

"Goose...." Matt grabbed the handles of the Gatling gun with sweaty palms.

"Dan! Barry! Turn the handle and light it up!" Goose hollered.

Dan, a thin man in his mid-thirties, dashed around the back of the house and sprinted toward the truck.

"What in tarnation?" Goose swore. "What's wrong?"

Dan skidded to a stop. He was gulping in air and held up a lighter. "Mine died." He gasped.

Goose swore a blue streak as he dug into the pocket of his overalls and tossed a Zippo to Dan.

"Thanks." Dan turned and raced back to the house.

Matt's eyes widened. Dozens of silhouettes crept out of the darkness. Some were small, most likely bone rats. The others were wolves.

"How accurate is this thing?" Matt said. His voice sounded so calm he almost didn't recognize it.

"It ain't a rifle, but a Gatling Gun ain't supposed to be. It's more spray and pray. And the second part is the most important." Goose bowed his head. "Dear God, I ain't ever think I'd ask you to protect me from a horde of demons, but I suppose it ain't that different from saying save us from the chariots in Pharoah's army. So, if you ain't too busy, we'd appreciate it."

A wolf howled.

The horde charged.

"Where's the barrier?" Matt shouted.

Goose shrugged. "Don't know. Something must have gone wrong. Go with plan B."

"What's plan B?"

"I call it raining lead!" Goose grinned. "Open her up!"

Matt peered through the sight and began cranking the handle. Bullets roared out of the barrel of the gun. His ears rang, and smoke and gunpowder burned his eyes and nose. Bright flashes blinded him.

In the gun stand to his left, Lou and Hector opened fire with rifles.

Two dozen wolves charged across the field. Their ears were flattened against their heads as their claws kicked up the dirt behind them.

Matt concentrated his fire on the lead wolf. It took three full turns of the handle to drop it.

Goose leaned forward and shouted, "Crank faster!"

Matt didn't need any encouragement; between Lou, Hector, and him, they'd only dropped two wolves. His right arm burned as he sped up turning the handle. Bullets spit from the barrel at a blinding pace. He dropped three more wolves, and the men in the stand dropped another.

But it wouldn't be enough. There were too many charging forward.

A glow and cheering to their right made Matt glance toward the house. Flames danced high into the night and streaked along a pipe running through the field.

"Ring of fire, baby!" Goose cheered.

The charging wolves skidded to a stop.

Matt exhaled.

It was working. Ridgecrest sat atop a huge supply of natural gas. And you didn't need electricity to use it. Goose had used the gas to create a barrier to protect the town.

"You're a genius, Goose!"

"No offense, but you ain't. Keep shootin'!"

Matt turned back to the gun and cranked the handle as Goose worked on feeding the belt.

The wolves approached the line of flames and quickly backed away. The bone rats chittered and scurried around.

"What are they doin'?" Goose asked.

Matt stared at the small creatures. They started moving in circles, like a dog looking for a place to do its business.

"EVERYONE GET DOWN!" Matt shouted as he grabbed Goose and dropped to the cover of the truck's bed.

Dozens of bone spikes arched through the air. Several pierced into the side of the truck.

Matt peaked over and quickly ducked back down as they fired another volley.

Someone in the tree stand screamed in pain.

Matt ground his teeth. "If we don't fire back, we're sitting ducks. You with me, Goose?"

"Let's kill some critters!" Goose nodded.

Matt helped Goose back up and got back on the gun.

The bone rats started their dance.

Bullets, smoke, and fire shot out of the barrel of the Gatling gun.

CLACK-CLACK-CLACK-CLACK-CLACK

More bullets rained down from up in the tree stand. Two people were firing shotguns now. Whoever got hit by a bone spike wasn't dead yet.

Another volley of spikes whizzed through the air but there were less than half the number as before. The windows in the truck shattered. One spike bounced off the Gatling gun, a sliver sticking into Matt's forearm.

Matt ignored the pain and kept cranking.

The line of bone rats turned and raced back into the forest.

Several wolves followed after them.

"We've got 'em on the run!" Goose cheered. "Oh, no..."

The fear in Goose's voice made Matt turn to look. But Goose wasn't looking forward anymore. Goose's gaze was fixed a few yards away from the open tailgate.

A huge bone-white wolf with smoldering fur and a burned face stalked toward the truck. The flames from the ring of fire gleamed off its black eyes. It pounced.

Goose screamed.

The beast's jaws clamped down on Goose's leg.

Matt let go of the gun and grabbed Goose's shirt.

The wolf jerked its massive head to the side.

The shirt ripped off Goose's back as the wolf dragged him out of the truck.

"Shoot it! Shoot it, Matt!" Goose shrieked.

Matt ripped out his revolver and unloaded it into the beast's back.

Bone splintered, but the creature thrashed Goose back and forth like a doll.

"Matt." Goose's voice was softer. He wasn't screaming anymore.

Matt grabbed the handle of the Gatling gun, spun it around, and aimed down. The gun was less accurate than a shotgun. He stood as much of a chance of hitting Goose as the wolf, but there was no other choice.

Matt prayed, "Please, Lord," then cranked the handle.

CLACK-CLACK-CLACK-CLACK-CLACK-CLACK-CLACK-CLACK

The wolf staggered sideways. It opened its mouth.

Goose fell unmoving to the grass.

Click-click-click.

Matt looked at the gun. The belt had fed all the way through. It was out of bullets. So was his revolver.

The wolf turned to face Matt. It crouched low and pounced. It slammed halfway onto the truck with its hind legs still on the ground.

Matt stumbled back into the Gatling gun. As the truck rocked, he slipped and fell onto the truck bed.

The wolf's jaw opened. Both of its canine teeth were broken off. It inhaled sharply.

Matt readied himself for the beast to roar and lung forward.

The wolf's eyes rolled back in its head, and it collapsed. Its massive chest rose once, then stopped.

Matt grabbed the side of the truck and climbed over, dropping to the ground.

Cheering erupted from all around.

"They're running away!" Hector shouted from up in the tree stand. "We won!"

Matt opened his mouth to join the celebration, but his stare fixed on Goose, lying face down on the ground. He rushed over to his friend's side and gently turned him over.

Goose's eyelids fluttered and opened. He groaned. "Did you get it?"

"Did I hit you?" Matt asked, checking him over.

"I feels like I got caught in a hay baler. That happened when I was five. I was with my Pa—"

"Did I shoot you, Goose?!?" Matt shouted.

"No need to get uppity." Goose sat up. "I don't think so."

Matt exhaled. "Sorry for shouting."

All around the town, more cheering filled the air. The church bells started ringing.

Goose smiled. "Sounds like we won." He gasped and pointed at his cast.

An enormous, broken wolf's tooth was stuck between the cracked concrete and rebar.

Matt chuckled and shook his head. Somehow, this ragtag group of misfits had held off the horde. But as he looked out into the darkness, he couldn't help but wonder if this victory would be short-lived. He had a feeling this was only a skirmish, and the real war had just begun.

32

A GOOD ONE

Cain Haight

Once I catch my breath, I crouch low and make my way to the shadow of the barracks. There are no lights on inside, but the windows are open. On the one hand, moving toward a building with sleeping guards inside is a poor choice. There's a chance the sound of my footsteps will wake them up. But I can't stay in the open with the patrols making their rounds. So I hide in the shadows cast by the barracks.

I creep along the side of the cement building until I reach the edge. One great thing about the lack of technology after the Dark is that I don't have to worry about motion sensors or night vision goggles.

I freeze. Sweat rolls down my back. They may not have technology at their disposal, but this is still an army base with soldiers on a military footing. My breath sounds loud in the silence as the hairs rise on the back of my neck. Something's off. I can feel it.

Kneeling, I scan the area between this barracks and the one next to it. I keep staring until my eyes start burning. The moon slips out from behind the clouds. The breeze is cool on my cheek. Something shimmers a few inches above the dirt.

Crawling, I move to the corner of the building, keeping an eye on the line vibrating in the wind. It's a fishing line tied to a couple of cans hidden by the drain spout. It's an old trick. They should have used a grenade.

Stepping over the trap, I keep going. I stop at the far edge of the building and check for fishing lines or any other DIY alarms, but the ground is clear.

From out of the darkness down on my right, footsteps sound on the tar.

I slink back into the shadows of the barracks.

Two soldiers appear. They're walking down the middle of the street in front of the barracks, but they're not behaving like they're on guard duty. Both are staring down, and one has his hands thrust into his pants pockets. Their shoulders are rounded, and they don't speak.

As they get closer, I see one is Chinese and the other is Russian. The Russian turns a little. He's missing his left arm. They're both carrying rifles slung over their shoulders, but that's it for gear—no belts or vests loaded with equipment and spare ammo.

I wait until they disappear into the darkness, and the sound of their footsteps is swallowed up in the night. My mouth is dry, and my muscles ache from not moving. Flexing my fingers to get the blood pumping back into them, I force myself to stand and casually walk across the street.

It goes against all of the action movies I've seen, but the way I figure it, if someone sees me walking, they'll believe I belong there. They'll think I'm heading to the bathroom or going someplace. If they spot me running fast and low, they'll start shooting. At least, that's what I'd do.

I reach the shadows of the building and stop. It's pitch black, and no matter how I angle my head, I can't see any traps.

That doesn't confirm that one isn't there—it only means I can't see it.

Creeping forward, I approach the front door. There's no guard outside. I'm about to start moving when my old drill sergeant starts screaming in my head about how rushing gets your butt shot off by the Russians. The man grew up during the Cold War, and I swear he thought the Russians were going to attack the US if he closed his eyes. Still, he was a good soldier and instructor, so I wait.

Footsteps sound at the corner of the building. A lone Chinese guard walks out of the shadows carrying a rifle and stops at the base of the stairs. He gazes into the night and wipes his hand down his face. From how his arms hang limply at his sides, he appears exhausted. After a minute, he leans against the column and sighs loud enough for me to hear. His eyes close. Suddenly, he jerks forward and scans around. His eyes are wide, and I can see the fear on his face.

I haven't moved, so he didn't hear me. Something else spooked him. Or he caught himself from falling asleep on guard duty, which is a big no-no even in the apocalypse.

He reaches into his jacket and unwraps whatever he has removed from his pocket—food. He takes a bite, carefully wraps it up, and sticks it back in. Then he stands at attention.

It looks like this is his post, and there's no way I'm waiting for him to go somewhere else. There isn't enough time for that, and a risk of being seen is too great.

I move like a lion—fast and silent. Unholstering my pistol, I take three long steps to close the distance. Pressing the barrel against his head, I hold my finger to my mouth as I grab his rifle. It's a QBZ-95 bullpup assault rifle favored by the People's Liberation Army.

He swallows, making his Adam's apple bounce.

I motion him inside and tap the side of his head with my gun for a little added emphasis.

He marches up the stairs.

At the top are two glass doors. Inside is a small room with an oil lamp sitting on a desk. I can't see much, but there doesn't seem to be anyone there.

I prod him through the door and over behind the wall. There is only the large counter in the back of the room and a door behind it.

"How many guards?"

The soldier shakes his head.

I press the barrel of my pistol against his forehead. "How many guards?"

"No English! No English!"

Just great. I point at him and then at the door.

He steps forward, and I slam him back against the wall. I point at him again, hold up his rifle, snap to attention, and then point at the door.

His eyebrows pull together, but he gets it—I hope. He holds up two fingers.

"Two?" I ask skeptically, hoping my tone expresses my doubts.

He nods quickly.

I press my lips together. I have no idea what to do with this kid. He's probably not old enough to drink. I should stab him, but I don't want to kill him—just shut him up. Pistol whipping only works in the movies. It makes a lot of noise, and there's as good a chance of my killing him as knocking him out.

His eyes widen, and he starts shaking. Looks like he's figured out what I'm debating.

I shake my head and take a length of paracord out of a side pocket of my cargo pants. I turn him around and pull his hands behind him. After securing his hands, I push him down and hog-tie him, wrapping the cord around his legs and tying that to his hands. I cut off one of his sleeves, gag him, and drag him into the corner.

Kicking myself for wasting the time, I hurry over to the door in the back. I holster my pistol but don't strap it. I'm hoping it looks like I belong. Firing a gun, even inside this cement building, would bring the whole base running. Holding onto the guard's assault rifle, I drop the magazine and check the chamber—it's empty, as is the magazine.

I shake my head and feel my upper lip curl. Who goes on guard duty with no ammo? The kid is young, but he can't be that stupid. I slap the magazine back in the rifle and hide it behind the desk. Thinking it over, I jog back to the kid and drag him behind the desk.

If someone were to stick their head inside the room, they'd see him in the corner but not under the desk.

I roll my shoulders to loosen up and pick up the lamp. I've got no idea what's waiting for me behind the door, but since Bri is in here somewhere, I've got to look. I open the door and stroll through like I belong. At the end of the hallway, a lamp flickers on the wall. Two men stand guard in front of a metal door. They look surprised to see me but don't raise the rifles they're holding.

I give a friendly wave as I start walking forward.

The soldiers are Chinese, but when the guy on my right opens his mouth, he says something in Russian—I think.

It must be because of the jacket Konstantine gave me. I nod, chuckle, and keep walking.

They exchange a puzzled glance.

The soldier repeats whatever he said before, only louder. Their hands tighten on their rifles. If they open up in this confined space, I'm gonna get shredded with lead.

I say the only phrase I know that's even close to Russian. "Du hast eine Zigarette?" It's German for *do you have a cigarette?* I hope it stalls them long enough for me to get closer and get the drop on them.

It doesn't work.

The guy on the right starts moving.

I drop the lamp I'm holding and fall onto my gut into a sniper stance. Darkness surrounds me, but I can see the guards clearly because of their lamp. I fire two rounds at the guy on the right.

He stumbles back and drops.

The soldier on the left has his gun raised and mashes the trigger. Bullets whizz above me as I fire three rounds center mass.

He seizes up tight.

I must have hit his head or heart because he goes instantly rigid. He falls forward like he was tased, and the rifle clatters across the floor.

I'm on my feet and running before it comes to a stop. When I reach the end of the hallway, it's clear both men are dead. I pick up the rifle, and smoke curls out of the barrel. I release the magazine. There's only a round left and one in the chamber. I eject that round and stick it into the magazine.

I check the other rifle. There's a round in the chamber, and the magazine is partially loaded. I quickly eject the bullets. Six rounds. The magazine can hold 30, but these guys only carried six a piece. I guess they really are that short on ammo.

I've got to get moving and fast. I'm hoping the gunshots coming from an interior hallway muffled the noise but who knows. I grab the handle on the steel door, but it doesn't turn. After searching the guards, I start going through a small set of keys I find. One works, and the lock clicks. I turn the handle and push. It swings gently open. The light on the other side makes me blink.

Behind the door is a foyer leading to a stairwell down. The lights are working. They have electricity. An elevator stands to the right. The doors are closed, and the lights are off. I don't know if it works, but I'd rather take the stairs.

I peer over the railing. The metal staircase leads down, and lights glow to the bottom far below. Glancing back in the hall-way, I stare at the growing bloodstains on the floor. I could shove the guards in the elevator, but there is no cleaning that mess up quickly.

Holding the rifle, I start down the stairs. A cool breeze dances across my arms, and the hairs on my neck rise. I don't know what it is, but I can feel it in my bones. Something's down there. And whatever it is, it's all sorts of bad.

At the bottom of the staircase, a long hallway stretches off in front of me. The floor is tiled white and covered with a red and gold carpet. Photos of the countryside hang on the walls with dark, wooden tables underneath them. It looks like I'm in a hotel, not the bunker of an army base.

Two closed doors stand opposite each other with more further on ahead. Behind me, just before the hall ends, is the elevator. I open the first door on the right. It's a supply closet.

The door on the left leads to a large room with empty shelves. Nothing is in it, and from the dust on the floor, it appears no one has been inside for a while.

I close it quietly and keep moving. My heart is pounding as I continue to the next set of doors. I shove open the door on my left and my breath catches in my throat.

Lucy is standing in the middle of the room, dressed in a white nightgown.

She gasps. Her eyes widen and she stares at me like she's seeing a ghost.

"Why am I not surprised?" I mutter as I slip into the room and shut the door behind me. "I expected to find you tied to a chair or suspended from chains hanging from the ceiling because they're torturing you, but no. Not you. You're like a cat that always lands on your feet." I glare at the bed with the covers pulled back. "Or, in your case, you land on your back on some guy's bed."

Lucy's eyes smolder. "You are the dumbest man who has ever walked the planet, Cain Haight."

"That's true. I actually believed there was a chance for you. Where are the kids?"

"I don't know. Sadie's here, but Mercy's dead. She got herself killed."

That news hits like a bullet to the chest. I grab the doorframe to steady myself and keep from falling over. I picture Mercy's face, and my eyes clamp shut. I can't even bring myself to look at her memory. I failed her.

I take a deep breath. There'll be time to mourn later. I've got to look to the living. I turn my back on Lucy. "Get dressed. We're going to find Bri."

"Like I said. You're the stupidest man alive."

I'm about to tell Lucy what I think of her when something busts over the back of my head. I stumble into the door and try to grab the handle, but my body isn't responding. I probably have a concussion from falling on my head after the balloon, and getting smacked again certainly ain't helping things. Like an old TV shutting off, the light dims in a circle until there's only a bright spot in the center of my vision.

I sink to my knees, but I'm not knocked out. Through the haze, I see broken lamp pieces on the floor all around me. Lucy must have cracked the lamp over my head. She did that the night she filed for divorce, too. It didn't knock me out then, either. She shoulda learned.

My head wobbles as I look up at her. She's got tears in her eyes, but her hand is balled into a fist and cocked back.

Running footsteps sound in the hallway.

Lucy swings.

I'm the one who taught her how to punch. Now, I regret I did. It's a good one. It catches me in the temple and jerks my head around. The darkness swoops back in. I'm falling forward...

33

MATES

Mercy Yoder

Mercy rode in the back of the wagon, watching the sky lighten. It was still an hour until sunrise. She closed her eyes and tried remembering how it would be back on the farm. A smile played across her lips as, in her mind, she watched a hundred different dawns. The weather and the seasons never mattered to Mercy; she found beauty in them all. From the frost sparkling like diamonds in the fall or the emerald green grass of summer blowing in the wind to the rainbow of colors in autumn or the blanket of snow in the winter, each season was as special to her as they were unique.

As the stars glimmered overhead, Mercy wondered if she'd ever see the farm again. Eve said she was taking her to a man who would kill her. Mercy was guilty of no crime, but Eve referred to her as a scourge. What a scourge was or what they had done to hurt this man and woman, Mercy didn't know. But the woman was clearly special. Somehow, she understood Mercy's thoughts.

Riding on the enormous bear beside the cart, Eve turned to scowl at Mercy.

Mercy smiled and politely nodded.

Eve's eyes blazed. Her lips curled back, and she appeared just as frightening as the creature she rode.

The bear trotted forward, leaving Mercy alone again and staring at the sky.

She lowered her head. Before the Dark, she didn't believe what others had told her about the world. John Mark had said it was a place filled with people filled with hate. "Impossible." Mercy had rolled her eyes. "The world has too much beauty in it for people to be angry all the time." But John Mark had shaken his head, and his eyes grew sad. "People out there don't get mad and hurtful—they're always that way. They walk around angry. They're filled with hate."

Mercy sighed. Haight. Cain Haight. He was an outsider, but he wasn't hateful. He was as tough as leather, but he was a good man inside. Her throat tightened as she remembered the truck disappearing under the water.

"Dear Lord, please let Cain be alive. Please let him have gotten out. Please." Tears streamed down her cheeks.

Paws raked the ground as Eve charged back to the wagon on top of the bear. Eve leaped off the bear and landed in the wagon with the skill of a gymnast.

Mercy gasped and pressed her back against the wooden side.

Eve stared at Mercy.

Mercy swallowed, waiting for the woman to speak, but she said nothing. Mercy's left temple throbbed like someone had stuck a splinter in her mind. She winced and looked away.

Eve roughly grabbed Mercy's chin and jerked her head up so the women were again eye to eye. Like sitting in the dentist's office getting a filling, Mercy's hands balled into fists as the pain in her head grew. It was too much. Too intense. Mercy grit her teeth. "Stop!"

Eve let go of Mercy's face. "Who is Cain?"

Mercy's chest rose and fell rapidly as she gulped in air. What had Eve done to her? Her head throbbed, and she had a terrible migraine. "How do you do that? Do you read my mind?"

"The man from the river. The one in the truck. Is that Cain?"

"It doesn't matter. He's dead."

"When?"

"A few days ago. He was in the truck when it sank. He couldn't get out, and he drowned."

Eve shook her head. "No. Is he your mate?"

Mercy sat up. "Did you say no?"

Eve nodded.

"Have you seen him? After? Recently? Have you seen Cain?"

Eve smiled. "If Cain were not scourge, I would mate him, too."

Mercy's neck lengthened, and her cheeks flushed. "I don't want to...mate him."

Eve leaned menacingly forward. "Do not lie."

"We're not married." Mercy stammered.

Eve shrugged, puzzled.

Mercy wanted to grab the woman and shake her but didn't dare. "Are you saying Cain is alive? Did you see him after the truck went into the water?"

Eve stood.

"Please, tell me!"

"He lives." Eve took a step and sprang out of the wagon, landing back on the bear.

"Wait!" Mercy scrambled to the other side of the wagon. "You saw him? You're sure?"

"Yes. He will come for you."

Mercy shook her head. "He will go to rescue his daughter."

"He will, but I read him." Eve touched the side of her head and then her chest. "He is fierce. He will not stop. He will go after his child, but when he discovers you are not with the others, he will come to rescue you."

Mercy shook her head. "It's too dangerous. He's smart. He won't come."

Eve huffed. "Even for a scourge, you are stupid. He has bonded with you. Once that happens, the alpha always comes for their mate."

34

FANS IN THE APOCALYPSE

Evan Green

Evan rolled over and winced. His side throbbed like a mule had kicked him. He opened his eyes. He lay on a couch in a living room. A huge TV hung on the wall with racks of movies on two enormous shelves on either side. The room was neat besides the mud-stained rug. The sky outside the window was starting to lighten.

He couldn't remember much after Sam finished stitching him up. Whatever that pill was that he'd taken had numbed the pain and knocked him out. He'd love another but couldn't take it. He needed to get moving.

Footsteps sounded in the hallway.

Evan held on to the back of the couch as he sat up. Brushing the hair out of his face, his eyes went wide.

Sam strode into the room, carrying a pistol in each of his hands. He stopped in the doorway and stared at Evan. His lips pressed together, and the creases on his forehead deepened as he frowned. "You've got two choices."

Evan stood and squared his shoulders. "I appreciate your

helping me, Sam. But I have to find my wife. I don't care if you threaten me. I'm going."

"Threaten you? What are you talking about?"

Evan eyed the guns. "You just said I had two choices—stay here, or you'll shoot me."

"Whoever said that last part? That's the soldier in you talking. I only meant what pistol did you want. You can choose between the Sig Sauer P226 or the Glock G29 Gen 5."

"Oh." Evan relaxed. "I'll take the Sig."

"Good choice. The guy at the gun store said Navy Seals use them. Out in the car, I've already got an HK MR556, a Mossberg 590A1, and a Remington 870 Tactical. I'm carrying the Glock and a TISAS 1911 Night Stalker Double Stack 9mm SF."

Evan took the Sig Sam handed him. "I wouldn't have pegged you for such a gun guy."

"I'm not, but I wanted to fit in when I moved here, and everyone said Tennessee is all about God and guns. I think I did go a little overboard on the guns part. But the gun store fellas are real nice."

"I appreciate the guns and you stitching me up."

"I'm only giving you the Sig."

"But you said all those other guns are in the car."

"They are. But I'm coming with you." Sam said, holstering the Glock.

"I can't ask you to do that. You said it yourself. I'll probably be dead by nightfall. There's no reason you've got to die too."

"If I stay here, I'll die of starvation. I don't even have anything for us to eat for breakfast. And I figure my chances are better going with someone trained by the military."

"I'm not a soldier."

Sam smiled. "My grandfather didn't like to talk about his service either. I get it. The car is packed, so whenever you want to go, I'm ready. What do they say? OORAH!"

Fifteen minutes later, Evan sat in the passenger seat of the

1972 Ford Cortina while Sam drove down the road. Evan had given up trying to convince Sam he had never been in the military. The more he denied it, the more Sam became convinced that Evan was not only a soldier but also involved in super-secret dark ops stuff.

Every few miles, they passed abandoned vehicles, but the worst part was the sets of clothes left behind. Bell Springs had been a small farming community, but it was now deserted.

"Can I ask you a question?" Sam asked.

Evan shrugged. "Shoot."

"What's the deal with all the clothes? Look over there next to that truck. See? It's like someone dumped out a load of laundry."

Evan took a deep breath. "These creatures. You call them nightmare squirrels, but we call them bone rats and bone wolves."

"Is that because it looks like they have some kind of exo-skeleton?"

"Yeah, and...they eat bones. There was this man from town who went out gigging frogs—"

"Gigging?"

"Catching them. Frog legs are really good."

Sam made a face but said, "They sound gross, but I'm so hungry I'd try them. I heard they taste like chicken."

"Not really, but they are good. Anyway, Gunner went out to catch some and never came back. My wife found him. What was left of him anyway. The monsters ate his bones. Lucy said it looked like a skin suit."

Sam turned white. "They eat the bones? While you're alive?"

Now, it was Evan's turn to make a face. "I suspect you're dead by the time that happens. It's still creepy."

"Are there more than the rats and wolves?"

"I don't know. We don't know where they came from either."

"I thought they were aliens," Sam said with a straight face.

Evan burst out laughing.

"That or a government experiment." Sam raised his voice. "They had to come from someplace, and there's that army base down the road. That's not much of a wild idea."

"The base is what I'd bet my money on. It's the same thing if a bunch of monkeys showed up outside the zoo."

Sam opened his mouth but didn't say anything. He stared out the windshield with a look of horror on his face.

Evan stopped speaking, too. In the distance, the city looked destroyed. A fire had devastated a large section of it, and other buildings appeared to have chunks blown off. Every structure they passed was heavily damaged, with charred walls and collapsed exteriors revealing their contents.

"Monsters didn't do this," Sam said as they drove on.

"Look at all the military equipment." Evan pointed at a downed helicopter. "Maybe the creatures attacked the city, and the Army fought back?"

Sam paled even more. "If the Army couldn't beat those things, what chance do we have?"

Evan didn't answer him. He stared out the window at the piles of rotting clothes—the only evidence remaining of the people who used to inhabit this city.

They continued driving, moving through streets that looked like a fire bomb had hit them. All of the cars were pushed out of the way. Something had cleared a lane through the clogged street large enough for a truck to drive through. Further up, some buildings appeared to be relatively unscathed.

Suddenly, movement caught their eye behind a flipped-over police car. Sam slowed down. As they approached, they saw a small figure dash across the street toward a four-story building with shops underneath.

"That's a kid," Sam said. "What should I do?"

Evan looked nervously around. "We can't leave them. Stop the car."

"Here?"

"You can stay. I'll be right back."

Sam stopped the car. He stared out the windshield, his knuckles turning white on the steering wheel. "I should go..." his voice trailed off as a black cat ran into the middle of the street.

The cat watched them for a moment and continued on.

Sam drew a shaky breath. "I think I should stay and guard the car."

Evan opened the door. The street was littered with crumbled cement and massive shell casings. Evan had never seen ones so large. He slowly made his way over to the building.

Brown eyes peered out of the darkness.

"Hi," Evan waved. "What are you doing out here? Are you all right?"

"Put your hands on your head and interlace your fingers!" A policeman shouted from the side of the building.

Evan stared at the man aiming a gun at him. He was clean-shaven and had close-cropped hair. He wore a green T-shirt and police pants with a policeman's belt.

"Put your hands up nice and slow," A woman ordered from the doorway.

Evan's mouth fell open. What he believed was a teenager was a short, thin woman in her late thirties with dark eyes. She held a pistol in her right hand and pointed it at Evan's chest.

Behind him, someone racked a shotgun.

Evan raised his hands.

"Tell your friend to come out of the car," the woman said as she pulled the sweatshirt hood off her head.

A man and woman armed with assault rifles stepped out from the corner of the building. From underneath the truck, another man emerged with a shotgun, followed by a large man with a bigger shotgun.

The woman nodded.

Everyone besides the cop slipped away and headed in Sam's direction.

"GO, SAM! DRIVE!" Evan's warning was cut off as the woman with the hoodie jammed her gun in his open mouth.

"One more word, and I blow your head off, and they kill your friend. Blink twice if you agree."

Evan blinked twice.

A few minutes later, Sam strolled back with the others. He was chatting away with a chubby guy with thick black hair. The woman took the gun out of Evan's mouth but kept it pointed at him.

"Hey, Evan!" Sam waved. "You won't believe who this is. It's Jerry Pace—the comedian."

"I've still got fans in the apocalypse," Jerry smiled.

"They check out." The huge guy said, pointing at Evan. "He's looking for Cain's crew."

The woman's eyes narrow. "Keep your hands on your head. You two are coming with us."

35

I HOPE I'M WRONG

Matt Browner

Matt sat in Dr. Harmon's waiting room with his head in his hands. Amos Yoder paced the floor, softly whispering to himself. Matt had gotten a couple of hours of sleep if that's what you call nodding off in a chair. After the monsters had retreated, Matt drove Goose here.

It turns out that Sarah Yoder had been helping the doctor all night. Between the doctor's son Lonnie taking a turn for the worse, Camila's blood pressure dropping, and Goose needing a new cast, neither got any sleep.

The door to the doctor's office opened. Doc Harmon appeared with Sarah behind him.

Matt and Amos rose.

Doc Harmon met Matt's eyes. The Doc's expression was grim. He nodded and headed for the door.

Matt moved to follow him, but Sarah grabbed his arm.

"Leave him be," Sarah whispered. "Lonnie didn't make it."

Matt inhaled sharply. He couldn't fathom how hard it

would be to lose a child, let alone if it had been yourself who had been trying to save his life.

"He lost too much blood. There was nothing we could do."

Matt nodded. In a way, maybe it was a mercy that Lonnie had died. He'd been involved with the group that killed the preppers and kidnapped Camila and Betsy. Who knows what the townspeople would have done to him if he had lived?

"How is Camila?"

"Her blood pressure is still low, but we stopped the bleeding. It's touch and go. She was so weak from having the baby, to lose that much blood after it is a miracle she's alive. She asked about the baby."

Amos stepped forward. "Gabby is taking good care of him. Your sister has been helping her."

Sarah smiled. "Esther certainly has the experience with nine kids."

Amos gently touched her back. "Can I get you anything?"

"Sleep. I can't keep my eyes open. Mary took over for me, so I'm heading to the guest bedroom if you want to join me."

"Before you two head off," Matt said. "What about Goose? Can I take him with me?"

Sarah shook her head. "That concrete cast protected Goose from getting bitten, but he broke his leg in two more places. Dr. Harmon gave him some pain medication. He'll sleep for hours, but he shouldn't be moved."

Matt opened his mouth and closed it before he swore. Goose's defense plan protected the town. With him out of the picture, how would they make sure the ring of fire kept working? "It is what it is." Matt muttered, "I better go and check on the perimeter."

"I'll go with you," Amos said.

"Get some sleep." Matt opened the door and stopped. "Who knows when you'll be able to get it again."

Sarah pulled on Amos's arm. "If you need me, you know where to find me."

Matt nodded and headed outside. The air was hot and sticky. His shirt clung to his back, and when he brushed his hair back, the palm of his hand came away drenched.

The center of town was deserted, but there was something odd about the stillness.

Matt stopped and glanced about. Everything appeared as it usually did except for the new barricades, but something was off, and he couldn't put his finger on it. Sweat rolled down the side of his face. His ears strained to pick up any foreign sound, but the town was silent.

He froze.

Where were the birds? None flew in the sky or flitted in the treetops. No squirrels darted beneath the oak trees. Even the bugs were quiet.

The door to Doc Harmon's office burst open, and Amos hopped out, pulling on his boots. Ani hid behind him. Her hands were moving frantically, and she was saying something to Amos, but she spoke so softly that he couldn't hear her.

"Hold on, Matt!" Amos called out. "Something's wrong. You need to come with me." Amos hurried over to the wagon with Ani following.

"What is it, Amos?" Matt jogged over.

"I don't know, but she said we have to go with her."

"Where?" Matt stopped beside the wagon as Ani climbed up.

"Come!" Ani patted the buckboard and pointed at Matt. "See. See with your eyes."

Amos climbed on board.

Matt shook his head. He was exhausted, and the last thing he wanted to do was go someplace with a woman who didn't make any sense. Then he looked at her eyes. They glowed a faint blue.

"Okay," Matt said as he pulled himself up and sat down.

Ani grabbed the horse's reins and shook them. The wagon jerked forward. Ani clicked her tongue and snapped the reins. The horse sped up.

"I didn't know she knew how to drive," Matt said.

"Neither did I," Amos answered.

The horse's hooves rang off the cement as Ani raced the rig across town. They passed Poplar Road and Figg Street, then turned right up Elm Street. The road curved slowly around as it rose higher and higher.

"Where are you taking us, Ani?" Amos asked.

"I can't be right." Ani's lips mashed together. "I hope I am wrong."

"Wrong about what?" Remembering her previous warning, Matt asked, "Are more monsters coming?"

Ani nodded and urged the horse to go faster.

"Can you tell how many?" Matt said. "We killed over a hundred last night. Can you tell if that cut down on their numbers?"

Ani touched her head and then her chest. "I hear them. I feel them. I hope I'm wrong about how many there are."

"Is it a hundred? More?" Amos asked.

"More," Ani said. "Many more."

Matt scratched his jaw in frustration. "How many more?"

They reached the crest of the road, and Ani stopped the wagon. Tears ran down her cheeks as she pointed.

Approaching the town from the highway, hundreds of bone rats raced beside packs of wolves. Behind them strode a dozen enormous bone bears. Sitting atop the horrifying creatures were what appeared to be men.

Ani's hand trembled. "Malik's army is here."

36

AIN'T DEAD YET

Cain Haight

I groan and open my eyes. I'm tied to a chair in the middle
of a room, and my neck is killing me from my head hanging
forward and resting on my chest. I rotate my head in a circle,
and it sounds like I'm backing over gravel on a tarred driveway.

The Chinese guard standing by the door winces.

I lift my chin in greeting.

He scowls.

I didn't mean to tick him off. Maybe I should have nodded. I
don't really care. My head is throbbing, my mouth is dry, and
my wrists and ankles are bound like I'm about to get the electric chair.

Besides me and the guard, we're alone in a large, empty
room. I'm bound securely to a heavy metal chair bolted to the
floor. There are no windows, and the twelve-foot ceiling is
almost invisible in the light cast by the four oil lamps. There
is only one door which is facing me. The walls are white,
besides the stains left by the soot of the lamps, which cast a
red and yellow glow throughout the room. The cement floor

is painted white—except for the large dark stain beneath my feet.

I'm strapped down with leather bindings. My hands are bound to the arms of the chair, a strap is cinched tight around my chest, and each ankle is held firmly against the legs.

The door across from me slowly swings open, and a thin Chinese woman backs into the room, pulling a cart covered with a towel. She's got this look that reminds me of Abbey Tuggle. In third grade, Abbey was really into bugs. She'd spend all recess catching them and then mount them on cardboard with pins like a junior serial killer in the making.

I sit up straight, feeling like I'm in a horror movie. The list of possible items on the cart is limitless.

The door closes behind her with a loud click.

"Well, I'd stand and shake your hand, miss, but I'm a little tied up. My name is—" I'm about to lie until I remember that Lucy is the one who clubbed me like a harp seal. "Cain Haight, and I'm only here to get my daughter. Have you seen her?"

The woman stops the cart next to me and smiles the way Abbey used to before sticking a butterfly in the head with a pin. She lifts the towel, revealing a car battery and wires attached to a rod with a leather grip. Next to them sits a bottle of water. She folds the towel and carefully places it on the corner of the cart.

"There seems to be a little bit of a misunderstanding goin' on here. I don't need a jump start to get talking. You ask, and I'll answer."

The woman picks up the rod.

"Pink. That's my favorite color. You might not believe me, but it reminds me of my daughter. Speaking of which—"

She presses the tip of the rod against my ribcage.

I grit my teeth as my muscles all go rigid. "Woo! That's got a bit of a kick. I gotta warn you, though."

The guard in front of the door shifts his hand so his finger crosses over the trigger.

Now I know he understands English. "I have to warn you that if you do that again without letting me go to the bathroom first, someone may have to mop the floor."

She chuckles and presses the rod against my leg.

That jolt gets me rocking back and forth. Sure, it hurts, but the truth is, I've gotten worse trying to fix the dryer at my house. But I'm not letting her know that, so I ham it up a bit and even let out a couple of muffled screams.

She doesn't say anything, ask me questions, make threats, or open her mouth except to grin. I'm losing count of how many times I get shocked, so I sit there twitching. I don't understand why it isn't hurting more. Maybe they used it on someone else before me, and now it's low on juice.

The door across from me opens.

A huge man fills the doorway as he lumbers into the room. His neck is thick, and from his bulging biceps, he must do roids. Behind him, a short man with thinning hair follows. His uniform is crisp and brimming with shiny medals. After them comes Lucy and Fen.

Fen and Lucy move to stand several feet away in the corner while the shorter man marches forward, the giant two steps behind him.

"You must be Tianzi." I nod. "Seems like you know my ex-wife. Pay special attention to the 'ex' part. You know that expression—how do you know an ex-wife is lying? Her lips are moving. I don't know what she's told you about me, but I'm only here to get my little girl, and then I'll go."

Tianzi turns to stare at Lucy. "He does bring up an interesting point. This is Cain Haight, no? The man you said drowned?"

Lucy pales. I don't know what she's seen so far but that woman don't scare easy. So, her being worried is definitely a point of concern for me.

"I was unconscious when the truck sank. I thought he drowned."

Tianzi walks over to Lucy. "Do not worry. I don't think you lied."

Lucy exhales.

Tianzi strokes the side of her cheek with the back of his hand. "Your mother lied to you. And in a way, also to me. She will have to pay a price."

Lucy gasped.

Fen placed a restraining hand on Lucy's arm.

I'm amazed Lucy keeps her mouth shut, but she does. It looks like she just sold out her own mother, too.

Tianzi crosses to the woman holding the cattle prod hooked up to the battery. He whispers something to her and smiles like a male version of Abbey Tuggle. The family resemblance is unmistakable.

"I don't know what you just said to your sister, but she doesn't have to keep electrocuting me. Just ask the questions, and I'll answer."

From the stunned looks on Fen's and the giant's faces, they had no idea the creepy woman and Tianzi were brother and sister.

Tianzi's face flushes a deep crimson.

The last thing I wanted to do was get him mad. I should have kept my big mouth shut but now I've got to figure out how to minimize the damage. I try for humor. "My apologies. I've got a thing for faces and seeing similarities. Maybe I should have taken that gig at the circus after all."

Tianzi punches me in the jaw.

I jerk my head to the side like it was a hard blow, but that right cross wouldn't win a plastic ring at the county fair punch machine. I lick my lip like it hurts. "Seriously, I'm sorry."

"I have need of your assistance, Mr. Haight," Tianzi says.

"Sure. I scratch your back, you scratch mine."

Tianzi glances back at the woman. "What is he saying, Pi?"

I'm not the most mature man, and the way he says her name makes me crack a grin.

Lucy is staring daggers at me.

I know she wants me to shut up. It has the opposite effect. I laugh.

Tianzi looks like he's going to punch me again until he sees I'm staring at my ex.

Pi reaches into her pocket, takes out a phone, and starts typing.

"You get cell service?" I ask, astounded. "Who do you call?"

"I scratch your back, you scratch mine." Pi repeats. "It is an American idiom. It means if we help him, he will help us."

"Excellent," Tianzi says.

"I was hoping you were calling someone to turn the electricity back on and maybe an extermination place to deal with all these creatures. Is all you can get is Wikipedia on that thing, or can you call in the calvary?"

Tianzi smiles. "We are both the calvary and the exterminators. We are the future."

I take a deep breath, ready to launch into my offer.

Lucy's eyes open wide, and she shakes her head like she's begging me to shut up.

"I hate to break the news to you, Tianzi, but you're not doing well on either front. The bone monsters destroyed your food and ammo, and your men look ready to give up. Now, I can help you out with both of those things."

Tianzi laughs. It's high-pitched and somehow even more irritating than nails on a chalkboard. "Always the arrogance of you Americans. What makes you think you can save the world?"

"Well, we've kind of done it a few times already. World War I. World War II." I smile. "And I can get you all out of this mess." As I speak, I lock eyes with the two guards standing next to the door. "I come from a land of milk and honey—plenty of food. No monsters. What more could you ask for? And I can lead you there."

The two guards exchange a glance.

Tianzi scoffs. "I know all about Ridgecrest. Soon, we will go there, not as beggars pleading for scraps, but as conquerors."

"The world has really gone into the toilet if you're acting like taking over Ridgecrest, Tennessee is like Napoleon conquering Europe. Ridgecrest is a dot on the map. You don't have to take it by force. There are Christian folk there who will share with you. And they have more than enough to share."

The guard on the left licks his lips and glances at his friend.

"I can lead you right there. It's a short ride."

Tianzi glances over his shoulder at the guards, who immediately stare straight ahead. "You take me for a fool. I have an army at my disposal."

"You have a few starved men who are low on ammo." I shoot back. "And this being the south, the folks in Ridgecrest have more guns, bullets, and firepower than you do."

Tianzi chuckled. "I am not speaking about an army of men. Ridgecrest will fall before me. Now that I have the boy, we can control the beasts." Tianzi's chest puffs out as he straightens up. He's posing now like a peacock, trying to impress everyone in the room.

The horror of what the experiments were all about slams me in the gut. They went from wanting to communicate with animals to controlling them. And the government did what it always does: uses its discoveries as weapons.

"It won't matter if you show up with a hundred of those monsters. Ridgecrest is your typical southern town. If you bring a herd of those bone things, all it means for them is more target practice and a huge party after. But there's no reason for it to break bad. If Jacob can somehow control these monsters, tell him to make them go away or kill each other."

"I finally have the ultimate weapon. Do you want me not to use it?"

"Look around, Einstein." I snap. "That's what everyone called Nukes. How did using those work out?"

"The leaders of the old order were fools. This new world will rise from the ashes with a perfect structure I will provide."

"What could go wrong with your plan to use a little boy to control a bunch of monsters that like to eat people?"

Tianzi backhands me across the face. "I wouldn't expect a simpleton like you to understand."

I look behind Tianzi at the guards standing before the door, hoping Tianzi sounds as crazy to them as he does to me. "You know what I ate before I left Ridgecrest? Two full plates of Southern barbecue: pork ribs and fried chicken with all the fixings, buttery mashed potatoes, collard greens, and okra. And corn on the cob with a sweet tea to wash it down."

The guards are practically drooling.

The giant eyes them nervously. He sets his hand on the pistol on his hip.

To my surprise, Fen is watching the giant and not the guards.

"I can lead you there. The people are nice. They'll—" I grit my teeth as Tianzi's sister jams the electric probe into my throat. Between the blow and the electricity, I can't breathe. I start thrashing around in the chair for almost a minute before she stops.

My head hangs forward, and I'm gulping for air. I think the lights are dimming until I realize I'm floating along the edge of passing out.

Holding the electrical rod with both hands, the woman steps back next to Tianzi. She stands so close that her back presses against his chest. Tianzi bites his lower lip and angles his head, his mouth inches away from her ear. He whispers something, and she smiles at him.

One look at their expressions and it's obvious they're more than just fishing buddies. When I remember they're brother and sister—my lip curls. I force myself to take a deep breath and raise my head. I meet Tianzi's cold stare, and my brain starts screaming at me to shut up and not push his buttons. But what do I do? I open my big fat mouth and say, "I didn't know you were knocking boots with your sister, too."

Tianzi glares at me and motions to Pi.

She takes her phone back out and says, "What does the expression knocking boots mean?" As she's reading, her eyes narrow, and her cheeks turn crimson. She shouts something in Chinese.

Tianzi starts wailing away at my face.

I gotta give it to him. When he's mad, he's got a good right. After the third haymaker, I do the only thing I can while tied to a chair. I angle my forehead into the punch.

Something in Tianzi's hand snaps. He screams. It's as high-pitched as I imagined it would be.

I can't help but smile.

Everyone in the room except Tianzi and I are looking at the floor. Maybe they think his breaking his hand on my face is as funny as I do, but they don't laugh. Me, on the other hand? I can't hold it back.

Tianzi is so mad he starts screaming at me in Chinese. I can't understand a word he's saying. Spit is flying out of his mouth. After a full minute of threats, he switches to English. "You think you're so funny, do you? Let's see how you laugh when Nian rips your heart out."

He turns and storms out of the room. Everyone except the guard follows. Before Lucy leaves, she shoots me a look and shakes her head like I'm the stupidest man on the planet.

I flash her a bloody smile. I may be a fool, but at least I ain't dying groveling. And who knows? I ain't dead yet.

37

MOMMA

Lucy Green

Lucy stumbled forward as Fen pushed her down the hall-way. She managed to keep from falling by grabbing hold of the wall. "You need to tell Tianzi that my mother didn't lie."

Fen shoved her. "It doesn't matter. Walk."

"It does matter. She believed Cain was dead. We all did. Momma didn't lie." Lucy stopped.

Fen slammed her hands against Lucy's shoulders.

Lucy pitched to the floor. Despite the carpet, the impact with the concrete beneath the carpet jarred her already battered frame. Frustration and panic fueled her anger, and she scrambled to her feet. "If you shove me again, I'll make you and your husband a matched set and take your hand off, too." Lucy stabbed the air with her finger and held it in Fen's face.

Fen seized Lucy's wrist and twisted.

Lucy gasped in pain and doubled forward.

Fen yanked Lucy's arm behind her back. Keeping hold of Lucy's wrist, Fen grabbed Lucy's hair and, like a bouncer, marched her through the open doorway at the end of the hall.

On the other side of the doorway, Fen spun Lucy around and slammed her against the wall. She covered Lucy's mouth and forced her to look up at the camera.

"I'm trying to save you, you fool," Fen whispered. "Shut up, do what I say, and I will try to get you and your daughter out of here."

"What about my mother? What about Cain?"

Fen made a face like Lucy poked her in the eye. "Impossible. It will be hard enough getting you and Bri out."

"I'm not leaving them."

"You don't have a choice."

With the speed of the five-time winner of the Ridgecrest Cowboy shoot, Lucy snatched Fen's pistol out of its holster and pressed the barrel of the gun against Fen's stomach. "I do have a choice. And my choice is we all go."

"You'll never make it out like this."

Lucy ground her teeth and glared at the camera above them. They were standing out of the viewing angle, but the guards would come running the moment someone saw them.

"Fine." Fen scowled. "I will try to rescue them, too. But we need to start walking. Give me my gun."

Lucy leaned forward so she was nose to nose with Fen. "You need to do better than try, or I promise you, you'll be the first to die." She handed the gun to Fen.

Fen exhaled. "Walk. Up the stairs."

Lucy marched forward but with a growing sense of unease. "Where are you taking me?"

"Tianzi wants me to confirm your story. He believes you are telling the truth about your mother believing Cain drowned."

Lucy's hope rose. "She did. We all did. Why would we lie?"

"Keep walking and shut your mouth."

Lucy's legs felt like they were on fire when she reached the top of the stairs.

Two guards were waiting there. The guards hardly glanced

their way as Fen marched Lucy past them, through the doorway and down the hallway to the front of the building.

The sun was rising over the trees in the far distance. The base was quiet, and the air was still. Today would be an oven as far as the heat was concerned. Lucy was already starting to sweat.

They crossed the grounds until they reached the single-story infirmary. There wasn't a guard posted outside, and to Lucy's surprise, there was none inside either.

Fen stopped at a desk in front of a tired-looking woman. They whispered, and Lucy couldn't tell what they were saying. But the longer the conversation went on, the paler the woman became.

"Thank you." Fen nodded, taking Lucy by the elbow, and marched her into the large room on the right.

Over two dozen beds occupied the room, but less than a dozen were filled. Chinese, Russian, and American soldiers lay silently in the beds. The odor of death and decay mixing with the spring fresh scent of disinfectant made Lucy want to vomit.

Many of the men were missing limbs. Most were asleep, but some stared at Lucy with haunted eyes as she passed.

Nearing the end of the row, Lucy stared at her mother sleeping in the last bed. She hurried to Sadie's side. "Momma?"

Sadie opened her eyes, and a smile slowly dawned on her face. "You look rough, baby. They hurt you?"

Lucy shook her head, then nodded. "Nothing I couldn't take. You don't look no better."

"Thanks." Sadie propped herself up on an elbow. She noticed Fen and the two women stared at each other momentarily.

"Do you two kn—" Lucy started to ask, but Sadie placed her hand on Lucy's wrist.

"Shhh. Where did you learn to whisper? In a sawmill?"

"I have a question for you," Fen snapped to attention and

fixed Sadie with a stare. "What happened to the man who left Ridgecrest with you? The one named Cain?"

Sadie glanced at Lucy.

"Do not ask your daughter. Look at me. Give me your answer now."

"We got attacked by a bone bear. Cain was driving the truck. We went into the river. I reckon the steering column broke and pinned his legs. I swam free, and he died. But you already know that. Why you asking again?"

"Did you see his body?"

"No offense, but that's a stupid question. The truck went underwater, and we went over the waterfall in the boat."

"So you did not see his body?"

Sadie rolled her eyes. "No. I did not see his body." She gasped and turned to Lucy. "He's alive, ain't he? He came, didn't he?"

Lucy nodded, and Sadie squeezed her arm. Lucy wanted to say something more, but the words caught her throat.

"He lives but will be dead by the time we return to the bunker," Fen said. "I'm sorry."

"Wait!" Sadie sat up and grimaced. "What are you talking about? We've got to do something."

Fen grabbed Sadie's shoulders and pushed her back onto the bed. She whispered something, and Sadie stopped struggling.

Sadie nodded. She turned to Lucy and opened and closed her mouth. Anger, fear, and pity washed across her mother's face. "We'll get out of here, baby," Sadie said. "Don't you worry. We'll get out of here."

Fen grabbed Lucy's elbow and yanked her off the bed.

"I love you, momma."

"I love you too, sweet pea."

Lucy choked back tears as Fen spun her around and marched her down the hallway. "I was telling you the truth. My mother didn't know Cain was alive. You have to tell Tianzi that."

"I will," Fen said, storming by the nurse's station without glancing at the worried woman. She shoved open the door and dragged Lucy outside. "And it will accomplish nothing. Your mother and Cain will both die today."

"What? No! Momma told the truth."

"Tianzi has no need for your mother. He only needs one of you to control your daughter and get her to keep the boy in line. The other one is dispensable and will be used as an example."

"Then we have to do something now. You said you would help."

"I need more time."

"We don't have more time!" Lucy begged. "Please, you have to save them."

Fen took a deep breath and stared at Lucy. There was genuine remorse etched on her face. "I will do what I can to save your mother. But there is nothing I can do to save Cain. He's already dead."

38

A TRUE THESPIAN

Evan Green

Evan sat in a chair in a medium-sized room with a desk and two old file cabinets shoved against the wall. Mismatched chairs were scattered about. The men named H and Bob stood with their arms crossed behind him. Angel, the woman who pretended to be a teenager, sat behind the desk.

"What's your name?" Angel asked.

"Evan Green. Where is Sam?"

"We're asking him questions someplace else. I want to make sure your stories match up, so you'd better tell us the truth. Okay?"

Evan swallowed and nodded. They'd taken his gun away. Without it, he couldn't overpower the armed men behind him and Angel. So far, he'd been treated fairly. Maybe there were good people still left in this world.

"Who is your father?" Angel asked.

"My dad? Why?"

"Answer the question," H's voice was deep and menacing.

"Martin Green. He's the mayor of Ridgecrest."

"What are the names of the people who left with Cain, and what are their relation to you?"

"Well, there's my wife, Lucy Haight—now Lucy Green. My mother-in-law, Sadie. Mercy Yoder. No relation. And Cain Haight."

"You married Cain's ex-wife?" Angel glanced behind Evan at the men.

"Yes. Not long ago. It was on the anniversary of the Dark. When everything shut down."

"Why would you get married then?"

Evan shrugged. "Lucy thought it would be a good day for a new beginning."

"And what did Cain think of you marrying his ex-wife?" Bob asked.

"He certainly wasn't happy about it. He didn't like me much before anyway."

"Then why are you going after him now?" Angel asked.

"I'm going to help my wife rescue her daughter."

"Her daughter?" Bob repeated.

"I told you we just got married. I've never had kids, and to say Bri idolizes her father is an understatement. I'm trying to give her time to get used to me." Evan leaned forward in his chair.

H made a rumbling sound in his throat that made Evan stop.

"All I want to do is find my wife. I don't know who you people are, but I don't want any trouble. Can I please go?"

Angel fixed Evan with a cold stare. "If you are so concerned about your wife, why didn't you go with them to begin with?"

Evan looked down at his hands. They shook in his lap. He pressed them against his knees and lifted his chin. "I made a bunch of excuses as to why I didn't go with her, but the real reason was that I was afraid. I still am. I feel like I've been kidnapped by aliens and dropped on a foreign planet. Everything's destroyed. You don't know if the people you meet now are going to kill you or help you. And there are monsters out here that want to eat your bones." Evan met Angel's gaze. "But I'm tired of being afraid. So I'm trying to find my wife."

Angel nodded sympathetically.

Evan smiled.

Angel lifted her hands and clapped. "Very good. Stellar." She looked at H and Bob. "We should get Jerry. Evan here is a world-class actor. A true thespian." She pointed at Evan, and her eyes narrowed. "I warned you not to lie to me."

Evan sat back in the chair and raised his hands to chest level with the palms out. "I don't know what you're talking about. Everything I said is the truth."

"You and your friend Sam didn't get your stories straight," Angel said.

"There's no story. That's why I didn't go with Lucy. I'm ashamed of it."

"Sure you are. You're just a coward. Stop lying!" Angel slammed her hand on the desk. "Sam admitted that you were a soldier. He said you were probably CIA. What agency are you with?"

Evan chuckled nervously. "No. Sam's got it all wrong. He's a coward, too. After he saved me from these guys who were trying to rob me, he thought I must be a soldier. I didn't correct him at first, but when he brought it up again, I told him flat-out that I'd never been in the military."

"Why would Sam tell us that you're special ops?"

"Because the more I denied being in the military, the more Sam thought I was lying."

"So you're saying that even your friend thinks you're a liar?"

"I'm not CIA. I'm not military. I didn't even finish the Boy Scouts because I didn't like sleeping in the woods."

Bob laughed. "I think he's telling the truth."

Angel frowned. "Why?"

"I found that when someone's story is so stupid it makes them look like a moron, most of the time it's true. When you add in that his pistol didn't have a round in the chamber, and neither of these guys have any food, but they packed wet wipes, I believe him."

"Wet wipes," H laughed.

"Sam packed the car," Evan admitted.

Angel leaned back in her chair. "Say I believe him." She spoke to H and Bob like Evan wasn't there. "What do we do with them?"

"The scouts haven't seen Cain since he left," H said.

"Cain was here? What about the women and kids?"

"I'm sorry to inform you that no one has seen Mercy Yoder. We don't know where she is or if she is alive or dead. Your wife, mother-in-law, and the children are being held by the faction controlling the east side of the army base. That faction is not friendly."

Angel continued to explain how the base had been split into two sides and how Lucy had been captured along with everyone except Cain. Evan's emotions ping-ponged back and forth between overjoyed and horrified. His wife was alive, but she was held prisoner.

When Angel finished explaining the situation, she turned to Bob. "How many vehicles have you rounded up?"

"We have enough to move almost everyone. H and I are going to make another run to try to find a couple more."

"With Cain kicking the hornet's nest, we must be ready to retreat," Angel said, rubbing her temples.

"Retreat?" Evan said. "To where?"

"Ridgecrest. That's why I'm sending you back up there to speak with your father." Angel's voice was steady and cold, like the ringing of steel.

Evan jumped to his feet. "I'm not going back to Ridgecrest

without my wife! You just told me she's being held captive by some crazed fanatic. Do you think I'm just going to leave her?"

"Settle down. Sit." Angel said.

Evan stayed on his feet.

H moved closer, his large biceps expanding as he balled his hands into fists.

Evan sat down.

"The situation in the city has become untenable. We can't stay here." Angel explained.

"I'm not going with you unless I get my wife," Evan said.

H stomped around Evan's chair and glared down at him. "I'm sorry for saying this so bluntly, but that's how I talk. If Cain fails, do you think you stand a better chance of getting your wife out of there? You'll only get yourself killed."

"More importantly." Bob placed a restraining hand on H's arm and pulled him back. "We'll need you to speak with your father. We want to ask him for sanctuary. We need you alive."

"I didn't come all the way to stay here and wait to see if Cain makes it."

Angel stood up, put one hand on the desk, and pointed to the door. "I have a responsibility to protect the survivors in that room. Ridgecrest is the best option for them, and Cain is the best chance you have of getting your wife back. You are going to stand down and give him that chance."

Evan glared at the floor. He hated to admit it, but they were right. "If Cain fails, I have to try to save my wife."

"We thought you'd say that." Bob grabbed Evan's right arm, snapping a handcuff around his wrist.

Evan pulled away, but H seized Evan's left arm, jerked it behind his back, and Bob clicked the handcuffs closed.

"I'm sorry," Angel said. "I truly am, but I have a room full of people to think about, and you too. I never should have let Cain go, but I won't let you throw your life away."

"Don't you get it?" Evan lunged forward, but H held him back. "I have to try. Please, let me try to get my wife."

Angel sat back down. "I won't do that. Take him to the holding cell."

39

AS NUTTY AS BOOTH GENTRY

Bri Haight

Bri sat on the bed, watching Jacob sleep. She couldn't understand how he could sleep so much. He was unconscious for days in the canoe. Maybe whatever drug they gave him was still making him tired. She hoped he was okay.

She glanced around the room. It was as big as the living room in her new house and filled with toys, comfy chairs, and a TV that worked. A week ago, she would have given almost anything to watch TV, but now all she wanted to do was get home.

Bri slipped out of the bed and silently crept over to the door. It was still locked. There weren't any windows either. She'd seen someone break open a door with a metal pole in a movie, but there wasn't anything like that in here. There wasn't anything she could use as a weapon, either. Everything was either plastic or squishy.

"Bri?" Jacob rubbed his eyes and slid out of bed. "What are you doing?"

"Trying to figure a way out of here."

"We should wait for your daddy."

Bri's lip trembled. "I don't think he's gonna come. They said my daddy is dead."

Jacob made a face.

"No, he isn't. He's close."

Bri glanced around, puzzled. "What are you talking about?"

"I heard him. And your momma, too. While you were sleeping."

"You couldn't have heard them. They're not here."

"Not with my ears." Jacob crossed his legs. "Hold on."

"What are you talking about, Jacob?"

"I have to tinkle." Jacob rushed into the bathroom and shut the door.

Bri chased after him. "How can you hear somebody without your ears? You're talking as nutty as Booth Gentry."

"Get out! I'm going."

"I'm not looking."

"But you can hear what I'm doing," Jacob said as he continued to go to the bathroom.

Bri swore and slammed the door.

"BAD WORD!"

"You're gonna hear a lot more of those if you don't get your butt out here and tell me what in tarnation you're talking about."

The door opened, and Jacob peered out.

"Did you wash your hands?"

Jacob shut the door. The water ran, and he came back out. "I don't know how to say it."

"You said you heard my daddy and momma but not with your ears. How can you hear without your ears."

Jacob touched the side of his head. "In here."

"Like with your mind? Like Professor X?"

"Who?"

"The leader of the X-Men," Bri took a deep breath and scowled. "Oh, you've never seen the movies. Did you dream it?"

"No. I heard them. Your daddy was really, really mad."

"What did he say?"

Jacob shook his head. "I'm not supposed to say things like that."

"My daddy cussed?"

Jacob nodded quickly. "A lot. And your momma thought he was the 'S' word."

"What's the 'S' word?"

"Stupid," Jacob whispered.

"That sounds like my momma and daddy. But how can you hear them thinking?"

Jacob shrugged.

Bri closed her eyes and pictured her horse. "Okay. Do me. What am I thinking?"

"Rainbow Glitter Magic Star."

Bri's mouth dropped open. "How did you do that?"

Jacob shrugged again. "I just listen."

"You have superpowers! What else can you do?"

"What do you mean?"

"Can you fly? Can you shoot lasers out of your eyes? Are you invulnerable?" Bri ran forward and punched Jacob in the arm.

"Ow! Why'd you do that?"

"To check your powers. Did that hurt?"

"Yes. I don't have any powers."

"You can read minds." Bri bit her lip. "Maybe that was just a lucky guess." She closed her eyes and pictured Copper with a birthday hat on her head.

"Copper," Jacob said.

"What's she wearing?"

Jacob's eyes narrowed and glowed a light blue. "A cone with stars?"

"Close enough. You do have superpowers. That means you can do special stuff. We need to figure out what you can do so we can get out of here."

The door to the room shook and opened. Tianzi, Pi, and Chao walked in. Tianzi's right arm was in a sling, and his hand was wrapped in a large bandage.

Jacob ran behind Bri to hide.

"I have something very exciting to show you," Tianzi said in a sing-song tone. "I need you both to come with me."

Bri didn't move.

Tianzi's lips pressed together. "I thought you would be eager to come and see your father."

Bri gasped. "My daddy is here?"

"Yes. And he has agreed to help us with a little experiment. But for that experiment to work, I need Jacob's help."

Jacob shook his head.

Tianzi fixed Bri with his cold stare. "Do you remember what we talked about, Bri? I needed you to convince Jacob that I am truly his friend."

Bri swallowed as she recalled the threats Tianzi made about killing Bri's mother and grandmother. She turned to Jacob. "I need your help, Jacob."

Jacob stepped away from her. His nose wrinkled, and his mouth twisted in disgust as a look of horror swept over his face.

"Please, Jacob. We need to help my daddy. You like my daddy, right?"

Jacob nodded.

"Then we need to go with Tianzi. He's our friend."

"Liar!" Jacob screamed and pointed at Bri. "He said he'd kill your Momma and Mawmaw."

Tianzi grabbed Bri's arm with his left hand and squeezed. "You broke our agreement."

"Ow! No." Bri cried. "I didn't tell him. I didn't tell him anything."

Jacob ran forward and kicked Tianzi in the shin.

Tianzi winced.

Bri punched Tianzi's bandaged hand.

Tianzi screamed in pain.

"Fry his brain!" Bri shouted.

Tianzi gasped and then, to her amazement, laughed. "Wait a minute. You're telling the truth. Jacob must have read your mind. He's already developing his new powers."

Bri grabbed Jacob's hand and ran for the door. They made it only three steps before Chao yanked Bri off the floor, and Pi wrapped Jacob in a bear hug.

Tianzi's smile broadened. "What a fabulous revelation. You have made me very happy, Jacob."

"I won't help you." Jacob struggled in Pi's arms. "You're bad. You're a bad, bad man."

"You don't understand, child. I will never harm you. I am not your enemy. I am your savior."

Jacob thrust out his little chin. "Mercy says Jesus is my Savior, and you aren't him! You're a poopoo head."

"Enough!" Tianzi snapped. "Bring them both."

Chao slung Bri over his shoulder like a sack of potatoes while Pi held onto Jacob's shirt as she ushered him out of the room. They walked in silence down the hallway until they came to a closed door with a guard standing in front.

Once the guard opened the door, the hallway no longer looked like a hotel's. This corridor was plain cement and wide enough for four people to walk side by side. But the group continued in a straight line.

They reached a large set of double doors, and a female soldier holding a large gun snapped to attention, saluted, and bowed low.

Chao and Pi returned the gesture, but Tianzi only nodded his head.

Jacob waved.

Bri exhaled. The little boy was the nicest person she'd ever met. What were they going to do with him?

The doors opened to a small room. Machines hummed, and the lights overhead made Bri blink. A control panel sat against the far wall with a long window behind it. But the window didn't look outside. She could see down into an enormous room with huge metal doors at the back. The room was so big it reminded Bri of the rodeo building at the fairgrounds. That room could hold the whole demolition derby ring and the stands with all the people.

Chao set her on the ground.

Bri gasped and rushed forward.

Beneath her, three men stood on the cement floor of the massive room. In the middle was her father. "Daddy! Daddy!" Bri screamed as loud as she could.

"Quiet it down," Tianzi ordered.

Chao grabbed Bri by the back of her neck and squeezed.

Bri's shoulders raised to her ears as she winced. "I'll shut up! Let go."

Chao released her.

"Puke face," Bri muttered.

Jacob ran next to Bri and took her hand.

Tianzi strode forward. He grabbed Jacob's shoulder with his left hand and turned him around so he could look down into the room. "What comes next is very important, child."

"Leave him alone!" Bri shouted.

Chao grabbed Bri by the back of her neck.

"If she speaks again, break something." Tianzi smiled at Jacob. "Do you know who that man is down there?"

"Bri's daddy," Jacob whispered.

"That's right. And you don't want your friend to be sad, do you?"

Jacob shook his head.

"Then do everything I say, or your friend's father will die."
Tianzi nodded to Pi.

She marched over to the console and began pressing
buttons.

Down in the room, lights flashed, and an alarm sounded.
Metal clicked and clunked. The two huge doors at the end of
the large room slowly swung open.

40

NIAN

Cain Haight

I'm standing between two men at the end of what looks like a small airplane hanger. They herded us in here at gunpoint and undid our shackles. The poor Chinese soldier on my left is covered in mud and blood. He's shaking like a leaf in a gale and keeps peering over his shoulder at the door we were led through, but it's locked now.

On my right is an enormous Russian about the size of the guy Rocky fought in Rocky Four. Or was it five? It doesn't really matter. The guy is 6'6" at least, but from the way he's swaying unsteadily on his feet and the lopsided smile on his face, he's as drunk as a skunk that got into the cider barrel. He reeks of vodka as he sings some song in Russian while we wait, staring at the giant doors at the end of the room.

Huge overhead lights hum. Between the alcohol drifting off the Russian and the dank smell of mud from the Chinese soldier, there's another scent I can't place. It's faint, but the deeper I breathe, the higher the hair on the back of my neck rises.

Besides us, the room is empty. Nothing. Not even a scrap of paper.

Warning lights flash, and an alarm buzzes. A loud CLACK fills the air and echoes off the cement—machinery whirls, metal clanks, and the doors in the back swing open.

The Russian's singing trails off.

A gust of air slaps me in the face, and I immediately recognize the smell I haven't been able to identify—death.

It's not blood I'm smelling or burnt flesh. You never forget those odors. But death has a scent all its own. I can't describe it, but it has a presence. It clings to you. You don't even have to breathe it in for it to get inside of you. And that's what it's doing right now to me. I'm like a fish swimming in an ocean of death. It's all around me and in me.

There are no lights inside the room that just opened up. The doors and wall above it block the light from creeping in, but something is in there. Something big stirs in the darkness.

The Chinese soldier whimpers. I'm surprised he doesn't run. Maybe if I were less stubborn or smarter, I'd run. A weird sensation ripples through my body. I stare down at my feet. My eyebrows travel in different directions. It's like my legs are locked in cement. I wiggle my fingers. They respond fine. But when I try to wiggle my toes, nothing happens.

The Chinese soldier is sobbing now. He's gulping in air and about to pass out.

Now I know why he ain't running. He can't.

Claws click off the cement. The shadows in the dark room shift—something enormous stalks forward.

I'm standing there, trying to make sense of what I'm seeing, but I can't. Whatever the creature is, it isn't human. It can't be. It stands over ten feet tall. It walks on two legs, but its feet are wide and clawed. Its arms are unproportionally long for its body. Like an orangutan's, they hang below its knees. Bone white scales cover its entire form but turn ashen on its broad chest, forming a pattern like rising flames. It struts forward and lifts a broad chin. Its face makes my breath catch in my throat. It's not human but a mix of ape and canine, covered in fine scales that shimmer in the light. The scales are black from the crown of its head to its wolf-like snout. It stares at us with snake-like, yellow eyes, gazing at each man.

The Chinese soldier loses control of his bowels.

"I am Nian." The creature's voice rumbles like thunder down from the mountain. "You are to be judged." Nian stalks forward and stops ten yards away. He studies the Chinese soldier for a moment and calls out. "Come."

To my amazement, the soldier doesn't hesitate. He marches forward. I can't understand why until I see his face. The man is terrified, and his eyes dart around like a man being swept out to sea. He's doing everything he can to stop himself from moving but helplessly marches forward.

The soldier stops a few feet in front of Nian.

"You are a coward," Nian says. "And a deserter. You opted to run away instead of fight. Your sentence is death."

Before the man can respond, Nian stretches out his long arms and seizes the man by his waist. He jerks him off the ground, slams him off the cement twice, and then flings him back into the shadows at the end of the room, where he lands with a wet smack.

It's hard for me to breathe. I've never seen anything that strong. He flung that soldier like a doll across the room. He could snap me in half whenever he wanted to.

Nian turns to the Russian.

The soldier nervously eyes the door.

Nian's snake-like eyes narrow. He raises a clawed hand and motions for the soldier to come.

The Russian turns and runs, screaming for the door. I can't tell what he's saying, but it sounds like a mixture of begging and cursing. He yanks on the handle and pounds the door.

Nian scowls and stomps forward. His long arm lashes out, smashing the soldier's head into the steel door. It sounds like a watermelon dropped off a building and hitting the sidewalk.

The Russian's body slumps to the ground.

Nian grabs it by the legs and hurls it across the room. The body lands about thirty yards away.

I force myself to take a deep breath. Whatever this thing is, it's not Superman. Its strength has limits.

Nian turns to me.

I stare back. I don't know what's going on with my legs, but I still can't even move my toes, let alone run. The only thing I can think of to save myself is trying to talk my way out of this. But what do you say to a monster?

"Cain Hate, you are here for me to pass judgment."

"Actually," I work up my most charming smile. "It's pronounced Haight. And before you get to judging me, I've got a proposition for you."

"You have violated the law by coming here."

"I came to get my daughter. Give me her, her friend, and my mother-in-law, and I'll go. You can keep my ex. She wants to stay anyway."

"Bri. She is your offspring?"

"Yeah. Despite that, she's a great kid. Let her go."

"Sadie," Nian says my mother-in-law's name like he's chewing on rocks. "She has killed many of my army. She is an enemy."

"Every soldier is an enemy until there is peace. After that, they're just people. She wouldn't have killed anything if it wasn't trying to kill her first."

"There is blood on your hands and hers. Both of your sins taint your daughter."

I try to open my mouth, but I can't. It's like someone is holding my mouth shut.

"Silence. There is one more you did not name. Your daughter's friend..." Nian lifts his chin and glares over my head at the back of the room.

I glance over my shoulder. There's a huge, tinted window on the floor above us, but I can't see through it.

Nian marches forward and past me. He stands with his legs apart and his arms stiff at his side, staring at the window.

I don't know if it's because he's focused on something else but my legs start working. I move away from Nian, but he's standing with his back to me, blocking the way to the door.

Nian staggers sideways like he's been punched in the head. He lunges forward, but his legs don't move. He glares at his feet and then lets out a roar so loud that I cover my ears.

I go to make a break for the door, but my legs stopped working again.

Nian turns to me and smiles. He stretches out a clawed hand, but I'm just outside his reach.

"Looks like we have a standoff," I say. "How about you just listen to me for a minute?"

"There is nothing you can give me."

"Really? From the way I see it, you're in a cage, too."

Nian's claws rake the air inches away from my face.

"I'm simply stating a fact. Here's another one. There's a big world out there. I want a tiny little piece of it. Ridgecrest. You can have the rest."

Nian lifts his head and stares down his snout at me. "Stop using your voice," Nian speaks inside my head.

This voice is even darker than his real one. My stomach feels like I'm on one of those rides that drop you fifty feet in a second.

"Why would you offer to help me?" Nian says in my head.

Not having a clue of how having a silent conversation works, I go for the easy option and just think what I want to say, "Because it's mutually beneficial."

Nian crosses his arms and puffs out his chest.

"They call you Nian, right?"

"I chose my title."

"Sure. Good choice. It fits. I don't mean any offense, but... what are you?"

"I am not a what!" Nian screams in my head—sending pain slicing between my temples. "I am Nian. There is none like me."

"That's fair. I can see that. What I'm getting at is the how. If I were to guess, I think that some scientists have been doing some experimenting and that never ends well. So, I can see how you're upset."

Nian chuckles. Even though it's inside my head, it rumbles so much that my teeth shake.

"I am perfection. The next step for the world. Why would that bother me?"

I rub the back of my neck. This thing sounds more puffed up about himself than Tianzi. "Again, that may be true, but right now, you're still a dog in a cage."

The analogy escapes my mouth before I fully think through how it will sound to a monster that is obviously part wolf.

Nian nods. "True. But my captivity is coming to an end. The scourge has long used what they deemed beneath them for their own purposes. In the Dark Ages, they would fling diseased rats out of catapults into besieged cities. In World War II, they used dogs strapped with explosives to attack tanks. But now they have perfected their weapon—me."

"And now you want to wipe out your makers. I get it. It's always the case. Do you know what happened to the armies who used the diseased rats? They got the plague, too. And it was the Russians who trained dogs to attack the Nazi tanks. But do you know what went wrong? The Russians used their own tanks in training and painted swastikas on them. But the dogs didn't care about the swastikas on the battlefield—they ran at the tanks that looked like the ones in training—and they blew up the Russian's tanks."

Nian laughs.

It's the creepiest thing I've ever heard. I want to wash out my brain to get rid of the memory of the sound already.

I click my tongue as I realize something. "So, the scientist created the bone monsters, and then they made the ghouls to control them?"

"Yes. But men are not strong enough. Their power is limited. But what really excited the scientist was the fact that these ghouls, as you call them, could almost also control man. For what is man but a beast?"

"And that's why they made you. You can control man and beast."

"For a scourge, you are somewhat intelligent."

"Seeing how you are now at the top of the food chain, why not accept my surrender? You want to be king of the forest? You got it. We'll stay in Ridgecrest, and you can have the rest of this big ole world."

Nian clicks the claws on his right hand together. He stares at me like he's peering into my soul. "Agreed."

I stumble forward. I can move my legs. I stare up at Nian and eye him suspiciously. "Seriously?"

"Yes. I will grant your request. I have only one condition. The boy must die."

Before I can stop myself, my thoughts betray me, and I give a huge mental middle finger to the monster standing in front of me.

Nian roars both in my head and aloud. It's deafening.

I sprint for the door.

"You're dead, Cain Hate." Nian screams.

The locks on the door turn, and it opens. Four terrified guards motion me to step out.

Why I do some things, I don't know. But I spin around, face

the real-life demon glaring at me, and smile. "Looks like you're the one still in the cage."

Nian roars.

One guard grabs me and yanks me back into the hallway.

Another guard slams the door shut.

"You're dead, Cain!" Nian's voice is so loud it is clear through the closed steel door. "I will take the boy and then kill you all."

41

MALIK

Mercy Yoder

Riding in the back of the wagon along a desolate road, Mercy stared at Fort Burgess in the distance. She'd seen pictures of the Army base in the past, but now, it was hard to recognize. Before, a huge flag flew atop a massive pole in the center of the gleaming rows of buildings. Row after row of soldiers stood at attention during a grand parade.

Now, it appeared empty and destroyed—a husk of its once vibrant existence. A long chasm ran like a scar through the center of the base. Its width varied from a dozen yards to places so large that the remains of three buildings rose from the water like islands in a river. Burned-out vehicles dotted the ground, and many of the structures were toppled or damaged. The transformation of Fort Burgess was a stark reminder of the loss that had befallen it.

Had the others made it there? Had they freed Bri?

"They are all inside." Eve's words made Mercy jump.

Mercy had never imagined someone being able to hear your unspoken thoughts. It was incredibly rude—

"You rude!" Eve snapped. "I didn't know why you were so worried."

"I'm sorry." Mercy stammered. "Can you turn it off and on?"

"I have to listen if that is what you mean. Sometimes it is hard."

"Hard to stop listening?"

Eve shook her head. "Hard to hear. Scourge's minds are jumbled. Scattered. Not like friends." Eve patted the bear's back. "They are nice to speak with. Simple. True. Honest. Not rude like a scourge."

"I apologize again. It's like..." Mercy struggled for the words.

"Seeing you with no clothes." Eve nodded.

Mercy blushed. "Yes, it's like that. It takes a little getting used to, but I will try."

Eve glanced up at the sun and shook her head. "No time. Almost there."

The wolves pulling the wagon sped up.

Mercy grabbed the sideboard to keep from pitching out the back. Her breathing sped up. Eve said this man she was taking Mercy to would kill her. Mercy had promised the Lord that she'd try to save Jacob's life. She had to try.

Holding onto the backboard, Mercy scanned the side of the road. Off to the left, on the same side as the base and about a hundred yards away, a chain-linked fence ran parallel to the road.

"You'll never make it," Eve said.

Mercy grit her teeth. How could she possibly escape with Eve knowing her every thought? "I have to try."

Eve shrugged. "Try. I can bring you to Malik with one leg."

Mercy gasped, but her revulsion turned to resolve—she had promised the Lord that she would do her best to save the children.

"Arrgghh!" Eve screamed. "Who is this Lord you speak of?

Every time you do, you don't picture anything but light. What does he look like?"

Mercy's brow pulled together as she tried to grasp the question and understand her own mind. Is that what happened when she prayed? Did she picture God as light?

"You are the most frustrating scourge ever!" Eve shouted as the bear moved so close to the wagon it bumped it. "How can you block out his face from me?"

"I've never seen His face," Mercy said.

"How does he give you orders?"

"I don't think of them as orders. I guess some are. There are the commandments, of course. But He wrote this book, the Bible, so—"

"I don't know how to read. And life more than just book. Does he make you look at ground? Does he wear a helmet?"

"Nothing like that. God isn't in one place. He's everywhere. I've never heard his voice audibly—"

Eve's nose scrunched up. "You've never seen him or heard him? He's not real."

"He is real. He speaks to me in here." Mercy touched her chest.

"You're crazy."

Mercy shrugged, closed her mouth, and thought, *Is it so crazy to hear God in my heart when you hear me in your head?*

Eve screamed at the sky. "Stupid scourge!"

The wolves howled, and the bear huffed.

Eve thrust out a finger. "Even if I want to let you go, I can't. Malik would know." She tapped the side of her head.

Mercy nodded understandingly. Her lips pressed together. "Thank you for considering it."

Eve snarled and urged the bear to the front of the wagon.

Mercy rode in silence as the wagon quickly sped along. The road curved and began to rise. A sign on the right announced SCENIC OVERLOOK AHEAD. Mercy grabbed the wagon's side and craned her neck to get a better view. The army base and valley stretched out before her. She glanced up the road and gasped.

Dozens of bone wolves and bears stood alongside the guard rail of the overlook, peering down at the base. The animals parted as the wagon approached.

A tall man dressed in all black, similar to Eve, stood with one boot resting on the guard rail. His long coat was worn and threadbare. His hair hung past his shoulders and was mostly gray, but streaks of black ran through it.

Eve sprang down from the bear and hurried over to the man. They embraced quickly and stood staring at each other. After a moment, Mercy realized they were having a silent conversation.

A group of wolves lingering near the back of the wagon scurried aside.

Two men, if she could call them that, crouched in the shadows of a large sign with a map of the valley printed on it. Their heads were bald, and their skin was greyish-white. Their large black eyes appeared even bigger due to their gaunt appearance. They wore no clothes and had no visible genitalia.

Mercy swallowed.

Their black eyes glowed a pale blue.

Pain raced between her temples. She grabbed hold of her head like she could somehow physically stop it, but the pressure increased.

"STOP!" The man speaking with Eve shouted.

Eve raced over, a knife in her hands, and leveled at the ghoulish men. "No hurt. She is for Malik."

The glow in the men's eyes faded, and they scurried behind the brick building.

Malik strode over to the wagon. His face was lined with age and scars. The right side of his head was peppered with several circular scars similar to craters on the moon.

"You are Mercy Yoder. I am Malik. You are Amish?"

Mercy nodded. "Yes, sir."

"You named my mate. She now wants to be called Eve."

Mercy's mouth fell open. "I ah...well, she asked me."

"She also said that you spared her life. Why?"

"I don't believe in killing another human."

Malik scoffed. "We are not human. Not any longer. Does that change things?"

Mercy shook her head. "No, sir. You still have a soul."

Malik's eyes shimmered. In his black pupils, a blue light sparked and flashed like electricity. "My father once thought like you. He believed in a God. But if one ever existed, it has abandoned this world. Go. You are not guilty. Return to your people."

Mercy couldn't believe her ears. She turned to Eve.

Eve smiled and nodded, but her stoic expression quickly returned.

"Thank you, sir. Thank you so much." Mercy climbed over the back of the wagon. She'd go to the base and try to reach the others. Then, they would all return to the farm. Her father—

Malik reeled like he'd been struck in the head. He staggered sideways.

Eve grabbed his arm to steady him.

He shoved her away and glared at Mercy. Hate marred his expression, and his eyes blazed a burning blue. "You lied! Your name is not Yoder. You are the spawn of Shawn Morgan."

Mercy glanced around, confused, but he was clearly speaking to her. "Me? No. My father is Amos Yoder. He is a farmer."

"Your father is Shawn Morgan. He is the soldier who betrayed me. Betrayed us. He is the reason for this." Malik pointed at the scars on his head. "He did this to me. You are a liar."

Eve shook her head. "Listen to her thoughts, Malik. She tells the truth."

"I know what she says, but the father in her mind is not named Yoder. I know him. He was my friend. Now, he is the betrayer. Put her back in the wagon."

"Wait!" Mercy cried, but Eve grabbed her arms. Mercy tried to struggle, but Eve yanked her off the ground and tossed her into the wagon like a bale of hay.

Pain sliced between Mercy's temples as Malik glared at her.

"I will free Nian, and then I will go to Ridgecrest. I have waited years to find your father. I will show him what true horror is. The pain he inflicted upon me and my friends, I will burn into him a thousand times hotter. Your father will die, but you won't see it. I will rip everything he has apart, including you, and then I will tear his mind in two."

Mercy's eyes rolled back in her head. She couldn't breathe.

Malik raised his arms over his head and turned to face the monsters. "Now is the time! Assemble your squads. Attack the base! Free Nian! Free our king!"

All around them, thousands of beasts howled. Bone wolves, rats, and bears all raised their voices in a thunderous cry.

The pain in Mercy's brain was blinding. Everything glowed a bright white, and then—

42

ASPIRIN

Cain Haight

My head feels like Babe Ruth hit me with a steel bat and used my brain for the ball. I can't see straight, and my nose is bleeding. Nian gave me a mental beating that somehow caused physical damage. I never want to go toe-to-toe with that thing again, but I can't get the echo of him screaming at me out of my mind. The really weird thing is it's not a memory. He's still yelling at me. He's faint and sounds far off, but he's threatening to kill me in some very imaginative ways.

The guards drag me into a room and tie me to a chair. I don't even think about escaping. I tried to walk a little, but my legs weren't cooperating. There's no way I could fight a teddy bear, let alone take on two guards.

After tying me up again, the guards move to stand by the door. They're both pale white and shaking. Neither of them talk. I can't blame them. That was like meeting the Devil. And Lucifer was having a no good, very bad day.

A few minutes later, the door flies open, and Tianzi, Pi, and

Chao storm in. Tianzi's right hand is bandaged, and his arm is in a sling.

That brings a crooked smile to my face. "Do you have any aspirin?" I ask.

Tianzi's eyes are lit up, and he's grinning like Abbey Tuggle, who just found another butterfly. "He spoke with you. What did he say? Why did he get so upset?"

His high-pitched voice makes my lips curl. "One, lower your voice. Two, if you want me to answer any questions, I'm gonna need a shot of whiskey and some aspirin."

Tianzi nods to Chao, who lumbers out of the room. "What did Nian discuss with you?" Tianzi says softer, but his words ring with excitement.

"I didn't mean to talk softer. Lower. Deeper. You sound like someone stepped on a cat."

Tianzi raises his left hand and thinks twice about smacking me. He motions to Pi, who slaps me across the face.

Blood sprays in the air from my still bleeding nose. "I've been slapped harder by a nun with the flu."

I close one eye. Where the heck did I come up with that one? Maybe Nian did some actual damage to my brain?

Pi raises her hand again.

I open my mouth like I'm ready to bite her, then burst out laughing. I've got to look crazy because they take a step back. "Nian wants to kill you even more than me. And that's saying something."

"Tell me specifics. Repeat everything."

I shrug the best I can while being tied up. "He didn't mention you by name, but—"

Tianzi's eyes widen. He turns to Pi in disbelief. She smiles sympathetically.

"Boy, do you have an ego," I chuckle. "Are you really ticked off Frankenstein didn't put your name on his arch enemy list?"

Pi rushes forward and starts slapping away at my face. Left, right, left, right, left—she gets five in before her hand starts hurting and stops.

I shake my head. In a weird way, the blows cleared the fog outa my brain and make me feel a little better.

Chao returns to the room with a bottle of whiskey and a glass. He approaches Pi, and she takes the aspirin from him and then holds the glass while he pours a drink.

"What is Nian's plan?" Tianzi asks.

"Give me the whiskey and aspirin first."

Tianzi nods.

Pi drops the capsules into my mouth, lifts the large glass to my lips, and pours. From the shocked look on her face, she expected me to cough and gag. I down it in one long gulp. Warmth washes over my body. "I'll take another."

Tianzi nods.

Pi takes the bottle from Chao and holds it to my lips.

I start sucking like a fat baby until she pulls it away.

"Enough!" Tianzi says. "What is Nian's plan?"

"From what he was talking about, it sounds like you guys created the bone animals so you could use them as weapons. Then, you experimented on people to talk to the monsters and created the ghouls. But that didn't work out so well, so you created Nian. And Nian can control both animals and people, right?"

Tianzi nods. "Exactly. But the handlers, ghouls as you call them, were not strong enough to control Nian."

"And that's where Jacob comes in?"

"His real name is Jaituk. His mother, who escaped, is Sentinelese. It's an untouched island off the coast of India. Her DNA is pure and uncontaminated. Her powers of control are impressive. Jacob's are off the charts."

Heat washes through my chest as the whiskey seeps through my body. Nian's screams in my brain click off. My eyebrows knit together. Did Nian finally shut up, or did something else make him stop talking?

"Jacob is the reason you are still alive," Tianzi reveals. "He saved you by preventing Nian from killing you. That was the purpose of my test. And it was successful."

"This is not going to end well," I say. "It never does. Read our history. What happened with the last arms race? Everyone nuked each other. The world as we know it is gone, and we're responsible. And now you keep creating weapons to control the previous weapon. So now they all want you dead!"

Tianzi leans forward. I've seen the same gleam of blinded lust in a drug addict's eyes, willing to sell his mother for a hit. "How does Nian plan to overthrow me? Is there any way to bargain with him?"

"It would be like trying to make a deal with Hitler. Nian hates all humans. He calls us scourge. You can't make a bargain with someone who doesn't have a soul. That's the whole lesson to be learned in dealing with the Devil—don't do it. Kill that thing while you still can."

"Without Nian, I would have to fight an army of bone monsters with only Jacob. He is not strong enough yet."

"What about the ghouls? They're using strategy to attack you. Try to make a deal with them. At least they were once men. Maybe they'd listen to reason."

"They want revenge for what happened to them."

"You're what happened to them. You created them. You turned them into freaks. Have you ever tried to communicate with them?"

"What would be the point?"

"What is wrong with you?" My anger and the whiskey make me break out in a sweat. "Haven't you learned anything from the end of the freakin' world? Not talking is what got us into this mess. No one fired an EMP. It was the sun. But everyone blamed everyone else and started World War III. And now those monsters are trying to kill what's left, and you're not even going to try to stop it?"

"I will stop it. With Jacob, I can control both ghouls, men, and beasts."

"You can control the boy now. But someday, he's going to get older, and he won't listen anymore."

Tianzi laughs. "You know nothing about control, and I am a master at it. Jacob will obey me, or I will kill everything he loves. That is why you are going to die today. Jacob needs an object lesson, and so does Lucy and your daughter. He will see that you will reap the benefits when you obey me, but there are consequences if you step out of line."

"If that's the case," I lift my chin, "then let me tell you what I really think about you."

Chao lunges forward and cracks me in the jaw. His hand is the size of a sledgehammer, and the right cross he delivers feels like getting hit by one.

My head jerks to the side. The last thing I want is another beating, so I hang my head, close my eyes, and pretend to be unconscious. I've had a lot of experience with that lately, and my act works.

Tianzi says something in Chinese, and everyone laughs.

I listen as they leave the room, and the door clangs shut. From the shuffle of feet, I know the guard is still here, so I keep my eyes closed. I'm still breathing, so there's a chance I can get to Bri. I need to be patient and wait for an opening. Tianzi wants to make a spectacle of my death. That means he'll take me someplace to kill me. When he does, that's when I'll make my move.

43

TRUST ME

Lucy Green

Lucy and Fen marched across the base toward the bunker. To the west, thunder rumbled. Puzzled, Lucy glanced up at the cloudless sky.

Someone whistled a melancholy tune she'd never heard before.

A Chinese soldier leaned against the remnants of a truck, smoking a cigarette. He inhaled deeply and whistled the song, the smoke carrying away on the wind.

Fen's eyes blazed. "Wait here." She stormed over to the man and smacked the cigarette from his hand. She spoke to him in Chinese. While Lucy couldn't understand what she said, she was clearly berating him.

The man bowed low and spoke to the ground while he addressed Fen. He talked quickly but softly.

When he finished, Fen continued to yell at the man while he stood silently before her. She turned on her heels and marched back to Lucy.

"What did he do, steal your lollipop? You really let him have it—ow!" Lucy winced as Fen grabbed her arm and dragged her back toward the infirmary.

"Shut up and listen to me," Fen ordered. "Somehow, Cain lived through his encounter with Nian."

Lucy grinned. "He don't die easy. That's for sure."

"His luck has run out. Tianzi has ordered his execution. He will gather everyone together in an hour to witness it. He wants to make an example out of Cain and your mother. They are to be shot."

Lucy yanked her arm free. "In a pig's eye."

"I have no idea what that means, but I have an idea to get you, your mother, and the children out."

"What about Cain?"

"You ask the impossible."

Lucy's hand balled into a fist. "I owe it to him to try."

"No. I will get the children. You will get your mother and the truck."

"And how am I supposed to do that?"

Fen and Lucy hurried up the stairs to the infirmary. "You are sick. I'm leaving you with the doctor. He will explain the rest of the plan."

The front door opened, and Dr. Kim held it ajar. He and Fen spoke quickly.

Lucy swallowed, and the knot in her stomach tightened. As Fen talked with her husband, the exterior mask of the hardened soldier Fen always wore, fell off. Fen's eyes were filled with concern. Her voice trembled as she pleaded with her husband about something.

Dr. Kim squared his shoulders, nodded, and turned to Lucy. "I am sorry that you are not feeling well," he said loudly and in English. "Come with me."

Lucy stepped in front of Fen, blocking her way. "You need to try to save Cain."

"There is no time to discuss this. You will have to trust me."

"Why should I?"

A gentle hand touched Lucy's shoulder.

Dr. Kim met Lucy's gaze. "I understand your hesitancy. Please understand ours. We are also trusting you."

His words hit Lucy in the center of her chest. The image of Fen pleading with him a moment earlier flashed in her mind. Fen had been asking him to go along with the plan. It was he who hadn't wanted to.

Lucy nodded and followed him inside as Fen headed across the base.

Dr. Kim walked past the now-empty nurse's station and to a room on the right. The examination room was small, with white walls and linoleum floors. The only decorations were military posters and charts on the walls and a small American flag on the counter. The exam table was covered in disposable paper.

"Undress." Dr. Kim said as he hurried over to a cabinet.

Lucy crossed her arms and scanned the room for cameras but saw none.

"This room is safe." He said. "There are no cameras or microphones. Get undressed."

"Get bent," All the goodwill she had felt toward the doctor vanished. "You know I'm not sick. I don't need an exam."

"We don't have time to argue." Dr. Kim pulled a set of scrubs out of the cabinet. "A guard checks in every thirty minutes. The one on duty is a Tainzi loyalist. We need to move quickly, but if anyone sees us, they must suspect nothing. Put these on. Can you use a manual transmission?"

"Is a frog's butt watertight?"

Dr. Kim's face scrunched up.

"If it's got wheels, I can drive it," Lucy said as she peeled off her clothes.

"The truck is ready and fueled up. We'll come back here to get your mother, and then—"

"Why don't we take her with us?"

"She is too injured to walk."

Lucy pulled the scrub bottoms up. "You don't know Sadie, Doc. She could be missing a limb and still go." She glanced at the stump where his hand had been and added, "Sorry for the analogy."

"No offense taken. But having her come with us to get the truck will draw too much attention. And call me Ru. Ready?"

Lucy grabbed a scalpel off the counter. "Now I am."

Ru led the way out of the room and down the hallway to an exit door.

Lucy followed beside him, trying to walk at a normal pace, but that was impossible as Ru sped on.

"Didn't you say we should play it cool?" Lucy said.

Ru exhaled loudly and nodded. He shifted to slow, but his eyes darted around like a startled mouse, looking for a way to escape. He wiped a hand over his sweating brow. "I'm not very good at this kind of thing."

"You're doing great." Lucy lied. "Keep it together, and we'll be eatin' chicken and grits tomorrow."

Ru grinned nervously. "As unappetizing as that sounds, I'm looking forward to trying your grits."

"Unappetizing? Trying? You've got to be kiddin' me that you ain't had grits before! They're a food group unto themselves. Of course, grits are made from corn, but Sadie makes a killer middlins dish. Middlins are made from rice. Middlins and shrimp are so good it'll bring tears to a glass eye, but since we got no shrimp, Sadie will use crawdads." She kept going on about the food and slipping into a southern tang to take Ru's mind off what they were doing. The more she talked, the more relaxed he got, and that was a good thing.

After a few minutes, they reached the motor pool. It was a large, fenced-in area with a shed-like building next to a closed gate. A single guard appeared.

Ru stiffened up.

"It is not okay. Shuchang is a loyalist." Ru smiled at the guard and marched toward him.

Shuchang eyed Lucy suspiciously. He spoke briefly in Chinese to Ru, who pointed back to the infirmary. The guard shook his head.

Sweat broke out on Ru's forehead. He turned to Lucy, and she saw the helplessness in his eyes. He didn't know what to do or say.

Lucy took a deep breath. What could she do?

Shuchang crossed his arms and frowned.

Lucy's mind raced. She slipped her hand into her pocket, her fingers tightening around the scalpel. Could she kill this man to escape? What would happen if she did? There were other guards around. Someone else would notice.

Ru said something else to the guard. His voice was pleading, and he thrust his arm toward the infirmary.

Shuchang leaned away and dismissively shook his head.

Lucy couldn't overpower him. She had to talk him into letting them have the truck, but how? Would he believe it if she said Tianzi wanted them to get the truck? Maybe he'd make them wait while he checked out her story.

It was times like this when she missed Cain the most. That man could talk the dogs off a meat truck. The memory of standing next to him in AutoWorld when he wanted to return a catalytic converter flashed in her mind. The salesman told him he couldn't get a refund without receiving the receipt. Cain didn't bat an eye or get upset. He said he'd talk to Gerald Hicks, the area manager. The salesman flipped on a dime and gave Cain the cash. Cain later explained that if he name-dropped the owner of the company, the salesman wouldn't believe him, but Hicks was known as a hothead who his underlings feared. And Cain knowing him was more plausible, so he went with that angle.

"Dr. Kim," Lucy whispered loud enough to be overheard. "Do I need to get Pi? She's not going to be happy."

Shuchang snapped to attention. "You should have told me that she was the one who requested this." He said, then marched back to the shed. A moment later, he reappeared with keys. He said something in Chinese, handed the keys to Ru, and bowed.

Ru returned the gesture and just stood there.

"What was I talking about?" Lucy said, placing a hand on Ru's elbow and nudging him toward the open gate. "Oh, yes. Middlins. Some folks like them as much as grits, but give me a big bowl of grits any day." She smiled as they strolled through the gate toward the trucks. "I grew up on them. That's what my Mawmaw used to say made me so tough. *All those grits you eat got stuck to your ribs, baby girl. That's why you got so much grit.*" Lucy stared up at the sky and smiled. "I guess Mawmaw was right."

44

THAT'S NO ANGEL

Bri Haight

Bri sat on the bed, stroking Jacob's arm. The little boy lay on his back, sleeping. After the guards brought them back to the room, he fell asleep the minute she got him into the bed.

Her hands were still shaking. She couldn't get the image of that monster, Nian, out of her mind. Her joy at seeing that her daddy was alive quickly turned to terror as that beast killed those men.

Jacob had tried to stop it from murdering the soldiers, but he couldn't. His eyes had glowed a light blue, but each time, he failed. When Nian had turned on her daddy, she thought he would die for sure. But Jacob's eyes blazed. He thrust out his arms and screamed. Nian stopped.

Their mental battle seemed to go on for ages, but it was only a few minutes. After the guards took her daddy out of the room, Jacob collapsed on the floor. Tianzi was so happy that he danced a jig and sang some song in Chinese. Then he ordered the guards to take Bri and Jacob back here.

Bri wanted to sleep, too, but couldn't. What was going to happen to her daddy now? Tianzi already tried to kill him once. Would he do it again?

Bri closed her eyes and prayed, "Dear God, I'm real scared. Please help Daddy, Mawmaw, Momma, Jacob, and me. We need a miracle to get out of here. And Mawmaw says that You provide—"

Something fell over in the center of the room. It was loud enough to shut her up but wasn't a big bang. Bri glanced around and saw that the block tower Jacob built had fallen over. She cocked an eyebrow. A red ball slowly rolled across the floor.

Jacob sat up and rubbed his eyes. "What's going on?"

The floor in the center of the room cracked.

"I think it's a miracle!" Bri hopped off the bed and pointed to the jagged line on the floor. "Did you ever hear the Bible story when an Angel broke Peter out of jail?"

"I love that one!" Jacob slid off the bed, too.

The floor vibrated and cracked. The split widened and spread like a jagged lightning bolt across the cement.

Bri grabbed Jacob, and they both jumped up and down. "An Angel is coming, Jacob! An Angel!"

A large chunk of the floor broke off and disappeared into the dark hole left behind. Dust and dirt rose into the air.

From deep in the hole, a chittering noise rose.

Bri gasped. "I know that sound. That's no angel."

Three bone rats appeared, followed by several more.

Bri shrieked and grabbed Jacob's hand. She dragged the terrified boy toward the door.

Inside the hole, something big, something huge, moved.

"Don't let them know you're scared," Bri said as she pulled Jacob across the room.

A dozen bone rats sat on their haunches on the other side of the hole in the floor, watching them. Their black eyes gleamed, and their tails slowly snaked back and forth.

"How do I do that?" Jacob whispered. "I am scared."

"Pretend you're not. Pretend you're brave."

"What are they? They don't look too mean."

A bone rat hissed, revealing terrifying rows of sharp teeth. It got up on all fours. All the others did the same. They chittered so loudly that Jacob covered his ears.

Bri grabbed a child's chair off the floor. She held it like a lion tamer and moved in front of Jacob. "Stay back! Get away!"

The door to the room rattled and opened.

A guard walked inside the room, first staring at the hole in the floor and then the bone rats. He reached for his pistol.

The rat's tails swooshed around, and a dozen bone spikes sailed through the air.

BLAM! BLAM!

The guard fired his gun.

Two rats flew backward as bullets struck them.

The guard dropped his pistol and stumbled backward. Four spikes stuck out of his chest. He wheezed and collapsed on the floor.

The bone rats turned to face Bri and Jacob.

Bri dropped the chair and shoved Jacob for the door. "Run!" She picked up the guard's gun.

The bone rat's tails swooshed around.

"STOP!" Jacob screamed, and the creatures did.

The monsters froze, their tails raised and their wicked mouths open.

Jacob's eyes blazed a brilliant blue.

"Are you doing that?" Bri kept the shaking gun aimed at the rats.

"I think so. Now, what should I do?"

"Tell them to go back in the pit. No! Wait. Make them turn around."

"What? Why?"

"It's a test. Just do it."

Jacob narrowed his eyes, and the rats turned to face the opposite wall.

Bri's mouth fell open. "Is my daddy in this building? And my momma? What about my mawmaw?"

Jacob shrugged. "I don't know."

"Try to read their minds."

Sweat formed on Jacob's head. "Your daddy is close."

The bone rats started chittering.

"There are two soldiers with him."

One of the bone rats lifted its head.

"He's in a little room. I've seen it before."

The bone rat started to shake as if someone were holding it down, and it was trying to get free.

"Hurry up, Jacob. Where is he? Where is this room?"

"I know I saw it. It's upstairs. He's upstairs!"

More bone rats moved. One turned slowly around and stared at Bri. It lifted its tail.

"Make the rats stop!" Bri shrieked.

Jacob's eyes blazed, and the rats closed their mouths and sat down. "I can't try to find your family and control the rats."

"Calm down. We don't want the rats to eat us, so concentrate on them."

Jacob nodded. "Should I make them jump in the hole?"

Bri looked at the gun in her hand. "No. We need to free my daddy. You said there were two guards, so this is what we do. We use the rats to get my daddy, and then he'll know what to do."

Jacob's outstretched hand shook. "Okay, but we better get goin'."

"Make those things go first."

Jacob raised his arms.

The bone rats scurried around the hole and darted out the

door. They stared at Bri with large black eyes that gleamed blue as they passed, sending shivers up her spine.

Bri held the gun tightly and smiled. "Mawmaw always said you never know if a thing is good or bad until it's over. And now that we have an army, even if it is creepy, maybe we did get a miracle after all."

45

AN OLD FRIEND

Cain Haight

I open my eyes as the guards are jerking me to my feet. My hands are cuffed behind me. I might be able to walk, but I don't even try. I hang there like dead weight and let these two goons do the work of dragging me.

I don't know where they're taking me, but I have a guess. Tianzi doesn't seem like the most patient of men, so I'm assuming he intends on killing me now. I would be flipping out more if it weren't for the weird fact that I'm okay knowing Bri is with Jacob. If that boy can control the monsters, he may be able to take care of her better than I can.

Not that I have much say in the matter anymore.

The guards shove open some doors, and the afternoon sun blinds me. They haul me down the steps, and my boots plow dirt rows in the ground.

They suddenly stop.

I lift my head and see Fen marching straight toward us.

"Where are you taking this prisoner?" Fen demands.

"The center of the base." The Russian guard on my right answers in English.

"You are to release him to me," Fen says. "Stand him up."

The Russian yanks me up to my feet.

The Chinese guard shakes his head. He says something in Chinese that sounds like he's turning down Fen's request.

Fen squares her shoulders and sticks her finger in the man's face. "You dare countermand Commander Tianzi's orders?"

The soldier pales. His bottom lip is trembling. He opens his mouth and closes it when something behind Fen catches his attention.

Everyone looks at the two-story building behind her. A large group of people are pouring out of the double doors. As the crowd marches over, it opens up, and Tianzi walks so fast that it looks like he may start running. When he catches sight of Fen, he slows down.

Pi and Chao catch up to him. Pi grabs Tianzi's arm and whispers something in his ear.

Tianzi nods.

Chao takes the lead, with Pi flanking the giant.

Tianzi walks five steps behind them as more guards move to form a protective ring around their commander.

Fen would make a heck of a poker player. She seems unfazed by this event, but I notice her hand moving slightly toward her pistol. Going for the gun would be a huge mistake. Being so outnumbered, she'd only get a few shots off. But if one landed between Tianzi's eyes, I'd be all for that idea.

"Captain Kim, what are you doing?" Tianzi asks as the herd of people stops.

"I saw only two soldiers escorting this prisoner. Being aware of how highly you value him, I thought it odd there was so little security assigned. I requested to take control of him personally."

Tianzi nods approvingly. "Excellent." He smiles but not

with his eyes. Those rat-like, little black specks, blaze with hate. "I am so glad to run into you. It seems a very serious matter has been raised and needs some clarification. I now find a part of your report regarding your mission to Ridgecrest troubling. Do you recall how you said Nicholi was killed?"

"A bone bear attacked us. He drowned. What clarification is needed?"

Tianzi snaps his fingers.

The crowd parts, and Nicholi strides out. He glares at Fen and flashes a wicked grin.

Tianzi cocks an eyebrow. "Well?"

"Bone rats attacked us. My canoe was damaged beyond repair. One canoe could not carry everyone, so as the mission commander, I decided who was more qualified to accomplish it. That was me. I make no apology for my actions except for the slight misrepresentation regarding how I notified you that he drowned."

"She tried to kill me," Nicholi shouts.

"And you wanted to trade the boy to Luka!"

The crowd gasps and moves away from the hulking Russian.

"She lies!" Nicholi shakes his head. "She is only saying such things to cover up the lies she has already told."

Tianzi looks back and forth between the two soldiers. His mouth is slightly open, and I can tell he doesn't know who to believe.

So I decide to stir the pot. "It looks like you've got a pretty big loyalty issue," I say. "How about I settle this? Everybody that wants to get out of here and go someplace safe, raise your hand—"

Chao punches me in the gut so hard he lifts me three inches off the ground.

I fall onto my knees, gasping for air. To my surprise, all the soldiers are holding their guns on Fen and Nicholi.

"You are mistaken, Cain Haight," Tianzi says. "My soldiers are loyal. They know the only safe place left on this planet is with me. They understand that they and their children will be fruitful and multiply to fill the earth with a new order that will last for a millennium."

I want to make a wisecrack about Hitler having a similar idea, but right now, all I can do is suck wind and try not to puke.

Several soldiers cuff Fen and Nicholi.

Once again, I'm yanked to my feet, and they start dragging me. Nicholi is pleading his case, slipping between English and Russian and a little begging in Chinese. I can't see Tianzi's face because he's walking in front of me, but I doubt Nicholi's crying has any effect.

"Shut up," I call over to him. "It won't do you any good, even if she is lying. Tianzi can't prove it either way, so he's going to put a bullet in both your heads. And it serves you both right for kidnapping my kid and her friend."

Nicholi starts shouting at me in Russian. I know a few Russian swear words, and he uses all of them and some others I've never heard.

They pull us toward the volleyball court. The nets are gone, and it's just sand now. Three wooden poles are stuck in the middle. They look like someone cut off telephone poles and drove them into the ground. Judging by the bullet holes already in the wood, this place has been used as a firing squad area before.

Nicholi is shoved toward the third pole. He head-butts one guard and kicks another one in the groin before a dozen men with clubs start wailing away at him.

I meet Fen's stare.

She doesn't look angry or resentful. She looks sad. "I am sorry for all the pain I have caused you and your family, Cain Haight." She bows low before the guards yank her up to a standing position. "I will take my shame with me to the grave."

I can't forgive her for dragging two kids into Hell, but there's something about the look on her face that is bothering me. I can tell that she wants to say more, but for some reason, she doesn't.

I nod. It's all I can do, but from the forlorn smile on her face, that little gesture meant something to her.

The guards slam my back against the pole. Three soldiers carry over ropes. They tie Nicholi and then Fen to a pole.

I take a deep breath. I know the odds are hopeless, but this is the last chance I've got if I'm going to make a break for it.

Toward the south of the base, there's a loud pop. I think it's a gun firing until I see the red flare. Even knowing it's a universal distress signal, I'm unprepared for the terror it causes in the soldiers around me. Everyone starts screaming and running. Pi and Choa grab Tianzi, and the three dash back toward the bunker with the circle of elite guards protecting them.

Machine gunfire erupts in the South.

The two guards standing next to me run in opposite directions.

I drop down and pull my handcuffed hands in front of me.

"Cain, wait!" Fen calls out. "Cut me free. I came to help you escape."

I laugh. I can't help it. "If you did, that was the worst attempted prison break I've ever seen."

"I'm serious. Lucy and my husband are getting a truck and Sadie. I was supposed to get the kids and try to get you."

"You're lying."

"I'm not. Tianzi would have killed my husband if I didn't do as he said. Please let me go."

Gunfire is getting closer, but that's not what makes me

break out in a sweat. The sound of men screaming and dying does.

I rush to the pole and start untying Fen's ropes. "Where are the kids?"

"They're in the bunker. Lowest floor."

A Russian soldier races across the volleyball field and starts hacking away at the ropes, holding Nicholi, with a knife.

"I've got no beef with you," I shout at the soldier cutting him free.

"Agreed." He reaches into his boot, pulls out another knife, and tosses it at my feet.

We both saw away as the screams and gunshots get closer.

I cut Fen loose just as a group of soldiers break from cover and run toward us. Two aim at me while a third sets his sights on Fen.

Fen raises her hands and starts shouting in Chinese.

I can tell from the look on the face of the guy who is wearing the most stripes on his uniform that he's not buying what she's trying to sell. He raises his gun.

Bone spikes sail through the air, slamming into the two soldiers aiming at me. They scream and fall to the ground.

The other soldier turns and fires at the dozen charging bone rats. He takes out a few of them, but they jump on him and start chewing. While he shrieks and flails, the other soldiers near him make a break for it and sprint for the barracks.

I run up and grab a gun while Fen gets the other. I'm ready to shoot the bone rats, but they're racing away, so I let them go.

"Daddy! Daddy!"

My breath catches in my throat. I can hear my little girl calling to me.

"Daddy!" Bri and Jacob dart out from behind a burned-out truck.

I'm blinking back tears as I run to meet them. Jacob's eyes

glow bright blue, but the little boy stumbles and the blue glow blinks off. His lips mash together like he's going to cry, and he pitches forward.

Everything in me wants to pick up my little girl who's running full out to me, but I know I can't. So I crouch and say, "Up on my back like a monkey."

Bri is bawling, and I can't understand what she's saying through the sobs, but she does as she is told. She wraps her legs around my waist, and her left hand grabs my shoulder. She tries to hold on with her right, but the 1911 pistol she's holding bashes me in the cheek.

"Careful with the gun, baby," I say as I scoop Jacob into my hands. It's hard to do while handcuffed and holding a machine gun, but I've got a feeling I'm going to need the firepower to make it out of here, so I can't drop it.

"Where's this truck?" I shout at Fen.

Fen lifts her chin towards the North. "Here it comes now."

I turn around.

An old Army truck with Lucy behind the wheel is barreling down on us. Sadie's sitting beside her, and there's another guy next to the passenger door. I've never been so happy to see my ex. I grin so much my face hurts.

We just might make it out of here after all.

46

TELL HER

Mercy Yoder

Mercy lost her balance and fell against the back of the wagon as the wolves raced down the road. Beside them, hundreds of bone rats chittered as they ran, hopped, and bounded over everything in their way. Ahead of them, Malik and Eve rode on top of their huge, bone bears. On either side of them, seven more bone bears moved with surprising speed. Perched on their back were more of the strange men. None of the men spoke, but Malik and Eve had an animated conversation. To Mercy's surprise, Eve was the one doing most of the yelling.

The road dipped down and then slowly began to rise once again. A bridge spanned the river. Mercy watched, amazed, as all the creatures headed off the road and toward two large pits on either side of the road. More of the strange men stood in front of the giant craters, ushering the bone rats and wolves inside.

The wolves pulled her wagon and headed toward the bridge.

Malik raised his arms and motioned to either side of the road. The seven strange men on the left steered their bears into the holes, and the men on the right did the same on the opposite side.

Eve raised her hand and the wolves pulling the wagon followed her up the bridge.

Mercy's gaze traveled along the river until it reached the Army base. The poor people there. They had no idea that a horde of monsters were headed their way. What could stop a force so powerful?

Mercy bowed her head. "Dear God—"

A gunshot rang out and the wood beside her splintered.

Malik rode on his bear, a smoking pistol in his hand. He glared at her.

"She does that," Eve said. "She calls on this person she can't see."

"I know the one she speaks to. He doesn't exist."

Eve made a face. "How do you know him if he doesn't exist? You speak as crazy as her."

Mercy bowed her head.

Malik fired again. This time, the bullet struck the wood only a few inches away from her arm. "Stop."

Mercy stared back into his blue eyes. "I can't. Lord, the people in that base need your help."

BLAM!

The wood splintered at her foot.

"Please protect them in their time of need."

BLAM!

A splinter sliced her arm, but she ignored the pain and the fear.

"Thank you for your mighty love."

BLAM!

The bullet whizzed so close to her right ear that her hair blew back.

"STOP!" Eve shouted.

Malik glared at her. "Are you ordering me?"

"If this Lord of hers doesn't exist, why do you care if she calls out to him? If he doesn't exist, so what? He won't answer."

Malik's lip curled. He holstered his pistol and rode his bear over beside the wagon. "Fine. Go ahead and pray. Your God can not help them. The time of the scourge is finished. We will remake the earth, and we do not betray each other."

"You're going to kill the people there, aren't you?" Mercy asked.

"You have no idea what they have done. They deserve to die."

"We all deserve to die." Mercy said.

"Spare me a sermon. I won't listen to your lies." Malik's chin tilted to the side. "No. Tell her." He pointed at Eve. "Tell her why your God failed to help her while she begged the scourge to stop. Tell her why your God abandoned her to the cutting, the drilling, and the burning pain. Tell her!"

Mercy stared at Eve, who gazed back at her with questioning eyes.

"If what he says true? Could your Lord have stopped them?" Eve asked.

"Yes. It's true. My Lord could have stopped your pain, but He didn't."

"Then your Lord is evil. Bring him here, and I will kill the scourge."

"God is not evil. I don't know why He lets some very bad things happen, but I know that he let his son suffer and die, too."

Eve turned to Malik with raised eyebrows.

Malik shrugged. "I told you that it makes no sense."

"To us." Mercy said. "I don't understand why God does some things, but I know He didn't abandon us. He came to earth and suffered, too. He died on the cross but rose—"

"You lie. Dead is dead." Eve shouted.

Mercy shook her head. "He came back to life. That was the whole reason He came."

"Then bring him here." Eve pointed at the ground. "I want to talk to him."

"It doesn't work that way," Mercy said.

Eve screamed at the sky. "You are so aggravating!"

"I told you," Malik said. "She lies."

"No. Read her. She believes what she is saying."

"That doesn't make it true," Malik said.

"Now you don't make sense." Eve shook her head. "You're both crazy. I go kill scourge. That is the right thing to do."

"Eve, don't!" Mercy called after her, but it was too late.

Eve's bear charged down the road and disappeared into the hole in the ground.

Malik slipped off his bear and walked over to the wagon. He grabbed the leather straps holding the wolves and pulled them free. "Stay here, Mercy Yoder. I have given you a front-row seat to the end of man as you know him."

"Please." Mercy begged. "Is there any way that all of this death can be avoided?"

Malik smiled. The scars on his face and head turned a darker red. "Of course there is." He climbed on the back of one of the wolves. "Call on your God. If he is really there, he will answer. When he doesn't, maybe you will finally see the light."

Tears rolled down Mercy's face as Malik and the other wolf galloped toward the hole.

The enormous bone bear lay down on the tar and stared at her.

She was trapped. Now, she would have to witness the people in the army base being slaughtered, and there was nothing she could do to warn them. And once Malik was done killing them, he would turn his horde to Ridgecrest.

Mercy sobbed and covered her face with her hands.

47

MY BACKUP PLAN

Cain Haight

I'm sprinting toward the truck with Bri on my back, carrying Jacob in my arms, trying to hold onto a machine gun, all while handcuffed. Gunfire is going off all around us, and the chittering of the bone rats and howling of the wolves is getting louder.

Fen runs beside me. She fires off two rounds from the pistol she picked up and stops. I think it's jammed, but then I see the slide is locked back. She's out of ammo already.

Lucy locks up the brakes and cuts the wheel. The truck slides to a stop five yards from us.

As I'm unloading Bri and Jacob into the back, the huge doors of a bunker swing open.

Fen stops beside me, her eyes wide.

A company of soldiers unlike any I've ever seen stream out the doors. They look like a futuristic cross of knights and samurai. They're all wearing red and silver armor with full helmets. The front row has shields. The second row is armed with machine guns, and bringing up the rear is a group with mini-guns.

A whistle blows—two loud calls.

Doors burst open from every building, and all of the regular soldiers taking cover make a break for that bunker.

"We better go!" I grab the tailgate and pull myself up and over.

Fen scrambles up beside me.

Lucy hits the gas and cuts the wheel.

I can't see into the cab, so I have to trust that she knows where to go. "Keep your head down, Angel," I motion Bri toward the front of the truck. "Get low behind that metal box. Take Jacob with you."

"Yes, sir." Bri grabs Jacob's shirt and starts dragging him to cover.

"You trained her as a soldier?" Fen asks, her brows knitting together.

"In the South, we call it obeying, being polite, and respectful."

"If we live through this, I'll have to share my experiences with your daughter with you."

Men race across the base, sprinting to make it to the protection of the bunker.

The super-soldiers march forward in three synchronized lines.

Wolves bound into view. They pounce on the fleeing soldiers.

"Why aren't they firing?" Fen says as much to herself as to me.

I don't know if they're conserving their ammo or don't want to risk hitting their comrades.

The first row of super-soldiers set their shields on the ground. The second flanks each soldier on the left side and opens fire. I expected them to go full auto, but they are shooting a round at a time. The rapport is loud, but the crazy part is that you can hear the rounds slicing through the air. The bullets make a high-pitched whine before slamming into the wolves.

The first wolf is rocked sideways. Chunks of bone fly off, and it whimpers in pain.

Another volley drops four of the monsters. The third round cuts down the entire front row of wolves. But there are more coming, and with them race a horde of bone rats.

The second row of super-soldiers steps to the side and begins to reload. As they move, the back row with the mini-guns steps forward. They open fire, and the air is thick with bullets. The bullets tear into the charging bone rats and the last of the fleeing soldiers. They twitch as they die in the hail of lead. The bone rats drop and litter the ground, but more and more take their place.

Loud howls fill the air, and the rats scatter, leaving behind hundreds of corpses on the street.

The man in the cab of the truck screams.

Lucy swears and cuts the wheel.

Metal crunches.

Suddenly, I'm flying forward toward the cab. The machine gun tumbles out of my hand. I try to grab Bri, but my back slams into something, and all the wind is knocked out of my lungs.

Fen bashes into my chest, her head smashing into my face and slicing my lip.

I'm seeing stars and coughing, but whatever went wrong ain't over. The truck is tipping over on its side.

Bri screams. She and Jacob are sliding toward me.

I grab Jacob in a scissor hold with my legs, and Bri wraps her arms around my head. Now I can't see.

The truck crashes onto its side. Glass shatters, and metal shrieks as the truck scrapes along the tar before stopping.

Outside, the super-soldier riflemen are back to firing another single-shot volley.

"Let go, Bri."

"No!" Bri shrieks.

"We've got to get out of this truck. It'll be okay. Trust me."

"I've got the boy," Fen says, picking up Jacob and heading to the tailgate.

We climb out of the tipped-over truck. We're a hundred yards from the main gate and fifty from the chasm and river dividing the Russian-held side from the Chinese. Lucy is outside the cab, standing on the ground, looking up. The man is standing on top of the passenger door, helping Sadie out of the side window.

A wounded bone bear is in the middle of the road. It stands and shakes, sending a cloud of dirt and dust flying. It takes a step forward and roars. The bear's front leg is dragging. It turns and hobbles away.

I move over to the cab, using it as cover, and Fen follows me.

The super-soldiers let out a cheer.

All the monsters have turned tail and are running away.

"That's good and bad," I say.

Lucy moves next to me. "Do you have a backup plan?" She asks.

"I've never had a plan to begin with. I'm making this up as I go." I grin.

Using the Chinese doctor as a crutch, Sadie limps beside me. She plants a grandmotherly kiss on my cheek and tussles my hair. "I knew you were too stubborn to stay dead."

Lucy points. "Our only chance is to make for the front gate."

I shake my head and notice Fen does, too. "Those miniguns will cut us down. Think you can swim with one leg?" I ask Sadie.

She grins. "Yeah, but I may go in a circle."

"It's not funny, Mom!" Lucy snaps. "Is that the new plan?"

Her eyes are blazing but watery as she stares at me. She's scared out of her mind, but I know it's because of Bri and Sadie. Still, seeing her freak out sobers me up. Before I can answer, a cloud blocks out the sun. I glance up, and a wave of panic washes over me.

Hundreds of bone-white birds streak out of the sky. The creatures are the size of enormous turkey vultures but have long whip-like tails. They dive straight toward the super-soldiers.

Mini-guns fire but not in the coordinated way they did before. There's panic among the ranks as men frantically sweep the sky to stop the attack.

Birds plummet to the ground, but several make it through and smash into the super-soldiers. Grasping the soldiers with their talons, the birds whip their tails around, slamming the spiked end against the armor. Once in position, the tails work like woodpeckers, rapidly chipping at the armor.

Some of the super soldiers begin screaming in agony as the spikes break through and slice into flesh.

"Cain!" Konstantin yells from the Russian side of the base. "Grab the ropes!"

On the other side of the chasm, several soldiers rush forward and heave ropes with small weights attached across the river, dividing the base.

"Who is that?" Lucy picks up Bri.

"My backup plan."

"Liar." Lucy smiles as we all run for the chasm.

A whistle blows twice.

The super-soldiers have formed a protective circle, and the front line is now using pistols in addition to their shields. Several soldiers in full armor lie unmoving on the ground, but the monsters are again falling back.

I grab a rope and tie it around Bri while Lucy ties it around herself. Once they're secure, I motion to Konstantin.

Holding Bri, Lucy dives into the water as Konstantin pulls them in.

Sadie, the man, Jacob, and Fen go next while I wrap the rope around myself.

A blinding light hits me in the back of the eyes. I cover my face with my hands and drop to my knees. Even with my eyes closed, the light is so bright it burns. Then I realize the light is coming from inside my head. Something like radio static arcs between my temples. Lucy is screaming, but I can't understand what.

An alarm blares. It's a deep-pulsing blast that reminds me of the sirens going off when Godzilla shows up.

The light in my head clicks off. I'm on my knees, and everything is blurry. The super-soldiers are all retreating into the bunker. I force myself to stand.

Wolves howl. Bone rats chitter, and the bears huff loudly.

In the middle of the base, Nian climbs out of a hole in the ground and turns his face toward the sun. He lifts his long arms high and, in a voice that roars like thunder, screams, "HAIGHT!"

I gasp as the rope around my waist tightens. I'm jerked off my feet and dragged across the tar.

Nian turns and glares straight at me.

I smile and wave before pitching backward off the chasm and into the river. Water rushes over my head. It's so dark I can't see. The rope pulls tight, and I'm getting dragged across the river.

The further I get away from Nian, the less the pain in my head is. But one thing is certain: with that monster free, there's only one thing we can do—run.

48

NO TIME TO SAY GOODBYE

Cain Haight

Konstantin pulls me out of the river and on the tar. My vision is fuzzy, but not from the water dripping in my eyes—Nian is still messing with my head. From the way everyone is staggering away, I'd guess whatever power Nian has, he's using it to scramble their brains, too.

"This way!" Konstantin points.

A long line of mismatched vehicles is parked in front of the barracks—old army trucks, civilian trucks, cars, and a few motorcycles. Soldiers are loading in supplies and wounded. We're surrounded by Russian soldiers who help us over to the convoy. Luka lumbers through the crowd and heads over to me.

Lucy's hand moves toward her gun.

"He's a friend, Lucy," I say.

She doesn't relax, but her aggressive stance doesn't faze the grizzled veteran.

"I dared not hope you would have made it. I'm glad you have." Luka holds his hand out to the convoy. "I place myself, my men, and my equipment at your disposal. We will provide safe passage for you to Ridgecrest in exchange for sanctuary there."

I stare at Luka, Konstantin, and a hundred desperate faces. His troops are primarily Russian, but many Americans and Chinese are among them. But how can I trust them? Things are already bad enough in Ridgecrest, with whoever is murdering the preppers and the Pickett's ready to start their own war. It would be crazy to bring an unknown army into town.

Someone tugs at my sleeve. I glance down at Bri and Jacob, who are standing beside me. Jacob is pale, and Bri has her arm wrapped around the boy's waist. Jacob motions for me to lean down. "He's telling the truth, Mr. Cain. They don't want to fight anymore."

I stare at his brown eyes and then at my little girl's. She smiles up at me. I turn back to Luka. "I guess we need to start trusting each other." I hold out my hand.

Luka lunges forward and embraces me like the father hugging the prodigal. The guy is as strong as a bear, and I think I feel a rib crack.

The crowd cheers, and I'm smiling until Luka drops me back to the ground. His eyes narrow, and he says something in Russian.

Behind me, metal scrapes on the tar. The bears are pushing the burned-out vehicles and rubble into the chasm.

"They're making a bridge," I say.

"Ready the trucks!" Luka bellows and then repeats it in Russian and again in Chinese. "Let them come. We have a big surprise waiting for them."

"We have to swing into the city on the way," I say. "There's a group of refugees holding up there. How much extra space do you have in the trucks?"

Luka shakes his head. "There are no survivors in the city. We've done some recon and have never found anyone."

"They found me. There's around a hundred."

"We don't have room for that many," Luka says.

"They may have some vehicles, but we'll need to make room. At least enough for the children and elderly."

Luka nods, and his brow pulls together. "There is something else you should know. I have debated telling you, but my silence is not right."

A knot forms in my stomach as Luka motions a soldier over. The soldier hands me his rifle.

"Look to the bridge downstream from the base," Luka says.

I press the rifle against my shoulder and scan through the scope until I see the road and the bridge to the South. The bridge appears empty until I catch sight of the enormous bone bear lumbering along the guard rail. I follow its path and see a wooden wagon. It's not hitched to any animal but—

Mercy.

My breath catches in my throat. For a moment, I think I'm seeing things. She's sparkling in the sun like an angel in the morning. Her chin is slightly lifted and the light is falling over her face and dancing in her hair. She's alive.

"Hundreds of monsters are moving down that road toward us," Luka says. "The main force of Nian's Army will cross at the base, and another group of monsters will try to flank us from the north. There is nothing you can do for her, my friend. But I thought you should know."

I hand the rifle back to the soldier who gave it. "The refugees are holding out in the old Macy's department store in town. Convince them to go with you."

"What?" Luka stands there for a moment, puzzled. "You will show us the way."

"I'm going to be busy. Angel, Bob, and H will take care of you." I march over to the convoy, and Lucy standing beside a truck.

She takes one look at my face, and her hands ball into fists.

"You've got that I'm gonna go do something stupid look on your face. Wipe it off, now!"

I can't help it, I smile. "I need you to take care of Bri for me. Luka spotted Mercy. She's on a bridge South of the base. I'm going to go get her."

"You left off the part about an army of monsters between us and her."

"I figure you knew that already."

Lucy slaps me.

It stings a little but doesn't hurt. She's going soft. There are tears in her eyes. I don't know why, but I kiss her forehead. "Take care of Bri."

Lucy stares at the ground.

I march to the convoy and eye a soldier sitting on an old motocross bike. "I need your ride."

The soldier opens his mouth, but Luka shouts something in Russian. The man snaps to attention, salutes me, and gets off.

I fire up the engine as Lucy runs up beside me. "I have to do this," I say.

"I know you do. I get it."

I stare at her as a thousand emotions spin between us. Love, hate, lust, betrayal, joy, pain, bliss, and agony crash like jewels in a kaleidoscope. But instead of the usual harsh light, this time, it's something not so bad. Beautiful even.

"I'm sorry for everything," She whispers and then she slaps me—hard, fast, and with a flick of the wrist that makes it crack like a whip.

My head jerks to the side, and I taste blood. I wipe my mouth with the back of my hand and wink. "Love you, too."

I flick up the kickstand, ease the throttle back, and head for the gate.

"Daddy! Daddy!" I hear Bri calling after me.

Tears wet my eyes. There's no time to say goodbye, and it's

better this way. Besides, once Lucy explains what I'm going to do, Bri will understand. She may never forgive me for throwing my life away, but she'll understand that I've got to try.

49

SURPRISE

Lucy Green

Brushing away the tears in her eyes, Lucy ran over to Bri, struggling with Jacob and Sadie as she tried to climb out of the back of the truck.

"Simmer down!" Lucy shouted as she placed a gentle hand on Bri's leg. "There's nothing you can do to stop that stubborn mule, and you know it. He's going to try and save Mercy."

"Mercy's here?" Jacob smiled.

Bri stopped fighting.

"She is here, but she needs help. Now, all of you listen to me. We've gone through the fires of hell to save you, and there ain't no way we're gonna lose you now. Sadie is in charge back here. Fen is driving, and her husband is riding shotgun. You stay down. Duck and cover. That's your job. Understand?" Lucy's voice was harsh and cold. She hated it, but there was no time to be nice.

"Yes, ma'am." Both kids responded.

Lucy kissed her hand twice and touched each child on the forehead. She looked at Sadie propped up against a box in the back, holding a shotgun. "You take care of them, Momma."

"No one is gonna hurt these babies."

Lucy jogged to the driver's side.

Fen gazed at the gate. "Where did Cain go?"

"He went after Mercy, but that's not our concern. You're in charge of this truck. If this convoy does something you think is stupid, use your own discretion."

Fen gave a tight-lipped smile and nodded. "I will protect the children and your mother. Are you riding in the front or back?"

"Neither. Keep them safe." Lucy repeated and headed toward the rear of the convoy.

On the Eastern side of the base, on the other side of the flooded channel, the horde of monsters grew. Thousands of bone rats chittered and scampered. Dozens of bone bears continued shoving debris into the ever-rising damn while the hundreds of wolves clacked their jaws, eager to reach their prey. They would be able to cross soon. If the convoy didn't get moving, they'd be overrun and ripped to pieces.

Lucy marched over to Luka. He sat on the passenger side of a jeep, shouting orders at a group of soldiers.

Luka pointed at her. "Get back to your truck."

Lucy stopped beside the jeep. She was done having men tell her what to do. "You're mistaken. This is a joint operation, and I have a say in everything. And we need to get moving."

"I made a deal with Cain—"

"Cain isn't here, and you need someone who knows the backroads, the choke points, and what you're going to face. I'm it. Besides, if you want sanctuary in Ridgecrest, I'm the only one who can get it, but we need to get there first."

"Good points," Luka shoved open the door.

Lucy got into the back seat.

Luka raised his arm and fired off three shots.

The convoy started moving.

"Cain wants us to meet up with survivors in the city," Luka said. "The scout drivers are familiar with the route. But we need to hold the monsters here for a little while longer. I have a surprise for them." Luka fired his pistol twice in the air, waited, and fired twice more.

Four trucks drove in the opposite direction of the convoy. They formed a line facing the Eastern front. The canvas tarps covering the back of the trucks were pulled off, and inside each vehicle sat 50-caliber machine guns.

The jeep parked to the right of the line of trucks.

Lucy turned to gaze at the clear sky. There wasn't any sign of the bone birds, but after seeing what they had done to Tianzi's super soldiers, she didn't want to face them even with the 50 calibers. She grabbed a bandage out of her pocket and started packing her ears. She had a feeling things were about to get very loud.

"They will cross at the shallowest spot. We figured they would. You see all the barricades." He pointed at the dozens of burned-out tanks, trucks, and cement barriers dotting the base.

Lucy's eyes widened. She thought they were randomly placed, abandoned where they broke down, but there was a clear pattern to them. The barriers were positioned to force whoever passed through to bunch up.

"Once we get them in the middle," Luka smiled. "I'll show them a little surprise. They thought they buried the ammo bunker, but do you see those pipes?" He motioned to some exhaust tubes next to a razed building. "Once we light the fuses, everything standing down there will go boom!"

The chittering grew louder. Thousands of the rats pranced and danced along the tar as the bears shoved a large charred-out bus into the chasm.

The wolves howled, the noise blending into one voice that seemed to shake the air.

"Get ready!" Luka shouted.

The bone rats charged. They swept into the chasm and then back up to the tarmac. They raced between the barriers and burned-out vehicles.

"Wait." Luka raised his arm. "Wait."

Lucy stared as the creatures swarmed. There were so many they blotted out the ground.

The wolves came next. They bounded through the rats like they were wading through a rushing river.

Luka swept his arm down.

"Fire!"

The machine guns roared to life, and the noise was deafening. Brass sailed into the air, and lead streamed forward. But it was like shoveling sand into the tide. For each bone rat that fell, several took its place. They'd never hold them off long.

Luka shouted something in Russian.

Soldiers appeared in each truck with a rocket launcher on their shoulders. Flames and smoke billowed out behind them as the rockets streaked into the horde.

Monsters blew to pieces, and small craters were blasted into the ground—only to disappear a second later like rocks tossed into a pond as the creatures continued to swarm forward.

"Light the fuse! Fall back." Luka ordered as the machine guns continued to fire.

A soldier dropped from the truck and used a propane torch to light a fuse. The green rope flamed to life. It snapped and crackled, the fireball streaking along the ground toward the exhaust pipes.

Lucy felt like she was watching Luke Skywalker's laser shot fly down the Death Star's trench. The energy ball reached a tipped-over truck and disappeared.

Luka laughed. "Do you know what the problem is with the Russian army? The Russian army." He laughed harder. "So be it. Out! Out!" He swatted the driver in the head and prodded Lucy toward the door.

Lucy attempted to protest, but the large man grabbed her shoulders, lifted her over the side of the jeep, and placed her on the ground. She opened her mouth, but no words came. Her eyes brimmed with tears.

"It is better this way. The old world is done. There is no place for old Russian soldiers. I give my spot on this earth to the children." The jeep rocked as Luka climbed into the driver's seat. "From now on, you are in charge." He pulled off his hat and set it on Lucy's head. He saluted her then, jammed the transmission into drive and punched the gas. "Go join the convoy. I will handle this."

Lucy stared in horror as he drove toward the oncoming horde.

The soldier who'd been driving the jeep ran toward the last truck.

All four of the trucks with the machine guns began to move.

"Halt!" Lucy shouted, drawing her pistol. "Stop you freakin' cowards!" She fired in the air as she ran toward the last vehicle. She climbed onto the cab's step, holding onto the large side mirror. "You three go!" She motioned toward the convoy. "We're providing cover for Luka. Open fire!"

The soldier on the machine gun gave a thumbs-up and pulled the trigger.

Luka's jeep swerved around the barricades as he raced toward the exhaust pipes. He clipped a cement barrier, sending pieces of metal and dirt flying.

The machine gun ran through one belt, and the crew raced to reload.

A whizzing sound split the air. Hundreds of bone spikes arced toward the jeep.

Luka raised his right arm over his head.

Metal shrieked, and bones snapped, but the huge Russian didn't cry out.

The machine gun roared back to life.

The jeep skidded to a stop beside the exhaust port.

Lucy raised her rifle and zoomed in on Luka. His right arm hung limply at his side, a half dozen bone spikes sticking out of it. As he limped toward the vent, she saw his entire right side was pierced with spikes.

Luka held a grenade in his left hand.

Another volley of spikes whizzed through the air.

The enormous Russian staggered forward. His left arm dropped to his side, and he fell to his knees.

The hand grenade rolled backward and underneath the jeep.

Luka pitched forward and fell on his face. He didn't move.

Lucy's stomach clenched. They had to delay the horde, or the entire convoy would be doomed. She turned and stared at the driver.

He was a young Russian soldier. His kind brown eyes met hers.

Lucy opened the door and climbed in. "Get out. I need the truck."

The man shook his head. "We have a better chance together."

He shifted the truck into drive.

The grenade exploded. Luka's jeep flew into the air and burst into flames. It crashed back to the ground as black smoke billowed skyward.

Lucy gasped. A sparkling red, white, and orange ball raced out from beneath the jeep's wreckage. The fire had reignited the fuse. The soldiers cheered as the burning fuse disappeared down the exhaust pipe.

Lucy held her breath.

One. Two. Three.

The seconds ticked by.

Four. Five. Six.

The horde continued to charge.

Seven—

The shockwave slammed into the truck and shoved it several feet sideways. The windows shattered. Lucy's hands covered her ears. Even with them stuffed with bandages, the pain was incredible.

She blinked rapidly. Everything around them was covered in a cloud of dust.

Lucy grabbed the driver's arm. "Go! Go!"

The truck vibrated and rumbled as he drove forward.

With the wind blowing from the West, the cloud quickly cleared.

Through the ringing in her ears, she could hear people cheering.

At least half of the Russian side of the base was gone. The site was littered with hundreds of monster corpses. The rest of the horde was in full retreat.

Lucy exhaled. They'd won some time, that was it. There was still a long way between them and Ridgecrest.

50

DON'T LET GO

Cain Haight

I've never been a defeatist. If I wrote a dictionary, words like quit and surrender wouldn't be included. But as I turn left out of the base, any glimmer of hope of reaching Mercy shuts off. Thousands of these bone creatures are along the roads and coming out of the woods. They're all heading toward the base, but there ain't no way of avoiding them.

Still, I've got no choice. I've got to go. I'd rather die right now than leave a woman so pure in the hands of things so evil.

I pull back the throttle and speed forward.

A few of the bone rats notice me and start flinging spikes.

I keep my head down and hug the side of the road. That's when I noticed the trail running parallel off to my right. I don't know if it's for hiking or dirt bikes, but either way, it's got more cover than being out on the street.

I twist the handlebars, cross the breakdown lane, and slip a little as I reach the grass. The off-road tires have excellent traction. I straighten her out and race up the embankment into the woods.

Trees streak by me as I zig-zag along the trail. It's wide and mostly free of rocks, so I'm making good time. With all the ups and downs and twists and turns, by the time the bone rats cutting through the woods notice me, I'm already heading around the next turn.

I slide around a corner and race past three giant wolves coming out of the brush.

They pounce and bound after me.

I shift gears and pull the throttle back. The speedometer hits thirty, but the wolves are gaining. Holding onto the handlebars feels like using a jackhammer as the shocks are going spastic because of the pitted terrain. My forearms are on fire as I fight to keep control. The rear tire slides off a rock and sprays dirt into the air, slowing me down.

The lead wolf is beside me. Our eyes meet. It opens its jaws, and I do the only thing I can think of and kick it in the ribs.

Pain races up my leg, and my bike jostles to the left.

Wood splinters and bone cracks as the wolf slams into a tree I narrowly avoid.

The path straightens out.

I shift gears and pin the throttle back.

The two remaining wolves are on my heels, but I'm pulling away and creating space. Soon, I lose sight of them.

Continuing down the path, I can see the bridge coming up on my left. There's a clearing ahead with an old billboard encouraging people to visit Lieper's Forge. I slow down and cut to the left.

The road looks clear, but I'm still breathing heavily, waiting for another group of wolves to come charging any moment. None do. I pull back onto the road, which is steadily climbing. Dropping the bike into second gear, I make my way around a few abandoned cars until I see the wagon come into view.

Then I see her. Mercy takes my breath away as she stands

with her hands clasped together, looking toward the base. I don't know if it's because of the sun or the beauty inside of her radiating out, but she has this glow about her.

My attention shifts to the largest bone bear I've ever seen lying on the road next to the wagon. It raises its head and sniffs the air. Then it plants its front paws on the ground and gets onto all fours. The thing is enormous—over twelve feet—and it's looking straight at me.

I skid the bike to a stop and pull out my pistol.

The bear starts lumbering toward me.

I smile. The wolves that just attacked me reminded me of a very valuable lesson—these creatures are fast, but they can't run forever.

"Come on, you big fat tub o' lard!" I aim at its head and fire.

The bullet bounces off its skull. The beast breaks into a jog.

"Faster, blimpo!" I fire two more rounds.

The bear speeds up.

"Come on, fatty! Show me what you got!" One. Two. Three. Four times, I fire.

The bear bursts into a sprint. It's fifty yards away and getting closer fast.

I crank the throttle and head in the opposite direction.

Not only is this bear bigger than any I've seen, it's quicker. Before I know it, it's so close behind me that I smell it.

I glance back and gasp.

The bear opens its mouth and chomps.

Pieces of the back fender shatter. The bike shudders, and I struggle to control it. I swerve around an old Lexus and shift gears again.

The bear lowers its shoulder and sends the wreckage of the Lexus spinning in a circle. But the move costs the bear speed.

I pull well ahead.

The bear slows to a stop, and so do I.

We're half a mile down the road from the wagon.

I gun the throttle. The rear tire spins, and smoke rises in the air. I do a 180 and steer for the right side of the street.

Before the bear knows what's going on, I'm past it.

I start laughin' and wavin' bye-bye as I speed back up the ramp.

Mercy is running down the middle of the road.

I race over to her and skid to a stop.

She looks confused at the motorcycle. It's a dirt bike and is meant for one rider.

"You're going to be riding backward," I say as I lift her up and set her down on the gas tank in front of me. "Wrap your legs around me, and don't let go."

Mercy buries her face in my neck. Wet tears dampen my skin. "I'll never let go again." She whispers, then stiffens. "The bear is coming back."

I crank the throttle, and we take off in the direction I've been heading. We reach the crest of the hill. On the left side of the road, I see a massive pile of dirt and a tunnel leading toward the base.

Two figures that look like men scurry out of the darkness.

I start shifting gears and speeding up. My temples start to throb.

Mercy moans. Her grip tightens on my back.

A colossal explosion sounds from the base. The bike shimmies as a blast wave washes over us.

The two ghouls howl and disappear into the tunnel.

A cloud of debris rises high over the Russian side of the base. I've got no idea what they just blew up, but whatever it was, I hope our side is the one who set it off.

Mercy hangs onto me as I drive down the highway. I've got no idea if Lucy, Bri, and the others have gotten away, but with the Russians helping them, they have a chance.

As far as Mercy and I go, I don't know. Right now, there's

still an army between us and Ridgecrest. But then I feel her breath on my skin, and the hope I lost comes rushing back. She's alive. So I don't care if I've got to run back through hell to get to Ridgecrest. I'll do it, seeing how I have an angel at my side.

JOIN THE FREE PREFERRED READER PROGRAM

Join the Preferred Reader program and get your _exclusive_ copy of *FIRST PATROL*

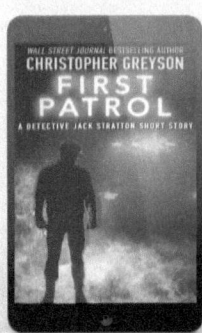

Preferred readers enjoy:

- Advanced Notification of New Book Releases
- The Christopher Greyson Newsletter
- Special Appreciation Giveaways
- The exclusive short story: FIRST PATROL!

Join Now! ⏷

Visit ChristopherGreyson.com to sign-up!

ALSO BY CHRISTOPHER GREYSON

The Girl Who Lived 1

The Girl Who Lived 2

One Little Lie

The Woman Beneath the Stairs

Pure of Heart

The Detective Jack Stratton Mystery-Thriller Series

The Case Files of Detective Charlie Westbrook

Kiku - The Rogue Assassin Series

The Dark - A Post-Apocalyptic Thriller Series

The Adventures of Finn and Annie - A Mini Mystery Series

ACKNOWLEDGMENTS

I would like to thank all the wonderful readers out there. It is you who make the literary world what it is today—a place of dreams filled with tales of adventure! Word of mouth is crucial for any author to succeed. If you enjoyed the novel, please consider leaving a review at Amazon, even if it is only a line or two; it would make all the difference and I would appreciate it very much.

I would also like to thank my amazing wife for standing beside me every step of the way on this journey. My thanks also go out to Laura and Christopher, my two awesome kids, and my dear mother and the rest of my family.

ABOUT THE AUTHOR

My name is Christopher Greyson, and I am a storyteller. Since I was a little boy, I have dreamt of what mystery was around the next corner, or what quest lay over the hill. If I couldn't find an adventure, one usually found me, and now I weave those tales into my stories.

My love for tales of mystery and adventure began with my grandfather, a decorated World War I hero. I will never forget being introduced to his friend, a WWI pilot who flew across the skies at the same time as the feared, legendary Red Baron. I love to hear from my readers. Please go to Christopher-Greyson.com and sign up for my mailing list to receive periodic updates on new book releases. Thank you for reading my novels. I hope my stories have brightened your day.

Sincerely,

THE DARK 3
Copyright: Christopher Greyson
Published: September 31st 2024

The right of Christopher Greyson to be identified as author of this Work has been asserted by him in accordance with sections 77 and 78 of the Copyright, Designs and Patents Act 1988.

All rights reserved. No part of this publication may be reproduced, distributed, or transmitted in any form or by any means, including photocopying, recording, or other electronic or mechanical methods, without the prior written permission of the publisher.

Any references to historical events, real people, or real places are used fictitiously. Names, characters, and places are products of the author's imagination.

No part of this book may be used or reproduced in any manner for the purpose of training artificial intelligence technologies or systems.

Find out more about the author and upcoming books online at
www.ChristopherGreyson.com.

v.1.1.06.16.26

www.ingramcontent.com/pod-product-compliance
Lightning Source LLC
Chambersburg PA
CBHW020415260626
47156CB00007B/2405